WEATHER WITCH

WEATHER
WITCH

Shannon Delany

ST. MARTIN'S GRIFFIN ⚞ NEW YORK

WEATHER WITCH. Copyright © 2013 by Shannon Delany. All rights reserved. Printed in the United States of America. For information, address St. Martin's Press, 175 Fifth Avenue, New York, N.Y. 10010.

www.stmartins.com

Griffin books may be purchased for educational, business, or promotional use. For information on bulk purchases, please contact Macmillan Corporate and Premium Sales Department at 1-800-221-7945 extension 5442 or write special markets@macmillan.com.

Library of Congress Cataloging-in-Publication Data

Delany, Shannon.
  Weather Witch / Shannon Delany. — 1st ed.
      p. cm
  ISBN 978-1-250-01851-9 (trade pbk.)
  ISBN 978-1-250-01854-0 (e-book)
  1. Witches—Fiction. 2. Fantasy. I. Title.
  PZ7.D3733
  [Fic]—dc23   2013003054

First Edition: June 2013

10 9 8 7 6 5 4 3 2 1

To the too-often overlooked and forgotten who were beaten down and enslaved by the desires of others and—more important—to the ones who still are: Be Brave and Rise Up!

Acknowledgments

I'd like to start these acknowledgments with a nod to the city in which much of this novel's action is placed: Philadelphia. I love Philadelphia and visit whenever I have the opportunity. Those of you who love history will understand why I chose Philly, and those of you who love fiction will understand why I've taken creative liberties with Philly's history, geography, and science.

I hope readers love both history and fiction as that will make this series more enjoyable. Some events mentioned in this story did actually happen; a few historical characters make appearances. If, by my treatment of the past, I encourage a few of you to research and read things beyond this series, I'll feel I've done a good job.

As always, thanks to my agent, Richard Curtis; my editor, Michael Homler, for giving this world a chance; the great staff at St. Martin's Press, including Loren Jaggers and the copyediting team; my son and other family members who know to steer clear when I have writing to do; my brother for chatting about this concept over Mexican food one day; and the original rock bands Autumn Fire and Just a Memory for inspiring a couple of scenes in the story thanks to their powerful music! Thanks also to Felecia Scialdone-Burchett, Marshall Kruse, and Heather Vanmoer for letting me borrow bits of their names for my characters.

A big thank-you to the very talented singer and songwriter Wade Mulvihill, who happily wrote and gladly provided the song "Reeling" that both Laura and Lady Astraea sing in this book.

Thanks to the folks at Maine's Bangor Museum and History Center and New York's The Farmers' Museum (Cooperstown), Nellis Tavern (St. Johnsville), and Hanford Mills (East Meredith) for gladly answering my questions; to Philadelphia's City Tavern for faithful reproductions of period food; and to Salem's Ye Olde Pepper Companie for keeping traditional candies available.

Special thanks to my beta readers for this project: Patricia Port Locatelli, Patrick Javarone, Steven Blaze, and the amazing Karl Gee (who has gone through this story almost as many times as I have now). Much love to you all!

WEATHER WITCH

Prologue

———⊰⊱———

I was born with a chronic anxiety about the weather.
—JOHN BURROUGHS

Holgate, Pennsylvania
1839

A banner snapped out on the pole high above the restrained seventeen-year-old boy, straightening to its full length. For a moment he thought he glimpsed his country's motto: *A Place for All*. The wind shifted and the banner fell limp against its long wooden pole.

The straps cinched tight across his chest and threatening to squeeze the breath out of him declared his place plainly. Sweat dotted his forehead and arms and had little to do with the bright orange sun hanging overhead. Attached to a broad set of boards that forced him on his feet at the very top of Holgate's tallest tower, Marion Kruse could see much of the bustling and walled compound below through the tower's crenellations if he just tossed his dark curls out of his eyes. But he didn't even try.

The view held no interest for him.

His focus was as fixed as his position—his mouth dry and his gaze nailed to the long, slender table that stretched nearby, covered with more than a dozen different blades and tools glinting ferociously in the unobstructed sunlight at the Eastern Tower's top. He tried to swallow but a lump wedged in his throat and stopped his breath.

The door groaned open, hinges protesting as a man not even a half decade Marion's senior—perhaps all of twenty-two—stepped onto the flat rooftop, briefly admiring the view beyond them. "You can see clear across the lake and the valley from here, you know? On days such as this I imagine a decent spyglass might let you glimpse as far as the rooftops of German Towne and Philadelphia itself," he said loudly enough that Marion heard. "What a *spectacular* day!" He raised his arms above his head a moment like an athlete warming up for competition and then clapped his hands together.

He smiled. A conventionally handsome man with a good jawline and a strong chin, his golden hair never fell into his eyes and his shirt and trousers always remained clean no matter what activity dirtied him. He took a moment to tie on his apron. The apron was a stark contrast to his perfect shirt and pants.

Marion shuddered at the colorful stains marring its fabric. Here a dark brown smudge, there a spray of rust-colored drops, there still more marks of a red so deep it put the bricks of Philadelphia's finest to shame. It appeared the apron had rested in a puddle of whatever *that* stuff was, it was so prevalent.

Marion found his voice but it was not the one he usually heard coming from his mouth. This voice was thinner, tighter, and squeaked out between his parched lips when he asked, "And you, who are *you*?"

"Brandon of House Dregard—Bran Marshall," the other said, long fingers drifting over the table and pausing to stroke the handle of one wicked tool before tapping the neck of the next in the long line. "But more importantly, I am the one who will free you from being Grounded. I am the Maker."

"I cannot be Made," Marion insisted. "I practice no witchery. I am no magicker. My line is pure. I am no Weather Witch." His broad hands balled into fists, he tugged at the leather straps pinning his wrists against the coarse wood, but the bindings would not give.

Bran pulled on a pair of thick rubber gloves and picked up something with a slender handle and a blade on its tip that curved like the most wicked of wolf's teeth. He held it up, admiring the way the light bounced off its edge. "Marion of House Kruse, ranked Fourth of the Nine, your rank is forfeit, your life is ours, our pleasure your duty, and that duty a great one." He took a slow step forward, his gaze passing through the blade between them and snaring the other man's eyes before he glanced up at the spotless sky. The ends of his mouth curled down. "Interesting." He shrugged. "Now we will Make a Conductor of you . . ."

Marion fought his restraints, his gray eyes wide as the blade pressed against the skin of his forearm and warmth wept slow and red from beneath it. "Have a care," he warned, the words forced through gritted teeth. "This thing you do Makes naught but revolution . . ."

Then the blade went deep and sliced wide and Marion howled against the pain. His head lolled back and, falling unconscious, he bled in silence.

Frost crawled out from around his body, creeping across his leather bindings and the rough wooden boards at his back, tumbling down to the warm stone tower's rooftop to fight the reality of summer with a chill so cruel its icy and prickling shards only withered in the hot dripping crimson that fell freely from Marion's arm.

Snow spiraled down lazily from a small gray cloud above and Bran shook his head. "Now what can we Make of *this*?"

Chapter One

Philadelphia, Pennsylvania
1844

The darkness of the alley rivaled the intent blackening the hooded woman's words.

As surely as dusk had fallen on Philadelphia, so too did it seem one of the city's great families would also fall.

"Are you most certain?" asked the woman's companion, a man of perhaps forty years. He snatched at his rioting hat as a breeze sliced down the alley, making both watchmen and lantern light shiver in its wake. He cursed the need to meet in such a place—one of the few alleys where the substandard candlelit lanterns were still required. Gas lines were too great (and volatile) a temptation for this neighborhood's inhabitants and too much a hassle elsewhere. And, while stormlight illuminated most of the city, no such technology was wasted *here*.

No one of Lord Stevenson's rank wished to be caught dead in the Below. And caught dead was certainly a possibility in this neighborhood considering the turf disputes between the Blood Tubs and Moyamensing Killers. "To storm such an estate on the Hill and be *wrong* . . . And on the night of young Lady Jordan Astraea's seventeenth natal celebration . . ."

The watchmen shifted at his words, woolen coats rustling as they raised their gazes toward the estate balanced on the mountain above. The Hill was the safest realty in Philadelphia.

When the Wildkin War had pushed the residents of what was briefly called Society Hill up Philadelphia's slopes and away from the hungry lapping of the waters (and the hungrier things swimming within their depths) the Astraeas had been the first family to stake a claim. Now there was no returning to the first properties the great families had owned. The recent influx of immigrants had turned the area's elegant original homes into squalid tenements and boardinghouses. Not that the wealthy would want to return with the water so dangerously close.

The hesitancy of the lord's words ill matched his desires to move against the Astraeas, and the young woman knew it. She had been careful selecting this Council member and contacting him through subtle means. His grudge against the Astraea family was long-standing, though most had forgotten it.

But, even so young, she had a gift for discovering the little things that either pulled men together or divided them. It was a precious and necessary family trait when one held her social standing. "I know this as well as I know my own name," she snapped. Moon-white gloves appeared long enough to tug the deep hood of her Kinsale cloak farther down, swallowing any hint of her face in shadow. A ruby flashed on one finger before her hands disappeared once more into rich folds of velvet.

The Councilman's gaze flicked from the mysterious lady

to the fluttering light of the smoke-stained lanterns near the alley's entrance. "One might suppose you, too, are a Witch—the way the wind cries when you are angered . . ."

"One *might* suppose," she quipped, the breeze playing with the heavy velvet hem, "that such words would be considered treasonous considering my rank. Go to the Astraea estate this evening. The Witch will be there, as I've said."

Light stuttered across his sharp features and he nodded. Shrinking against a fresh chill, he pulled his tall hat's brim lower over his brow. "And who—?"

She held her hand up, silencing him. "Bring a Tester. He will know the Witch easily enough."

He waited in silence with the watchmen—with no Weather Wraiths currently in Philadelphia proper he had settled for using simple men—until the lady disappeared from the alley and the sounds of a carriage rattling across cobblestones told of her departure.

He did not need her surname to guess her rank. From the noise on the street he knew her carriage was horse-drawn by a single, calm steed, like the carefully tended cavalry's or the privately owned ones barely afforded in the city—not like the wild-eyed and panicky survivors of Merrow attacks. A steed such as hers would have been well protected, stabled, and that took significant money.

She was at least a member of the Fourth of the Nine and that was good enough for him.

Finding another Weather Witch at the Astraea estate meant further lessening old Morgan Astraea's influence by casting doubt on the high-ranking Councilman. He'd do anything to peel one of Astraea's fingers back from the reins he held, anything that would put himself a step closer to achieving his goals.

"We must hurry. Call in the nearest Tester and a Ring of Wraiths. There will be some nearby Gathering. If we are to do this we must do it well and professionally."

A watchman split from their group, jogging to obediently do his duty.

The dying light of sunset streaked across the public's promised clear sky, illuminating the fat-bellied airships hanging overhead as they awaited instructions for their coast into the Eastern Mountain Port. It would be a clear night for docking cargo, with rain scheduled to fall on Tuesdays and alternating Fridays only.

Lord Stevenson reached up to his hatband to adjust a metal and glass contraption nestled there, bringing its system of lenses and scopes over the hat's brim and down to sit on the bridge of his nose. Blinking as he rolled a finger across a small brass gear by one of the two scopes, he flipped through a series of tiny lenses, watching the atmosphere high above him come into sharp focus. Faint and feathery disruptions overhead manifested as wisps of clouds, which slowly edged their way across the evening sky, pulling in from all directions to draw together above Philadelphia's most desirable real estate: the Hill.

And remarkably near the Astraea estate, which sat at the Hill's crest like the king of the stone-faced mountain.

Holgate

The newspaper folded near Bran's elbow was a distinct temptation with its headline of *Unseasonable Frosts Frustrate Phil-*

adelphia. Bran ran the back of his hand across his forehead and tried to focus on the books lying open before him. *A Genealogy of Witches, Wardens, and Wraiths* was heavy enough reading, but writing the blasted thing? Even worse. He tapped his pen's steel nib to clear it of ink and set it down.

But the only way to track the Weather Witches was through their lineage—family lines meant much as magicking was one of the traits passed to one's offspring. Whereas one might attribute a propensity for headaches to pale blue-eyed people living in very sunny climes, connecting physical traits to witchery was not so simple.

Were brown-eyed brunettes more likely to trigger and demonstrate witchery than green-eyed blondes? Statistically speaking, no. But redheads . . . gingers . . . they were fiery in more ways than one.

He blew on the page and tenderly lifted its corner, lingering on the memory of a redheaded girl from his hometown. More trouble than he had ever expected. He grinned, but, catching himself, squashed the expression and refocused on his task.

Gingers and anyone from Galeyn Turell's line seemed particularly prone to witchery. It was as they said: "The apple does not fall far from the tree."

Luckily, all Weather Witches manifested their affinity for magicking before the age of sixteen.

His desk lantern's brilliance ebbed, its glass panes reflecting equal amounts of shadow and light. He leaned forward to inspect it. The glowing double-terminated crystal powering its interior seemed constricted, producing only a soft, wavering glow. He glanced at the lanterns lining his library walls. The fire hazard of candles and brief monopoly of gas had been replaced years ago in most of the country by storm-light and their energy source: stormcells, tiny crystals that held power and eased it out slowly.

But even that technology was not without flaws. It did have a distinctly human origin.

His room still radiated a soft white light, each stormcell bright and steady except for the one on his desk.

The one that mattered most.

He shook his head and picked up the set of bone keys resting on his desk's corner. A Maker should be afforded plenty of light for his work.

He snatched up a smaller journal and opened it, running one finger down a list of names and times. Someone was not doing what they needed to . . . Ah. His finger stopped on the name of a freshly Made girl.

Age six and recently Gathered from Boston.

Most people would expect little from a child—yes, a sense of decorum and proper etiquette, of course that, but usually they had another year or two before they were thrust into some form of necessary employment. But Witches were different little beasts. Age was of far less importance than proper training.

Witches Burned Out. Best to train them up, Make them, and pull all the power from them as quickly as one could—harness the energy before it dissipated—before they died, leaving only one final stormcell, one specially colored crystal, their *soul stone,* behind.

This child was too young—too newly Made—to be Fading. Either she wasn't trying or she wasn't Drawing Down enough.

He pushed his chair back, picked up the lantern, hung the keys on his belt, and grabbed his small journal. Tank

Five. Best go and deal with the problem now rather than suffer the consequences of not solving it later.

Out the door and along the narrow hall he went. Down seven flights of stairs. That was the real headache of maintaining rooms in the Eastern Tower's upper apartments— traveling so far up and down just to reach the Holding Tanks. At the eighth floor's landing he peered through the narrow strip of smudged glass at eye level and, steeling himself, opened the heavy wood and iron door. He paused there, nose stinging at the thick scents of chamber pots, old hay, sweating rocks, and perspiring people.

The Tanks were worse than any stable he'd ever been in, especially in the crawling heat of late summer, and the Tanks Witches stayed in before their Reckoning? Not a thought he liked to dwell on. Night only faintly dulled the rankness stabbing his sinuses and left him a little less dizzy than day. Frankly, had there been no problem with any Witch, he would never venture down to the Tanks. But he was the Maker and a Maker's reputation was built on his successes.

Or destroyed through his failures.

But, he had made enough changes in his system since the escape of the Kruse boy.

He raised the nearly dead lantern, its rectangular glass panes shimmering more from other lanterns' lights than its own power. He slipped on a pair of thick gloves hanging by the door with a snap of rubber, feeling them fall into a proper and clinging fit.

Bran tugged out his journal and found the girl's name. He called, "Sybil! Sybil, do you hear me?"

A moan drifted to his ears.

His lantern flickered in response.

He stood before her door in an instant, his hand fumbling

through the bone keys. He found the one he needed and popped the door open. In the dark cell the child lay flopped like a rag doll in the straw of her bedding. Moonlight streamed through the bars in the only outside-facing window on Floor Eight and he scrambled forward, reaching a tentative hand toward her forehead.

Fever could spread like western wildfire in the Tanks and wipe clean an entire season of Witches before racing through the compound, murdering the Grounded populace, too. Even through the gloves, the touch of her flesh reassured Bran there was not enough heat to prove fever. He shifted his hand, clamping it more tightly to her brow.

There was barely enough heat to prove life.

Sybil's flesh was cold as the water in the claustrophobic cell's corner bucket. Bran stretched the distance and dragged the sloshing wooden pail to him with a grunt. "You aren't drinking," he muttered, noting the volume of water remaining. "You can't Draw Down if you don't drink. And you can't Light Up if you don't Draw Down. Sit," he demanded, grabbing her arm in an effort to right her.

He dragged her limp form up until she nearly appeared seated normally against the damp stone wall—although her head lolled on her slender neck and her eyes remained unfocused and dull.

The lantern in her Tank was as dead as her expression. She hadn't even managed to keep her personal lantern powered. Or perhaps she no longer cared to.

Bran reached into the bucket, fishing for the awkward thing at its bottom that was both spoon and cup. His fingers towed it up, gloves coming back slick with a rainbow's oily sheen. "Dammit." He kicked the bucket over, water splashing toward the sluggish drain in the room's center, and he stormed out the door, fist curled tight around the empty container's handle.

The watchman at the hall's end raised his head in question.

"When was the last time the Witches had fresh water?"

The man blanched, shrugging his shoulders. "They have *water* . . ."

"*Fresh* water," Bran demanded. "They cannot Draw Down properly if they don't drink. And they can't drink *slime*." He whipped the bucket out at the man, clipping his chin with the bucket's edge. "Do right by me or your reputation will suffer."

The man rubbed his jaw but nodded.

"As will your face," Bran added. He shoved out the door and jogged down the last flights, coming out onto Holgate's main square.

By night the compound was an eerie sight. Built by a Hessian with a penchant for castles and Old World architecture, it was in stark contrast to almost every other place in the Americas. Which was why it was perfect for Making Witches. Close to a large freshwater lake but far enough inland from the bay to make Merrow attacks difficult (Holgate and Philadelphia being determined not to suffer as Baltimore had), the place provided all he needed. Water to make weather, height to catch air and lightning, and rock so chances were less they'd catch fire and burn.

Chances being *less* were, of course, far from a guarantee.

The base of what the occupants called Tanks and Tower was broad stacked and mortared rock that shimmered when flecks of mica and pyrite caught the moonlight, making the place ripple at night like some otherworldly locale. Bran shook the thought from his head.

There was no otherworldly *anything*. He was a man of science. His reputation depended on it. The fairy tales and things that still held sway in rustic churches and around fires late at night had been proven to be of *this* world.

Yes, there were things that stole children from their cribs at night and monsters that ate his fellow men. There were misbegotten and misshapen beasts that haunted deep forests and abandoned houses and there were certainly devils seemingly drawn from man's darkest desires. And magick. Grim, dangerous magick that tore families and empires apart. But none of that magick was here.

Not in the truly civilized parts of the New World.

The Wildkin, including the Merrow, Pooka, Kelpies, Gytrash, Oisin, Wolfkin, Kumiho, and a host of others were as firmly of *this* world as the other natives that called themselves the People.

And they were just as unwanted.

Magickers were expressly forbidden in the New World. The only ones that had crossed the ocean were the result of Galeyn Turell's bizarre Making when the Merrow—naturally occurring beasts only a few distant cousins beyond the normal human family—attacked the ship the girl had been on after an accident that had killed one of their princes.

If Galeyn hadn't demonstrated her strange weather-wielding powers as the Merrow slithered their way across the boat's blood- and gore-slicked deck the winds would never have kicked up and hurled the Merrow away, and the ship would've never vaulted into the air and made it to the colonies.

And there would be no Wildkin War.

How eagerly since then had foreign authors turned a blind eye to the true nature of the Merrow—Hans Christian Andersen the worst offender, using fiction in an attempt to fashion peace.

Unbidden, Bran's eyes went from the well and pump in the town's square to the descended portcullis, and the lake and bay not far beyond. The Merrow were never more than a heavy flood away from Holgate's lake . . .

He hooked the bucket onto the heavy faucet's head and, grabbing the pump's handle, filled it in one long stroke. He was back inside and up the stairs nearly as fast as he'd come down, the burden of the water secondary to the fact that a dead Witch would mar his record.

Nearly as much as the escape of a previous Witch had.

The Witches were all he had. For better or worse they were his only go at immortality. His was one of the most important jobs in all of the Americas. His might be a name to continue on along with those of other great men. Like that of presidents or generals, or like his father.

Or he could be forgotten, leaving nothing of note behind.

He could fail.

"Here," he said, scooping the water and pressing the ladle against her thin, pale lips. Water poured across her cheeks and chin, spilling down her throat to soak into the linen shift she wore.

She shivered and choked, but she swallowed. She drank. So he scooped more and poured more and she sputtered, her already large eyes going wider. He slowed the flow of liquid, letting her catch up with a few eager swallows before she shook her head and mumbled something.

"What?"

Her eyes, now slightly brighter, remained unfocused and her lips fluttered before she had air enough behind her thoughts to form words. She blinked at him, coughed, and tried once more.

Her voice strained and small, she said, "They come. And there is naught to be done for it."

She gasped and the stormcell in his lantern blazed so bright blue he fell backward, blinded. The lantern flew from his hands, glass splintering as the thing burst into pieces, the glaring soul stone tumbling free and into the thick and dusty hay.

By the time it returned to its normal intensity and most of his vision was back, Sybil was the cold of death, the very same cold as wildly running water.

"The stone," Bran hissed, sifting through the wet straw and grime, his fingers blackening with filth as he hunted for the elusive sparkle of a soul stone. "Aaah!" he exclaimed, pulling his hand up to his face, glass sticking out of it like porcupine quills. "Damnnn . . ." Bleeding and cursing, he pulled the splinters free, and stood to sweep the floor with his booted foot instead, fingers plunged into his mouth and filling it with the taste of iron and dirt.

His stomach dropped when he heard the distinct sound of something scraping across the last bit of a grate before clinking its way into the darkness of the room's single and filthy drain.

The soul stone was as good as gone.

Chapter Two

For there is no friend like a sister
In calm or stormy weather...
—CHRISTINA GEORGINA ROSETTI

Philadelphia

In the generously appointed rooms that Jordan Astraea called her own, there was a flurry of activity in preparation for her natal day celebration.

"No. No!" a young woman in a fine gown snapped, swatting away a servant's hands as they tried to fix her friend's hair just so. "Laura, leave it be," Catrina demanded.

The seated girl spoke, her voice soft, nearly shy. "Chloe . . ."

Another servant, this one older than the first by a dozen years and larger by at least the same number of pounds, stepped forward, her hands flying up to adjust the calico bandana always knotted crisply atop her head. "Yes, Miss Jordan, milady?" She curtsied, spreading her heavy broadcloth skirts with hands the color and scent of exotic spices and more tropical climes.

"Please do go see to my good lady mother."

Chloe nodded. "But your hair . . ." she said in echo to Laura's earlier protestation. "You have not all your ribbons in place."

Jordan groaned, leaning back on her damask-padded bench as far as her dress's snug bodice allowed. "Leave it be," she requested.

"Indeed," Catrina added. "Leave it be. Surely we can handle such a mundane task."

Chloe blinked. "If miladies so desire."

Drawing each word out with a separate breath Catrina Hollindale, ranked Fourth of the Nine, said, "We *so* desire." She clapped her gloved hands together. "Do go on now," she urged the servants. "I daresay women of our status can finish placing a few ribbons."

Chloe again nodded. "Far be it from me to argue with her ladyship, but it is precisely due to your superior rank and status that we merrily dress your hair for you."

"Chloe." Catrina's tone was thick with warning. "Go now before I become quite cross and throw something at you."

Both the servants and Jordan glanced at the walls, papered with boldly alternating stripes and vines and covered in numerous equally bold nicks and dings from the girls' frequent tantrums.

Jordan's gaze slid back to Catrina.

"I will do it," Catrina's pitch rose, her tone going shrill as her hand stretched out to the silver-plated brush on the mahogany dressing table before her, her eyes narrow and fixed on the servants.

Laura raised her hands and scurried for the door, Chloe close behind, but her eyes never left Lady Hollindale's twitching fingers. The door slammed shut, and, for good measure, Catrina hefted the brush and whipped it, a wicked grin twisting her full lips when it popped against the door and the servants gasped on the other side.

Jordan watched her best friend—a girl more like a sister to her than her own two sisters by blood, young ladies who would most likely not even bother being in attendance at the evening's festivities—warily.

Clearing her throat, Catrina brushed her hands down her skirts, rearranging them so the pleats lay perfectly.

Jordan stood. "One day someone will pick up whatever you hurl and throw it back at you," she warned, briefly crouching to snatch up the discarded brush. She set it down on the tabletop and tugged the last strands of hair free from the brush's bristles, pressing the hair into the hole atop the small sterling box on her vanity.

"If someone *dared*," Catrina said with a huff, "then they would glimpse the true fire of my nature."

Jordan returned the brush to the silver tray holding her tortoiseshell comb and sat again, turning on the bench to better examine her face in the newest of two freestanding mirrors.

Catrina had once remarked that a beautiful lady could never have too many mirrors.

So Jordan had asked for a second mirror.

And a third.

Catrina had quickly pointed out she herself had seven— imported from Germany, no less!—arranged about her room so she might examine herself from every viewable angle before going out. Such things were necessary when one was of Hollindale rank.

But Jordan need not worry about examining herself so fiercely, not when she had a friend like Catrina. "And where are your fine parents on the night of my seventeenth birthday?" Jordan asked. "Still abroad on diplomatic assignment?"

"Still, yet, and always," Catrina said. "I would miss them sorely except most days I barely even remember what they look like."

"Is your uncle at least in attendance?"

"As much in attendance as a drunken letch can be . . ." Catrina stifled a sigh and picked a ribbon off the tray. "I should not complain. It is through their absence and generous allowance that I have the freedoms I do." She twirled the ribbon between her thumb and forefinger. "You look lovely," she said, tucking it into Jordan's dark tresses so it coiled down by the top of her ear and bounced. "Oh. Oh dear."

"What is it?" Jordan bent closer to the mirror.

Catrina frowned at her reflection, pondering. "Nothing really . . ."

Jordan's eyes widened as she viewed herself as critically as she could. Her nose was too broad, but that hadn't changed. Her eyes were set slightly wider apart than perfection dictated, but that, too, was nothing new. She ticked off her list of flaws: eyelashes too short, lips too thin and long and falling far too readily into an *easy smile*, ears a bit too obvious, freckles marring the bridge of her nose because she was occasionally slow to put on a bonnet or hat . . . But these were her standard imperfections. "I do not see it—what is the problem?"

"Never fear, I will remedy the offense," Catrina volunteered. She tugged out the single drawer in the vanity and found a tool she had demanded Jordan could not be without.

Tweezers.

Her hand darting out serpent-quick, she yanked a single hair from Jordan's eyebrow and stood victorious while her friend hissed in surprise.

"Ouch! You are a fiend of the highest order," Jordan declared.

"But you are far more lovely for my cruelty. *Nearly* perfect."

"I will never be perfect," Jordan mumbled.

"Perfection, like beauty, must be worked at in order to be obtained. You do not work as hard as you should. Hands?"

Catrina's inspection of Jordan continued. Her nails needed filing and however did she manage to get dirt up beneath them? Her face required a bit of powder to smooth out her troublesome complexion, but she also required a bit of Lady Salvia's Wonder Salve to relax a faint line appearing in her brow. After much primping and a hefty dose of criticism Jordan was far closer to retiring for the evening than greeting guests. But as harsh as Catrina's attentions might sometimes be, they were still attentions and invaluable in that way at least.

Even a fine house on the Hill could be lonely if no one bothered paying attention to you. And Jordan's father was a very important member of the Council, only having time to pay attention to politics. And Jordan's mother only paid attention to Jordan's father.

So Jordan was fortunate to have Catrina.

"Now, wherever is the dress I sent you?" Catrina asked. "I was hoping you liked it enough—"

"Oh—it's quite beautiful—"

"But not lovely enough to wear tonight? For such a special occasion?"

"No—that's not it. It's just . . ." She glanced down at her hands. "It's too much, Catrina. It is far too grand a gift to accept."

"Too grand a gift to accept? From one friend to another?"

Catrina shook her head, her pinned-up curls a mass of trembling gold corkscrews. "How long have we been friends, Jordan?"

"Years."

"I seem to recall it being *twelve* years. And who introduced you to Rowen?"

"Well, *you* did . . ."

"And you two have—well, done whatever it is you call this relationship of yours for how many years?"

"Three."

"So I call that equivalent to fifteen years. There is almost no gift too grand for a friend of fifteen years." She tipped her chin up imperiously and gave a sniff of disappointment.

"Well, I suppose . . ."

"You *will* wear it, then?"

"Yes. Yes, of course."

"Excellent. I had it made special for you by Modiste du Monde."

"That shop on Second Street by Elfreth's Alley, run by that odd little seamstress?"

"Odd and a bit churlish," Catrina admitted, "but a very talented *mantua maker*. Where is the box, Jordan? It *is* still in the box, is it not?"

Jordan blushed.

"Precisely as I feared. How well I know you. Where is it?"

Jordan threw her hands into the air. "However should I know? It is wherever servants put such things."

"You do not know where your things are kept?"

"Must I? Servants dress and undress me, bathe me and brush my hair. It is a wonder I know anything, they do so much for me."

"I see." Catrina reached out and yanked one of Jordan's

curls so she yelped. "You are spoiled as badly as month-old milk!"

In a sudden show of spark, Jordan said, "And yet there are several young men interested in having a taste of me."

"Oh! You naughty little beast!" Catrina laughed. "Well, I expect the dress to be in here . . ." She strode to the large armoire and pulled open its two doors. Its interior sported a row of pegs on which hung an assortment of skirts, blouses, and dresses that would not do well in the drawers along its bottom. On the armoire's floor was a paper box. Catrina scooped it up.

"Well, at least the string is off it," she muttered, turning to face Jordan again. In three very unladylike strides she was before her best friend removing the box's lid to reveal the delicate dress sparkling within. With a quick move she dropped the box and, grabbing the dress by its shoulders, pulled it free of the tissue paper and gave it a good shake. "It is amazing, is it not?"

"It is," Jordan agreed. "Quite truly."

"Well then. But perhaps . . ."

"Perhaps what?" Jordan asked, a hesitant finger tracing the thick flounce of lace trimming each of the sleeves' wrists. "Do you now think me not deserving of this dress and all the attentions it might bring me?" Jordan stood and Catrina laid the new dress across the bench and set about undoing the back of the dress Jordan already wore. Each hook was separated from each matching eye as her corset was revealed to the warm evening air inch after inch. When it was opened to her hips Jordan tugged on the shoulders and sleeves, loosening the dress's bodice so she could peel free of it.

The gown puddled at her feet, gossamer and silk taffeta, ruffles and ribbons, and Jordan carefully stepped out of it to stand before Catrina in only her petticoats, stays, stockings, shoes, and chemise.

The dress at her feet was wonderful, but it was most definitely last year's style, whereas Catrina's gift was as fresh as fashion got in the New World.

The bell in the main square's bell tower sounded, echoing out one deep and penetrating peal, and Catrina rested a steadying hand on the dressing table, confessing, "I lost track of time."

"It seems a bit inconsistent recently," Jordan agreed, nodding.

The lanterns in Jordan's bedchamber dimmed, fading to pinpricks of white, and the girls closed their eyes against the Pulse's coming flare. The sky stretching beyond Jordan's balcony window splintered as a hundred fingers of lightning stabbed along the Spokes from the central Hub, screeching across the lower atmosphere to find reaching metal rods that topped each ranking family's slate roof.

Houses hummed, power drumming through narrow wires and refreshing the crystals in lanterns, wall sconces, and chandeliers until there sounded an audible sizzle and Jordan's room blossomed stark white as the Pulse recharged all the lights in the connected city.

The Pulse retreated, the glare ebbing back to its normal cheerful warmth, recharged for another few hours.

"Why do you think that is?" Jordan asked, her voice soft.

"What? The Pulse?"

"No . . . the inconsistency. If the Pulse is powered by the Weather Witch at the Hub, why . . . ?"

"Perhaps that Witch is dying," Catrina said, picking up the new dress.

Jordan blinked. "Perhaps . . ."

Matter-of-factly, Catrina said, "They do that, you know. Die."

Jordan blanched. "You say it so coolly. As if their lives mean little."

Catrina pulled back, examining her friend's face carefully. "You're Fifth of the Nine. Witches are unranked."

"Yes, but they . . ."

". . . are Weather Witches. They provide a service. They make sure goods are delivered. My shoes? Brought on an airship Conducted by a Weather Witch. Your perfume? The same. They are trained up *Made*, and taken care of. They live their lives so we may live ours the way we deserve. Because, you know, Jordan, we always get what it is that we deserve."

"Like this gown?"

"Yes, like a gown, a handsome *beau* for a beautiful belle . . ."

"You deserve all that," Jordan agreed. "Where is your handsome *beau*?"

Catrina moved aside, her lips puckered. "I have my eye on someone. And yes. We do get what we deserve if we take the steps needed to obtain it. Such things require work, Jordan. Thought and planning. Careful consideration."

Jordan slipped into the gown—all satin, silk, and splendor. She swayed, helping settle the fabric over her petticoats. "And you believe I deserve every attention this amazing dress will fetch me?"

"Most certainly so."

Jordan did a little spin before her mirrors, admiring the way the sleeves fluttered and the golden fabric lay against her skin in a neckline cut to dazzle Rowen.

Her hand flew to her chest. Dazzling Rowen was not necessarily the best strategy.

"What are you doing, you silly goose?" Catrina asked, pulling Jordan's hand away.

"I—*Rowen* . . ."

"What about you and Rowen?" Catrina's tone sharpened, her eyes narrowing the faintest bit. "You two aren't having trouble again, are you?"

"No, I mean . . . I don't know. I think he's going to . . . He said he has a special surprise for me tonight."

Her eyes still thin, Catrina whispered, "Surprises can be good."

"I think he's going to ask for my promise."

"Oh." Something in Catrina's features tightened. "Well, isn't it about time?"

Jordan's nose crinkled. "I'm not certain . . ."

"You're not certain about *what*?"

"What if he's not the right one for me? I mean, should I not know if Rowen Burchette is meant to be mine and I his? Should it not be as Shakespeare wrote—with 'sweet pangs—Unstaid and skittish in all motions else, Save in the constant image of the creature, That is belov'd'?"

"You feel no pangs?"

"No. Not a pang nor a twinge."

"And no skittishness . . . no sensation of being off balance?"

"No."

One of Catrina's slender eyebrows arched. "You are full of doubt, poor little dear." Her lips twisted but her eyes sparked. "Are you afraid he might ask for your promise in an effort to climb rank?" Catrina's eyes popped wide open. "Not that Rowen would *ever* do something so callous—using you merely to raise his status."

"No," Jordan whispered, though the thought had occurred

to her shortly after they'd first met. Rowen was a beautiful boy and rank could never be far from mind when someone like him came into the life of someone like her. His family was a class below her own—still perfectly acceptable as marriage material, but not the step up the social ladder her parents wanted her to take.

Promising herself to Rowen was only a gain to him. And a misstep could be disastrous to rank—a badly planned marriage, a social faux pas, magick discovered in one's heritage . . . Many things could send a family hurtling toward ruin. But magick—it was the worst—it was a nearly inescapable taint and the only thing that did more than ruin a family's reputation. Magick was even worse than being a Catholic in Philadelphia.

Magick ruined *everything*.

"Then you must tell him *no* should he ask," Catrina said to their reflections. "And perhaps it is best if you do not draw undue attention to yourself. Step out of the dress."

"What? No. I am in the dress and wish to remain so." Jordan set her hands on her hips.

"It is so . . . *showy* . . ."

"It took so long for you to convince me to wear it and now you change your mind? I think *not*. Perhaps you are jealous?"

Catrina's eyes grew small again.

"I jest!" Jordan grinned. "This dress feels delightful," she whispered. "It feels like *destiny*."

Catrina peered at her from beneath long eyelashes. "You are right," she said, turning Jordan around so she could better pull taut the lacings that ran up her corset. "This dress is destined for you. Now suck in your breath," she urged.

Jordan obeyed, holding her breath so long as Catrina fumbled her fingers around the lacings that the room swam in her sight and her knees went soft. Catrina tugged the dress closed and smacked Jordan on the back, so she hauled in a fresh breath. Cinched so tight her stomach felt tucked in with her lungs and her décolletage defied more than gravity—it defied *reason,* she realized, glimpsing herself in the mirror—Jordan stumbled forward.

"Fantastic!" Catrina said with a little clap. "Now a final spin . . ."

Jordan obliged, stopping so fast her layered skirts swayed out like they'd continue without her. She laughed. "The skirts are so thick I don't imagine I'll fit through a single doorway."

"But it shapes you marvelously. You are a bell-shaped belle. You've always had nice breasts, but now it looks like you have hips, too, and a waist so distinguished a wasp would be envious." Catrina stepped around her, touching her hair to gather up little strands and let loose others. "Your necklace?"

Jordan handed her the black velvet band with its butterfly wing pendant glinting under glass.

"Perfection," Catrina announced. "Just . . ." She reached out, pinching Jordan's cheeks so fast Jordan had no chance to block her.

"Ouch! What—"

"A real blush is far better than any rouge the Old World might manufacture."

"Then get me to blush, not *bruise,*" Jordan suggested, pulling on her gloves and sliding on a few bracelets.

Frowning, Catrina yanked two bracelets off. "You mustn't look garish."

"Why must you change me," Jordan snapped before slapping a hand across her own mouth. "I apologize. That did not come out as I intended." She lowered her eyes. "It is merely . . . I am happy the way things are. I am content as one might be being imperfect and understanding I may never love Rowen— well—not in the way most want. I don't want anything to change. I am comfortable."

"Fine, fine. It is your party. If you want to be comfortable and wear too many bracelets to be seemly, be my guest. If you want to blush, perhaps Rowen will recite a limerick . . ."

Jordan clicked her tongue at her friend as they squeezed out the door together, skirts shifting awkwardly in too narrow a space. "Rowen would do no such thing—"

"Ha! You're blushing even now, you little liar. Here. Take your shawl."

Jordan settled the sheer shawl around her shoulders. It did nothing to hide her bosom.

"Stop frowning," Catrina demanded.

Down the hall they went, pausing at the top of the stairs to observe the crowd milling about in the hall and foyer below.

The walls were painted the rich sunset hue of Spanish Red and trimmed with bone-colored chair rails. Wainscoting lined the lower third of the foyer, so bright against the deep red it nearly glowed, and hiding every seam between ceiling and wall hung meticulously carved wooden molding the creamy color of whalebone ivory so perfect no scrimshander had dared yet carve his art into it.

It made for a powerful scene, filled with powerful people.

Jordan sighed. "You're right, of course. Rowen is always good for at least one questionable joke or song."

Catrina adjusted her skirts, and, scanning the crowd, announced to Jordan, "And there he is now. Speak of the devil."

Rowen stood spotlighted by the wall sconces just inside the foyer, the glow of their renewed stormcells stroking the angles of his jaw and turning his normally golden hair into something otherworldly.

Jordan's breath caught and silently she cursed her too-tight stays for the lack of air.

"Come now. We must make a grand entrance," Catrina urged. She took Jordan's hand and led her a few feet farther down the hall, to the item that first set the Astraea estate apart from all others on the Hill: the elevator.

When Jordan's grandfather's occasional limp had become pronounced one especially cold spring, he had hired a displaced craftsman with ties to Russian Empress Catherine and her remarkable shop of royal wonders. The eldest Astraea had the inventor re-create the lift originally designed for St. Petersburg's Winter Palace. That lift carried him to his chambers on the house's upper floor when his knees no longer managed the stunning marble stairs. That lift was the same glass and crystal-lined elevator, now refitted with brass and bronze and powered either by the ingenious screw mechanism invented for the frigid palace or by stormpower, that hung suspended like a giant diamond and carried his granddaughter and her closest friend to the guests gathered below.

The lift's door slid open and the crowd clapped as Jordan and Catrina stepped out.

Rowen bowed with a dramatic sweep of his arm and crossed the broad hall, his hand raised, awaiting hers.

But her father was the first to greet her, slipping between Rowen and herself and grasping her waist to swing her out of the young man's path. Lord Morgan Astraea pulled her near, setting his large, warm hands on either side of her face and saying, "Do nothing rash, daughter. Make no irreversible decisions on this eve." He looked long and hard at Rowen before returning his gaze to his daughter. "Your rank is all you have." He paused then, eyes scouring her face. "Your rank and your beauty."

She glanced down, gaze pinned to the careful stitching of his close-fitted frock coat. He was the picture of perfection with his broad shoulders, manicured mustache, and bold eyebrows. His jaw had the same strength as that more commonly found in Rowen's lower rank, but she thought him even more striking because of it. Here was the man who had dandled her on his knee when she was but a babe, the man who wanted nothing but the best for her.

The man warning her away from what Rowen might offer.

Jordan sighed. "I will make the appropriate choice if and when it is offered."

"That's my girl," Lord Astraea proclaimed, dropping his hands to her arms. "You will make a fine match. To a fine fellow." He leaned in and kissed her, his whiskers tickling her cheek so she smiled. "Now go, have a wondrous time!"

Rowen stood statue still, hand yet extended waiting for her.

With a swallow, she got her racing heart under control.

"My lady," Rowen whispered, his eyes snaring hers as he caught and raised her hand, his lips skimming the top of her knuckles. A tremble ran the length of her arm.

Her dress was too tight—it was obviously cutting off circulation to her arm and causing it to shake.

"Don't you look dashing," Catrina said, raising her hand for Rowen.

He released Jordan's hand long enough to pick up Catrina's, give it a cursory kiss, and drop it again to retrieve

Jordan's. "Come, my lady," he said, guiding her past his parents, her parents, and many of the gathering guests.

Catrina trailed behind them.

Everyone had arrived as expected. Although the Astraeas were Fifth of the Nine, their parties were touted in the papers as events to be seen at. The entertainment was always first-rate as no expense was spared.

If you weren't known for your rank, you had to be known for something. The Astraeas chose to be known for their hospitality.

Jordan, knowing her limitations, chose to be known for her beauty.

Such as it was.

Both seemed to work in the family's favor, lower-ranked guests curtseying to Jordan and Rowen as they passed by and offering hearty compliments on her hair, her visage, her grace . . . as higher-ranked guests inclined their heads ever so slightly and murmured quiet words of praise for what promised once again to be a memorable event.

"So how long have you been here?" Jordan asked, adjusting her arm to drape more comfortably across Rowen's. It was not hard to be comfortable with Rowen. He was well-shaped enough by the muscles he'd developed fencing, hunting, and horse riding but still a little soft from imbibing on his evenings spent socializing with his fellow gentlemen. Potentially tending toward a slight jowliness like his father, Rowen was still quite pleasant to look upon now.

Jordan tipped up her chin. Considering her well-proportioned features and appropriate bone structure, and respectable rank, she could choose nearly any man of like rank she wanted.

Still, here was Rowen. Already attained. Safe, bright

enough for pleasant conversation, and good enough looking to provide her with a suitable escort to events. And—she looked him up and down from beneath her eyelashes—the man knew how to dress. If nothing else could be said of Rowen, he at least cut a sharp figure in trousers, vest, and coat.

Catrina cleared her throat.

"Oh. Yes, Catrina made a gift of this dress for me."

Rowen raised his eyes to Catrina for a moment. "It's lovely. French lace and metallic thread from the Orient, yes?"

"You're so perceptive, Rowen."

His eyes narrowed. "Thank you, Catrina."

A seventeenth birthday celebration was one of the sweetest events of a young person's life, so sweets were showcased in quiet recognition of a person's escape from a most ominous possibility—that of being a Witch. And their caterer, an ex-slave named Thomas Dorsey, had proven to the Philadelphia elite that events he catered were quite sweet!

A fountain burbling with wine stood in the center of the main hall so guests coming in could quickly imbibe the intoxicant of choice. On a central table jumbles smelling of lemon were stacked beside a jiggling velvet cream molded in the shape of the old Independence Bell. Small chocolate custards topped with Caledonian cream peeked out of porcelain dishes, ladyfingers lined a silver tray, and dainty French cakes sporting tiny spots of champagne jelly vied for guests' attention among German puffs and gold and silver puddings aplenty.

Not far beyond the buffet of delicacies stood several young gentlemen (some Rowen's friends) who called on Jordan occasionally. Rowen guided her away from them, smirking. Also nearby were cages filled with all manner of exotic bird and beast, making for a colorful menagerie.

Closer, though, someone glimmered in the light beneath the main chandelier, and Jordan could not help but stare.

Catrina leaned in, whispering, "Well *that* is a bold fashion statement! Who does he think he is—a cast-off of some distant maharajah?" Tiny cut crystals wound round the young man's throat and wrists, creating twisting streams of softly glowing purple light, the shimmering ensemble finished off with a subtle (if one might call such a thing subtle) circlet of gold holding one last, larger crystal between his dramatic brows and raven-dark hair.

Jordan glanced from her best friend to the boy she had always adored—the boy everyone adored. The black sheep of his conservative family, Micah Vanmoer dressed in the clothes of a mourner and had poetic and musical leanings of a nearly riotous sort, and that was precisely what Jordan adored most about him. Micah was a younger (sober) Edgar Allan Poe.

While she was often mute, young Micah was an orator of the most expressive sort. If his new choice in adornment was yet another reflection of his personal taste, then more power to him.

Rowen watched her reaction before clearing his throat and patting the hand she rested on his arm. "Let us go greet our friend, Micah." He led her so it appeared it was not *she* who made the choice to support the boy, but Rowen.

Jordan smiled at Rowen, knowing somewhere her father let loose a sigh of disappointment.

Their conversation was brief and oddly stilted considering Micah's normal verbosity, and he apologized, saying, "I fell ill recently and still have not returned to rights." As the trio turned from the boy to mingle with others, Jordan noticed that if Micah glimmered with jewels then Lady

Liradean dazzled as if she were constructed only of light. It must be a growing trend, Jordan supposed, noting several other guests sporting jewels.

"She glows like an angel," Jordan murmured, her mouth close to Rowen's shoulder.

Catrina overheard and sniffled in contempt. "If she appears to you an angel, I daresay all Heaven is far gaudier than ever I expected."

Jordan's brows knitted together at the assessment. Rowen bent so his face was between the two girls' faces.

"Should not all angels sparkle beyond mortal means? If Jordan judges her to be angelic, I second the notion, for there is no lady here closer to heavenly than our own Jordan Astraea."

The words were a clear challenge to Catrina's attitude. And her social standing. Yet, uttered by Rowen, they were a challenge she chose not to accept.

Instead Catrina sniffled again, her gaze locking with Rowen's as she muttered, "Too true," an instant before looking away.

Men of the highest ranks mingled nearby, chattering on about things they felt important. Whereas they often frequented the city's coffeehouses for stimulants and stimulating conversations, on evenings of social occasions they brought their debates along, regardless of the beverage lubricating conversation.

"I do so wish they would overlap the timing of the Pulse. We are *the Athens of the Western world*," Lord Liradean said. "How truly difficult is it to be a Weather Witch? Are you not essentially *kept* by our own good government, your needs supplied for, food, clothes, and shelter never a worry? Considering such things you might assume they could overlap so that there is no stutter of power associated with the Pulse."

"True, true," his companions muttered, nodding.

"Have you seen a Weather Witch, Lord Liradean?" Micah's voice cut through the amiable conversation like a knife.

Lord Liradean sputtered into his wine glass. "I daresay *not*," he answered tersely. "It is not my place to deal with such a class of characters. Of this one can be certain—they are far better treated now than their forbears in Salem village."

"Do they even have a class," Micah wondered aloud, "or do we strip them of that as well as rank when they are declared a Witch?"

"You, lad, do nothing related to them either," Lord Liradean's voice rang out, "and nothing related to anything else of any true value to society from what I can tell."

Micah raised and lowered one shoulder in a lazy shrug. "I merely suggest, gentlemen, that we know of what we speak before speaking."

"And where would the fun be in that, Micah?" Rowen challenged. "I daresay"—he briefly adopted Liradean's tone and timbre—"that adopting such a suggestion as the rule would lead to the quietest parties upon the Hill." He winked at the blustering Liradean and dropped Jordan's hand to grab Micah and steer him from the muddle of older men in a joking fashion that left the group chuckling.

"You seem to be recovering your old self now, but you, dear Micah," Rowen whispered, "must needs learn who to encourage into thinking new thoughts and who has never had a thought in his head."

Micah nodded. "Are you then of the opinion that one cannot teach an old dog new tricks?"

"More strongly of the opinion that one should let sleeping dogs lie. Because that is all politicians do anyhow. Lie."

"True, true. Perhaps I should sit and relax. I feel a bit off," Micah mentioned. "Even my complexion's coloring seems off of late."

Rowen nodded while behind them Lord Liradean continued to bluster, "And that boy Rowen of yours, Burchette, when is he due for service?"

Rowen ducked his head at the question, retrieving Jordan's hand.

"Soon, soon," Burchette returned. "He is on the cusp."

"He'll make a fine enlisted man," Liradean assured. "With his jocular attitude he could keep them laughing as both ball and bullet fly."

"We hope for a bit more than that," Rowen heard his father confess.

Liradean's volume dropped but Rowen and the others still heard him. "Surely you do not expect him to be a leader of men . . ."

Burchette's response was slow in coming. "I simply expect him to be the best that he can be."

"Come," Rowen said. "Let us step away from these animals of a purely political variety and see what more noble beasts the menagerie has provided for viewing."

Jordan nodded, saying, "Oh . . . Rowen, remember . . ."

"I know, I know . . . You must be seen. Showcased." He winked at her. "People watch you no matter where you go, Jordan, you need not seek their attention so hungrily."

She pressed her lips together. "When attention is all you are good for . . . "

He stepped away from her suddenly, pulling her arm to spin her back into his side.

She laughed.

"You are good for far more than you give yourself credit."

"No. I am as useful as a single butterfly's wing." She touched the pendant hanging at her throat. "Beautiful to look upon and worth a comment here or there, but with not even the ability to take flight."

"Oh, do hush," Catrina said, closing the gap between them. "You have value, Jordan."

"How so?"

Catrina paused to consider as they walked past a gaggle of younger girls gossiping.

". . . old man Biddle's boy has fallen in love with a serving girl!"

"I saw them once from my window late at night as they were winding their way down the Hill together. She on a white horse, of all things!"

"Wherever were they off to?"

"I watched them go all the way to the water's edge!"

"Well. That will be a short-lived romance if they go on in such a carefree manner. And rightly so," the girl added, seeing they were being observed by the three friends. With a curtsy to Jordan and a wink at Rowen she said, "One should stick to one's own class and know well one's own place."

Remembering the girl was Sixth of the Nine (as was Rowen), this time it was Jordan who guided him away from the too obviously interested members of his same rank.

"I am not as clever as you," Jordan complained. "I cannot do more than simple arithmetic in my head. I am utterly beyond hope in all but the simplest card games—"

"They are not suitable pastimes for a lady of fine rank," Catrina scolded.

Rowen gave a bemused snort. "Then we must needs oc-

cupy our hours alone in other ways," he said, raising an eyebrow so that Catrina was quite thoroughly scandalized.

Jordan swatted at him.

"Hours alone?" Catrina squeaked. "*Unchaperoned?* You do
know that is the thing most certain to ruin a young lady's
reputation—other than witchery . . ."

"It was only the once," Jordan chided.

Rowen coughed.

Catrina was incensed.

"And for but a few hours . . ."

Catrina's eyes widened. "A few—"

"Why whatever might a young man and a young woman
do together in but a few hours?" Rowen asked drolly. "I cannot *possibly* imagine . . ."

Catrina sucked in a sharp breath. "I daresay you *can*
imagine, Rowen Albertus Burchette . . . oh! And you probably *have!*"

"Are we not instructed to use the gifts we have been provided by the Divine, Catrina?" Rowen asked, raising his eyes
to the ceiling and clasping his hands together in the most
perfectly pious of poses. "It just so happens I intend to use
well those things I have in a most impressive size. Like my
disproportionately large imagination. As well as other things
of"—he coughed—"*substantial* size that the good Lord saw fit
to gift me with."

Jordan thought the grin that twisted his lips was most as-
suredly cocky. She tore away from his arm to cover her
mouth with her hands, her eyes suddenly as disproportionately large in her head as the things of more than sufficient
size he alluded to. Her gaze strayed to his trousers and she
twirled away, blushing and coughing when she realized what
she was doing.

Rowen laughed so hard the sound startled the beasts in the menagerie, sending them screaming, screeching, and rattling their cages' bars. Jordan snatched Rowen's arm once more, peering around him at the assorted cages. Something with sharp teeth pressed its mouth between the bars, gnashing needlelike fangs in her direction.

"Oh! How awful!" Jordan whispered, tugging on Rowen's arm to maneuver him away from the menagerie. "Dangerous things should be kept under lock and key!"

"They are only little and surely not as frightening as the orangutan that inspired Poe—" But Rowen allowed himself to be led away by Jordan.

Jordan shook her head.

"You must be more careful with what you say in public, Rowen. People will talk . . ." Catrina scolded.

He shrugged. "Jordan craves attention."

She swatted at him again. "Not of *that* type. Women will be staring at you, wondering . . ."

"Do you think so?"

"Why yes, of course," Jordan said, thinking sometimes they were as different as their favorite candies: he as bold as the smoky-flavored Black Jack, and she as sweet and understated as Salem's lemon Gibraltar.

"Hmm. Well. You should know, Jordan, that I also crave attention from time to time," he admitted, his voice going lower, softer.

Jordan picked up the fan hanging at her hip and snapped it open. The gown was far warmer than she thought it would be.

"Rowen," Catrina warned.

Jordan turned to look at her friend. "Fetch us drinks, please?"

"What?" Catrina blinked. "Do I look the part of a servant?"

she asked, rolling her hand down before her to draw attention to the finely wrought gown she also wore.

"N-no," Jordan stammered, "but neither is there a waiter or butler here."

"You are the hostess," Catrina said. "Perhaps you should go and fetch drinks for Rowen and *my*self."

"I am the guest of honor," Jordan protested.

Catrina blinked again. "Fine. I will tote and carry." With a flick of her wrist she opened her fan and traipsed off toward the fountain, glancing over her shoulder but once.

"You are far too anxious, Jordan," Rowen whispered, his eyebrows lowered. He ran a soothing hand over her forearm and she rested her other hand atop his.

"I'm sorry. You know . . ."

He nodded. "I do. And you hide your nerves well from everyone but me. If they only knew that is why you act the way you do. People love you, Jordan. You are more popular than you know."

She glanced down at the floor but something about her brightened. "At least, adorning your arm I am well presented and better loved for people's love of *you*. You are so much better than me, Rowen."

He snorted. "Sixth of the Nine here."

"Does that truly matter?"

He looked startled. "Yes. I think it must. Our society is built around rank and order. Rank is the most important thing we have."

She stiffened, hearing something so closely akin to her father's justification for rejecting Rowen coming from Rowen's own lips.

"If certain things weren't in their place . . ." he continued.

"There'd be chaos."

He nodded.

"Spoken like a true military man."

A waiter carrying a tray full of hors d'oeuvres paused before them and Rowen took a fistful, popping them into his mouth and barely chewing between bites. "A truly *hungry* military man."

Jordan was far enough into their friendship that such moves no longer stunned her. "Rowen," she admonished softly as the servant drifted away.

Rowen blinked at her. "Did I take too many?"

She smiled. "Actually I half expected you to clear the entire tray. And lick the poor waiter's hand for crumbs." She winked at him and he straightened. "You've already been to the kitchens to see Cook, haven't you?"

He grinned, for a moment looking all of twelve. "You are stunning," he said, dragging her toward the broad French doors and onto the veranda that stretched along one side of the estate's back, hemming in the gardens and ending where the property dropped suddenly away.

They walked all the way to the end of it, Rowen striding like a man on a mission.

The Below spread out at the Hill's foot, buildings seemingly alive and creeping with flickering lights through the shadows the deepening evening threw.

Rowen interlaced his fingers with hers.

"This is—*improper*," she protested.

"Improper?" He arched an eyebrow. "You're afraid of what someone may say about being this close here—*now?*"

"We are—again—unchaperoned . . ."

"Exactly." He leaned in, his eyes closing, and she dodged away from his willing lips, neither of them aware of Catrina standing inside the distant doors and seeing all.

Rowen caught Jordan's wrist and drew her close, encircling her waist with his arms.

A breeze blew up from below, rattling the topiaried tree branches and bending them toward the raised veranda's floor. Green leaves snapped off and spiraled around the pair's feet as a storm built in the sky above.

"Come. Let's go back inside," Jordan said.

Rowen's eyebrows drew together. "What is wrong?"

"You said you had a surprise for me . . ."

The metallic threads in her dress sparked like lightning traveled their careful stitches, and the wind tugged at her hair, pulling free one of her many curling locks.

With quick hands, Rowen caught the rogue curl and held it a moment, running his thumb along its silky length before tucking it behind her ear. "Yes." He unfurled a smile. "I do have a surprise for you. Would you like it now or shall I draw you out more publicly for my presentation?" he asked, straightening from where he leaned against the veranda's banister.

"No, no . . ." She slipped her fingers free of his and clutched his arms, standing a good distance from the French doors and the crowd surely wondering where the party's hostess had disappeared to with her most regular gentleman caller.

He grinned. "Make up thy mind," he whispered. "Chaperoned or . . ." He skimmed her lips with his thumb. ". . . not?"

"Not. But only for a moment longer," she promised. "Rowen, you know I adore you."

His back went ramrod straight at her choice of words. "Yes."

"You are an absolutely amazing and talented man of fine breeding and nearly noble rank. Socially speaking we would make a fine pair, but . . ."

"I'm sorry. Are you . . ." His eyes searched her face, confusion plain. "Are you telling me we are . . . finished?"

She sighed. "Not so much finished as—"

He crossed his arms over his chest and did his best to peer down his nose at her although she was dressed in the high-heeled shoes the wealthy deemed fashionable for such parties. "It's your seventeenth birthday and you're ending things with me."

"No. No. Wait!" She reached for him, grasping at his arm. She could not tug it free.

His chin tipped up in defiance, he watched her struggle with a coolness in his gaze she had never seen before.

"Rowen, I'm confused," she apologized, wrapping her arms around him and leaning her head on his chest. His stance softened, his arms sliding out from between them to wrap her up once more. "I was so worried you'd ask for my promise and that I wouldn't be able to give it to you with everyone watching and . . ."

"Is that all this is?" he asked into the top of her head. "You were in a panic because you thought . . ." His arms tightened around her. "Be brave, sweetheart. I'd never embarrass you that way—no matter how much I tease," he promised. "I do have a surprise for you, but it has nothing to do with asking for your promise. Not just yet." He cocked his head. "I've brought you a fine gift . . ."

"Wait." She searched his face. "So we are well?"

"Yes, darling girl, we are well. Now for your gift—"

The French doors swung open and the party burst onto the veranda, Catrina and Thomas Dorsey himself at its head, bearing drinks. "You cannot monopolize the party's guest of honor for the entire event," she scolded Rowen, handing them both a cup. "Things are about to become quite hot," she promised, waving her hand so the move ended with her pointing back the way they had come. The ruby on her ring finger flashed.

Chapter Three

Dame Fortune is a fickle gipsy,
And always blind, and often tipsy;
Sometimes for years and years together,
She'll bless you with the sunniest weather . . .
—WINTHROP MACKWORTH PRAED

Philadelphia

Entertainers streamed onto the porch, men and women in parti-colored outfits that clung to their forms in all the most interesting places. It was at once scandalous and delightful—and utterly foreign. Rowen grinned, leaning back against the porch's railing and taking Jordan with him.

A man wearing a hat that shadowed his eyes with fat fabric tendrils topped by bells stretched into a bow so low only the most supple of dancers might do it. "My lords and my ladies, most gracious hosts and hostesses," he said in an accent Jordan had only heard the day Rowen dragged her down to the Cutter docks to watch the men make sails and the ships go out, "tonight we will delight and astound you by setting your senses *afire*." He tugged a lit torch out from behind him and the crowd jumped back.

"I assure you, though, that what we do here may look like

magick, but it is merely science, spit, and spark!" He tossed the torch high into the air and tore his strange hat off, throwing it into Jordan's astonished hands as another costumed performer tossed a second torch his way. Both torches flew into the air and tumbled down, were caught and tossed back up as another was thrown into the fray, so quickly three fiery torches flew before the gasping crowd.

Two of his compatriots jumped in with three more torches, three men juggling nine torches, each in turn thrown to the man in the middle, who then hurled them high, caught them, and spun them back to his friends. He tossed all but one of them away, the other performers extinguishing each in turn. With a fluid movement their leader caught the final torch, and, taking a swig of something from a flask that appeared in his hand, he rolled the lit torch along his open mouth.

The crowd screamed and Jordan pressed the hat close to her stomach, eyes wide.

Flame danced across his tongue and he snapped his mouth shut, snuffing the fire before taking another swig of the clear stuff in the metal flask.

He bent, leaning so far back his hair nearly brushed the veranda's floor. He brought the flaming torch close enough to his lips he might have kissed it . . . but instead he sprayed liquid past its flaming head, and the crowd fell back, shrieking, as he breathed fire.

Swinging the torch, he passed it off to be snuffed and the screaming became wild clapping. With a gracious bow he grabbed his gear and he and his cohorts dodged away.

"Stunning," Rowen murmured.

Jordan looked up at him. "It was a brilliant display."

"I was referring to *you*," he corrected.

She rolled her eyes.

His gaze drifted from her eyes to the place on the veranda occupied by a well-dressed man sporting a leather mask in the form of a fox's face. At his side stood an attractive female assistant in a fine silk robe decorated with rolling waves. Her hair was long, straight, and as dark as ebony and her eyes were slanted in a distinctly Oriental style.

Between them rested a large and colorfully painted wooden trunk.

"So what is this, do you suppose?" Jordan asked, motioning to the man and woman. The crowd had quieted, seeming to wonder the same thing.

"Good evening, friends. I am the Wandering Wallace," the man said, his arms sweeping wide to encompass the entire crowd as if they were all personally invited by him. "Tonight I will entertain you and challenge your senses and powers of observation with tricks that will both astonish and amuse."

There was no response from the crowd. They withheld judgment, cautiously waiting. He looked suspiciously like something one would have seen before taking the boat to the New World. With his trunk painted brightly with stars and strange symbols and his beautiful assistant with her foreign features, he nearly stank of something they knew better than to become entangled with.

Magick.

"Let me first assure you that the tricks I perform tonight to entertain such fine folks as yourselves include no magick at all. Nothing will truly disappear and nothing will actually manifest. These things are but simple illusions brought to you as the result of years of training in sleight of hand. Can I make it appear that something has manifested out of thin air . . . ?" He slid his hand across the empty space before them and opened it, a ball popping into existence between his finger and thumb.

A few ladies in the crowd jumped back and a few men bristled. Some even turned their faces to the rumbling sky overhead, disapproval obvious. "Yes, yes. But wait," he instructed. "When I slow the move down . . ." He turned his back for a mere moment before starting all over again, hand flat and before them. ". . . and loosen my fingers . . ."

The same ladies who had gasped before gasped again, but this time in delight, as his fingers parted and they glimpsed something the color of the ball between them moments before he slipped it sloppily into his palm and showed them how it appeared in its final position. "I use no magick in my performances, merely well-practiced sleight of hand."

The crowd clapped.

"But, as the hand is quicker than the eye"—with a flash of movement he launched three doves into the air and people shrieked—"I think I might yet be of some entertainment value."

Rowen brought Jordan a little closer, getting comfortable for the show.

He grunted when something jabbed his ribs. "Oh." Jordan's mother withdrew her closed fan from his side and flicked it open before her face, leaving only her glaring green eyes visible.

Rowen corrected his slouched position.

She raised both her eyebrows and fluttered her fan slightly.

Rowen scooted Jordan a little away from him.

With a wink that made Rowen straighten further, Lady Astraea stepped back into the crowd.

"Some simple trickery now—my lady." He beckoned to

Serafina duBois. "You seem a clever lass. Might you assist me?"

Serafina nodded, flouncing her way to the illusionist.

Jordan stiffened, watching her. Of all the girls in Jordan's circle of friends it was readily agreed that Serafina was the prettiest. With her rosebud mouth, petite nose that turned up perfectly at its tip, and a head full of soft golden curls, she looked as angelic as her namesake. It could not be denied that Serafina was lovely to look upon. But clever? Hardly. This was the girl who had drunk ink, mistaking it for tea. If the illusionist could make Serafina appear clever it just might be the finest illusion ever witnessed.

Serafina dipped a little curtsy to the crowd and all the young men clapped.

Even Rowen.

Jordan's too-wide lips pressed together in a frown.

Catrina tapped her own forehead lightly, her gaze drifting to Jordan, who forced herself to relax and erase the faint crease of worry that would eventually deepen into a wrinkle. Sighing, she focused on Serafina.

The illusionist's assistant pulled a piece of paper from the decorated trunk, passing it to her master with a flourish. It was the same stuff used to wrap packages at Wilkinson's. Nondescript, brown, and of a sturdy weight. Rectangular in its proportions. Another flourish and scissors were handed to the illusionist, their handles and body black except for the silver sheen of the blades themselves.

"I shall now issue a challenge," the Wandering Wallace declared. "If anyone here can cut a perfectly proportional five-pointed star from this paper without drawing a single line and using these scissors, I shall allow him to choose any item from my trunk of tricks."

His assistant gasped an obviously rehearsed response, her slanted eyes widening and her small mouth drawing into a perfect o in a parody of shock.

No one had successfully taken the illusionist's challenge.

But, wine flowing freely and Rowen's friends in attendance, it was only a moment before the challenge was accepted.

And lost.

Another accepted, another piece of paper was butchered, and another young man returned to the crowd perplexed.

They grew still and the illusionist grinned, waving another piece of paper, taunting them. "Is there no other taker? No other among you to take my challenge?"

"It cannot be done," a disillusioned member of the aristocracy declared. "A perfectly proportioned star is too difficult a shape to construct without the aid of proper tools and appropriate mathematics."

"That is nearly precisely the argument our country's founding fathers used against dear sweet Betsy Ross when she suggested five-pointed stars to adorn our nation's flag! But Mrs. Ross was an enterprising soul and, in the same spirit, with my help, the good lady—"

"Serafina," she volunteered.

"The good lady Serafina," he said, "will help me show not only that it can be done, but it can be done with only a single cut of the scissors!"

Skepticism flooded the crowd in barely audible gasps as the Wandering Wallace took one last piece of paper, waving it before the crowd. He handed it to Serafina.

"Now we shall fold this paper. Here," he instructed, adjusting Serafina's fingers on the paper. "And here. Now unfold . . . Now fold here . . . And here and here . . . Here, unfold. Here. Unfold. And cut from here to there!"

Serafina did each thing as he prescribed and with a hiss of the scissors and a moment of unfolding, the promised star was produced. Everyone clapped, and Serafina curtsied once more and danced her way over to Jordan. "For the true star of the evening," she said, handing over her paper prize.

Jordan smiled, finding Serafina quite clever indeed. Gently, Jordan refolded the star and slid it up her sleeve.

The illusionist, finishing some card tricks and a few more bits of bird work, glanced at Rowen, and cleared his throat.

Rowen leaned over Jordan, whispering, "Back in a moment."

She tilted her head and watched as he strode out of the crowd and stood front and center with the illusionist.

Lightning crackled in the clouds overhead.

Rowen cast a wary look at the sky but grinned for the crowd. "I have studied with the Wandering Wallace and have learned a few things from him, but not, of course, the face of the man beneath the mask. Some things, it seems, are to remain secrets—but not all," he said. "And this evening, as a tribute to the lady who has me bewitched—"

The crowd gasped.

Micah laughed at them, saying, "He speaks figuratively, not literally. Had he truly been bewitched he would be unable to talk about it. Everyone knows that."

Rowen smiled, adding, "She has bewitched my imagination, and so I shall share with you a special trick." He motioned to Jordan. "Please step forward."

Lowering her head, she did so.

Rowen threw a hand out to her and, as she took it, he proclaimed, "My lovely assistant!"

The crowd clapped and Jordan raised her head, straightened her spine, and put her shoulders back.

"I said I had a surprise for you."

"Rowen." Her eyes darted to the crowd and back. "Not here . . ."

"Have a little faith," he said, the words tight. He grinned at the crowd, all showman, and said, "That is a lovely hairdo. Do you fine people not agree?" Clapping answered him. Rowen stepped up beside her to seemingly examine her hair. "Elegant. Wrapped very tightly and yet with so much body to it . . . Colorful ribbons weaved in . . ." He reached up and tugged one slightly, his grin tilting when the ribbon bounced. "But what's this? One seems different . . ." He turned her so one side faced the crowd and his hand closed gently around one ribbon and then he yanked his hand back, trailing a long set of colorful handkerchiefs after it.

Jordan's hands flew to her mouth and the crowd rioted with laughter.

"Look at you," Rowen mused, "you're so beautiful there's beauty wrapped up inside you that no one has glimpsed until now." He looked away from her then, addressing the crowd once more. "What would a young lady want on her seventeenth birthday but . . ." He drew the last word out so it became the longest single syllable ever uttered as he bowed before her and, on the ascent, produced a bouquet of ". . . flowers."

Jordan clutched them to her and blushed.

"And, as I would not dream of doing anything but sharing such a delightful lady with all of her friends and family . . ." He towed her forward gently, lowering his face so his lips came level with her ear. "Be brave, Jordan," he whispered, and swallowing, she held tight to the smile smeared across her face for the good of the guests. The crowd parted for her and, taking her hand, Rowen led them back inside, pausing in the main hall where three waiters held a large silver platter on which balanced a cake in three dramatic levels.

Seventeen candles burned in a fiery ring around the cake's top tier and the waiters lowered it with aching care so the entire thing balanced just before Jordan's smiling lips.

"A wish, a wish!" the crowd chanted.

Jordan blushed and nodded. She turned from the cake, clutching Rowen's hands, closed her eyes and screwed her face up in her most thoughtful look before whipping around and blowing the candles out with a puff of breath that left her dizzy.

The guests burst into cheers and raucous clapping.

But everyone fell silent when the Wardens marched in.

Heavy boots slapped out an intimidating rhythm on the marble floor, drowning out every sound except the rush of blood filling people's ears at sight of the Wardens invading their festivities.

Tall, broad, and dressed in hip-length charcoal-colored cloaks and sleek trousers tailored to slide over black boots, the Wardens were the most elite of guards. Unshakable, undaunted, and irreversibly silenced by a mysterious event rumored to be called "Lightning's Kiss," their faces were carved with crimson fern-shaped tattoos recalling their arcane path to power.

Behind the Wardens something else whispered with movement, things so tall they were more *long* than tall, more *sleek* than slender, and a more accurate description than saying that they *walked* would have been to say that they glided, they drifted, they *haunted* the space between the Wardens and the walls.

Until the Wardens parted and, black as a heartless sea, the Wraiths flowed forward.

Wearing relentless black, from their strange soft boots and long frock coats to their tall crowned top hats shrouded with mourner's black, the Wraiths cut imposing figures against the backdrop of the crimson-and-bone hall. Still as stone they stood, faceless beneath the dark veils hanging along their hats' brims; even their hands were robed in gloves the color of a moonless sky.

Deaf as doorstops, they were a sharp contrast to the Wardens. To many it seemed all they had in common was witchery. And the power of flight.

Everyone in the hall stood mute, their eyes fixed.

Everyone except Morgan Astraea—the man whose youngest daughter's extravagant birthday party was being ruined.

"What is the meaning of this?" Jordan's father stormed, his face purpling as a vein rose by his hairline.

The Ring shifted, the Wardens took one stomping step to the side, and Astraea immediately recognized the Councilman. Though a range of emotions slid across his face in rapid succession, surprise was not among them. But *rage*? It settled on his features and he thrust a pointing finger toward the foyer. "We shall speak. There."

The Councilman nodded, following old Morgan Astraea, the Wardens marching behind, and after the Wardens drifted the Wraiths, every piece of them swallowed up in fabric and unimaginable. The crowd hissed, seeing one last person in their ranks.

A man so thin he seemed nearly skeletal, ceremonial robes hanging off him like draperies from a pole, slunk in amongst the Wardens, a slender cane wrapped tight in his gnarled hand, his other hand sheathed in metal—a contraption more mechanism than man. For a moment he turned, icy eyes scanning the crowd.

They gasped again. Although most had never seen one before, all the party's attendees knew him by his manner as much as his clothing.

Tales of the Testers were not easily forgotten.

Holgate

After he'd returned to the library adjoining his laboratory and withdrawn the journal he kept hidden in the false-bottom drawer, he tucked it into his belt, then stoppered his ink bottle, picked up his pen, and laid them both into his travel bag. The bag had served his father well as a rifleman's pouch, but as Bran benefited from the lessons his father had imparted as the Maker before him, so he also benefited from the scant remainders of the dangerous wartime exploits that helped make his father's name immortal.

Taking a lantern from off his wall he walked to the Tanks more slowly now, no need to rush as the dead certainly didn't.

With barely a moment's hesitation, Bran slipped his arms around the child and carried her out of the compound, beyond the unassuming door beside the main gate, and down to the small slope where the dead were buried. She felt lighter in his arms than he'd expected, like something had left her— some heaviness connected to life. He set her on the grassy ground and, raising the lantern that now shown with a steady white light, looked around for a shovel.

Briefly.

Burying the dead was not his job.

But filling her spot in the Tanks *was* and as suddenly as the request for a Tester and a Ring of Wraiths had come into Holgate, he knew at least one Tank wouldn't remain vacant long.

He pulled the journal out, sat down only a few feet from the body, and began to write.

The girl in Tank 5 has expired under strange circumstances. She was not in my care for long, showed strong potential and was most easily persuaded to work when introduced to the cat. Death was not fever-induced and yet she said the strangest thing and seemed quite convinced of the reality of her words. "They are coming and there is naught to be done for it." It causes me to speculate on the cause of her untimely death. She was not broken to the point of d

The pen stilled in his grip, a breeze rallying and lifting off the water. It moved like a specter up the slope, slinking around the dead girl's body and ruffling her dirty hair before stroking its cold, damp touch across the Maker's face and dissipating.

He squinted at the corpse. Had she stirred? Setting aside his journal and pen he leaned across her, holding the lantern to her face. No breath moved within her. But the breeze came back, this time running icy fingers through his hair and stroking the back of his neck so its every hair stood straight up. Something slipped along his ears, chilling even the insides of them with what sounded distinctly like words. "Murrrrderrr." He shuddered, tilting his head. "Murrrderr," the wind sang again. Then something new followed and, heart racing, he listened. "They commmmme," the wind hummed. He rubbed his ears. "Soooooonnnn they commmmme . . ." He pawed frantically at his ears and stood, the journal and pen falling into the grass, his gaze wary on the water.

Last summer's cattails waved in the wind, whistling an eerie tune. Surely that was all it had been—the wind through the rushes. Still, he gathered his things and gave one last glance to the body before walking much faster to the compound than he'd walked on his way out.

His returning speed was not because he felt lighter being relieved of the burden of the body. It was rather because the wind chased him like a hound snapping at his heels.

Philadelphia

Pushing his way through the astonished party's crowd, old Morgan Astraea addressed the uninvited men who now stood in his foyer. "What precisely are you doing here?"

Jordan's mother stroked a careful hand down his back as they huddled as near the door as he could maneuver them.

"We've received reports of a potential Conductor being in your household."

"Why would you presume a Witch is here?"

Thunder cracked so loud the huge house rattled.

Morgan Astraea nodded. "An unpredicted storm would raise questions, I suppose." He groaned. "You discovered one just two years past—and we were as surprised as you," Morgan assured. "We need no taint nor the blasphemy of magick in this household," he assured. "Root the devil out!"

The Councilman smiled, signaling the Tester with a simple sweep of his fingers. "Signal the servants," he suggested. "Such trouble is nearly always breeding in their ranks."

The servants were gathered and although Rowen did a tremendous job keeping most of the guests focused on him—one of his more stellar abilities—Jordan could not help but slip from his grasp and make her way toward the staff that waited for the Tester's verdict.

Behind her Rowen paused in the midst of telling some joke and she sensed the crowd breaking apart, watching her and watching him equally. Footsteps followed her—his boots covering the distance quickly, Catrina's heels clopping in a harried fashion.

Jordan stood at the edge of the circle of Wraiths, Wardens, and servants, watching the Tester's eyes rove in a strange, unceasing manner. Two years ago the Councilman had come and taken Marisca, Cook's daughter. There was no Tester needed. And, much as her parents had adored her, no one dared hide her from the Council's eyes. The punishment for Harboring was swift and sure.

They all heard tales of the posses that rode, rooting out anyone using magick or displaying magickal abilities. This was the New World. A world free of the taint and trouble magick brought.

A world unlike the one across the Western Ocean where magick tore dynasties apart and brought wars of epic proportions to crush commoners and nobles alike. Everyone knew the most dangerous of the magickers were Weather Witches. Well, nearly the most dangerous . . .

But all people, young and old, rich and poor, ranked and Witches, knew tales of Galeyn the Weather Witch and the way, at only eight, she saved an entire ship of colonists from a vicious Merrow attack. Compared to the multitude of Weather Witches, other magickers seemed only rumors.

The Tester's eyes found hers and held them until no one else in the room dared speak, dared move, dared breathe . . .

His hand reached out, long and thin with fingers that curled more than bent, turned palm up, and slowly slid in the air before them like a hunting hound scenting the air.

Someone whispered, "He is preparing for the Touch Test," and another voice behind her agreed, "Said to be as *simple as Salem* . . ."

His hand paused a moment, fingers twitching like they'd been tickled by some invisible feather . . . then his hand darted out, fast and sure.

Jordan jumped when he grabbed her arm and sparks flew between them, the scent of something in the air burning, and he yanked her forward with a rudeness no one would ever show a member of the Fifth of the Nine.

"No," she yelped.

Most were no longer seeing her because they all—the best of the higher ranks of the Nine—watched as Morgan Astraea's face crumpled and fell, realizing what it meant that his daughter was a Weather Witch. That magick ran in *her* blood and not his wife's.

And certainly not in his own.

"No . . ." Lady Astraea whispered, her face twisting in a mirror of his agony. "No. It cannot be," she protested. "He is wrong!" Her voice rose as she took a sudden step forward. "No," she said again, regaining control of her voice. "The Tester is wrong. There is no chance that she is what he claims. My blood is without taint and Lord Morgan Astraea's blood is without taint and . . ." She raised her head, tipping her chin up nobly, but her hands trembled at the unspoken accusation. "It is utterly impossible due to my spotless reputation."

Lord Astraea was still frozen, pain etched deep in his features, when the Councilman puffed out his chest and announced to the assembled crowd, "The Tester is beyond reproach. But it appears her ladyship is not."

"No," Lady Astraea protested. "I would *never* . . ."

But her lord turned away, his face drawn and his attention fixed to a glowing wall sconce by the doors, and the Tester shoved Jordan into the waiting hands of a Warden.

The Wardens spread out, snapping the steel-ringed butts of their heavy-handled canes on the marble floor so the sound rang through the hall. The servants stepped back, eyes lowered—thankful it was not one among their number this time.

Standing in the foyer, the Warden's grip tight on her, Jordan swallowed hard. The carefully framed paper cuttings of the previous Astraea family members' profiles all seemed to be pointing at her, their sightless silhouettes weighing her. Her grandmother, quite the debutante of her time, peered down her aquiline nose at her grandchild while Great-grandmother Silicia tipped her head heavenward as if to avoid the distressing scene being playing out beside her picture. Jordan even imagined that the silhouettes of her sisters (who seldom cared a whit for her) looked away, aware Jordan's profile would never hang beside theirs.

Wringing her hands, Lady Astraea repeated a single word: "No." It ran from her mouth so fast and smooth, over and over again so that soon it was just a trilling noise somewhere between a choke and a cry.

Jordan's gaze latched onto her mother and she swallowed

hard, uttering the one word that held all her emotion in its two soft syllables. "Mother?"

"No," Lady Astraea snapped, head shaking, the word firm. "No. You are mine and you are *his*. Have faith, Jordan. The truth will out," Lady Astraea insisted. Her eyes were wide, wild, and she took an unsteady step forward. "Test her."

The Tester's head jerked up, his eyes glinting at the challenge. "Test her?" he asked. His lips twisted into a grim smile. "Test your child? Here?"

"Test. Her."

Catrina and Rowen both stepped forward.

"Be brave, Jordan," Catrina said. "Yes. If you are so certain—test her. Before us all. Prove you are correct or leave this house."

Rowen's head lowered, but he caught Jordan's eyes.

It was the surest way to prove her innocence.

The Warden released her but when the Tester drew his blade, Jordan pulled back, "No" tumbling from her lips as well.

Catrina stomped forward and looked Jordan in the eyes.

So many eyes were on her, so many intense stares seeking her out she had no idea who to turn to. So she chose the one closest. Catrina. Her best friend. The same one who had introduced her to Rowen. The girl who was so much like her sister . . . Jordan swallowed again and nodded.

"I will hold your hand," Catrina offered. "It will only be a little cut—nothing that will mar your perfect skin for long," she assured. "Surely it will not leave her scarred, will it?"

The Tester said, "One can never tell."

Jordan trembled. All she had were her looks . . . and her rank.

The sky rumbled overhead and everyone jumped.

"But what harm is a small scar when it proves you're innocent?" Catrina said, so close to Jordan's face their noses nearly touched.

"Yes," Jordan agreed. "Yes. Hold my hand," she asked so gently the crowd stepped forward to hear. "Test me so my mother's good name might be restored."

Catrina clutched her hand and the Tester changed his position ever so slightly, the knife glimmering. Jordan closed her eyes and bit down on her lower lip, her fingers going white around Catrina's as the blade nipped her right forearm.

Sparks flew up from Jordan, Catrina fell back, her face contorted in horror, and above them all the heavens opened and dumped rain until there was no noise save the rush of water.

Catrina trembled, clutching at Rowen, and Jordan fell to her knees, sobbing the one word on everyone's lips—*No.*

The downpour stopped as fast as it had started and the brief silence that followed was somehow more deafening.

"The girl is seventeen, is she not?" the Tester asked.

Nods came from all around.

"The Astraea family is hereby found guilty of Harboring."

"Noooo!"

The Wraiths swooped in with a keening cry, and, grasping Jordan by her arms, lifted her to her feet once more. Although her shoes scraped the floor, for a moment she stood only by the Wraiths' will, her legs loose as rubber beneath her starched petticoats. Her eyes squeezed shut and tears trembled on her lashes, threatening to fall. But she drew in a ragged breath, found her feet, and forced her eyes open under the realization that this might be the last time she ever saw her home.

Her family.

Her friends.

Her Rowen.

"No!" Rowen shouted. "You cannot take her . . ." He protested, lunging across the space between the party guests,
the Wraiths and the rest of them. "She is my—"

Meal-ticket, Jordan thought. *If he were honest, that's how
the sentence would end. We are not lovers, we have never even
kissed* . . . And the idea they might exchange promises had
set her nerves trembling just two hours before as she was
laced into her gown by her best friend.

The Wraiths paused, their fingers tightening on Jordan's
upper arms as they hauled her farther from him. The Wardens cracked their canes' butts against the floor in unified
warning.

Rowen worried them. Jordan might have snorted at the
idea had snorting been acceptable ladylike behavior. As it
was not, she merely tilted her head in her best imitation of
appropriate curiosity. It was imperative she maintain some
dignity even when being placed under arrest.

But the idea of Rowen being worrisome to Wardens and
Wraiths?

Rowen? The man best suited to matching the buttons on
his waistcoat to whatever pocket watch he wore on a given
day? Rowen—the one who could only duel with a sword if
he stood on a designated piste?

Rowen, to whom "alpha" was merely the beginning of
"alphabet"?

She had known him since they were five and six and the
only thing worrisome about Rowen was his willingness to
sneak alcohol into the teetotalers' punch bowl and dance
like a mill worker. Or curse like a sailor for the sake of mak-

ing her blush. Or sing a song he'd heard attending a minstrel show . . .

"You cannot take her," he repeated, fiercer than she'd ever seen him.

His mother stepped forward, resting a hand on his arm.

He shook it off and took another step.

"Do not act the madman!" his mother scolded. "Let her go."

Jordan raised an eyebrow. So that was how it would be now, yes? The accusation made, her family's reputation already tumbling to ruin not even ten minutes since the Wardens' arrival.

A few guests slunk toward the door the Wandering Wallace's assistant held open for their escape. Best not to be remembered as having attended *this* particular party. Rank by association meant being part of the wrong group at the wrong moment might mar your standing irreparably.

Jordan should not have blamed them, as she herself would have been among the first to sneak away in similar circumstances. Still, she blamed them whether she *should* or not.

"You cannot take her," he insisted. "I haven't given her her birthday gift yet."

Don't do it, she thought, scrunching her face up to be as unappealing as possible. *Don't dare ask for my promise now—it would be social suicide . . .*

With one more step he was toe-to-toe with her. He leaned in—*down,* she realized, suddenly struck by Rowen's height. She was certainly no delicate flower but Rowen was . . . a *tree* by comparison. His shock of blond hair brushed against her forehead and his lips found hers with a homing ability she would have never imagined in someone who got turned around window-shopping!

When his lips moved against hers the panic filling her head died away to nothing and she was left with only silence. And sensation.

That was when he sneaked his fingers into the heavy folds of ruffled lace trimming her sleeve and pierced the fabric there with something cold.

Her eyes popped open and she gasped but he hardened his kiss as his hands drifted back down her arms and paused to clasp her wrists. Pressing his cheek to hers he whispered, "When you are alone and only then—look. Someday you will learn to more readily wear such a thing in such a fashion." He broke away then, resting his forehead against hers, his eyes searching her own.

"Now," the Tester snapped, and they dragged her out the front door of her family's mansion.

The last glimpse she had of her seventeenth birthday party was of Catrina stepping up to Rowen and slipping her hand around his to lead him away from his view of Jordan.

His taste on her lips, Jordan understood a new way Rowen might yet prove worrisome.

The doors closed behind them and Jordan's vision faded in the grip of night. She stumbled on the wet herringbone walkway, only held up by the Wraiths' fierce and biting fingers. They tugged her forward a moment until she remembered the quality of her shoes and forced her feet to catch up with the rest of her so as to not scuff their brocade satin.

The smell and the impatient stomp of a beast with shoed feet announced another presence even before she glimpsed them under the soft glow of the street light.

Horses.

A carriage was hooked to them, its body rounded and

trimmed in molding that reflected the wavering light. Tall wheels and high windows glinted.

Even she had only ridden in a carriage drawn by real horses for weddings and funerals. Horses were a dangerous commodity with the Wildkin War still raging. Their meat was a Merrow delicacy so few made it over the sea in any-thing but a Cutter or an airship. And any that had the misfortune of grazing near a body of salty water . . . Jordan shivered. Bloody trails marking the disappearance of an entire herd of horses by the bay made it known that Mer-row—at least when hungry—could slither more than a quar-ter mile on land to pull a horse back to a watery end.

When the other water-loving Wildkin joined the Merrow cause in some strange sense of watery camaraderie, not even freshwater was safe. There might be no magicking allowed in the New World, but the beasts that existed here naturally (or stowed away to cross the Pond) seemed happy to thrive as fiercely as if magick had given them birth instead of the natural world.

Jordan watched the horses—might one be something more sinister in disguise? It had happened more than once accord-ing to Catrina. Wealthy men had lost more than pride when a Pooka replaced a horse in a herd and allowed itself to be ridden or hooked to a carriage.

But, noting the heavy adornments of metal and bars on both doors and windows, Jordan realized her transport was both carriage and cage.

Chapter Four

All sorts of things and weather
Must be taken in together ...
—RALPH WALDO EMERSON

Philadelphia

The doors closed and Rowen looked down at his hand, his gaze lingering on Catrina's fingers, wrapped round his own. He yanked free of her and, taking a step back, nearly trod on his own mother.

"We really must be going," his mother said in a stage whisper so loud the entire party heard. "It is not appropriate for us to be seen in the company of such . . ." She paused, letting the sentence hang so anyone might fill in the blanks.

Rowen stepped away from her as well.

"She nearly ruined your future, Rowen!" she scolded, no longer wasting good graces on a gentle tone of voice.

He shook his head.

"She lied to you, Rowen," his mother said, the pitch of her voice rising.

He shook his head again. Jordan would have teased that

if he did that much more people would surely hear rocks rattle.

Damn it.

Jordan's mother sniffled by the servants, eyes and nose running as Chloe tried to dab the moisture away and was swatted at for her attempts.

Lady Astraea's husband had stalked from the room, glowering, after tearing her modest silhouette from the foyer wall, the accusation of Jordan being a Weather Witch impugning his wife's morality. She must have slept with someone with a tainted bloodline to conceive Jordan. She had betrayed his trust and their vows. She was an adulterer. A fornicator. And having been intimate with her, his reputation was ruined as well.

None of it made any sense.

Rowen's brow furrowed in thought.

Lady Astraea was as blindly faithful as a wife could be. She overlooked all her husband's imperfections—the squirrel hunts that never resulted in squirrels being brought to the kitchen but inevitably required the servants to help walk a tipsy Lord Astraea to his bedroom, the money that disappeared whenever he and the boys played cards but never ("I swear on my life, Cynthia, never!") bet, the fact he still could not dance a proper waltz. It seemed to Rowen she loved Lord Astraea even more for what was certainly only the abbreviated list of quirks he had observed or been told of by Jordan.

Lady Astraea was not the type to fall under another man's spell.

And Jordan had never manifested powers—or even shown the slightest affinity with the weather—until tonight.

None of it made any sense.

Catrina's hand once more found his and with a growl

Rowen shook her off and vaulted across the distance to Lady Astraea.

Wide-eyed, she stumbled back, but Rowen caught her sleeve and, closing his eyes (and trying to equally close his ears against the screeching of his mother), pulled the disowned Lady Astraea into his arms.

He said exactly what she needed to hear—a lie.

"It will be all right," he assured as she snuffled into his shirt.

"Rowen Albertus Burchette!" his mother shrieked, and he jerked upright, hearing his middle name invoked in public.

The clomping of her heels across the glossy marble tiles only gave him a moment's warning before her hands caught his arm and she tried to wrench it away from Jordan's mother.

Rowen stood his ground, tucking his head closer to Lady Astraea's and whispering the lie again.

"This is unseemly!" his mother declared, grasping Lady Astraea's arm instead.

Lady Astraea yelped, but hid in the shelter of Rowen's arms with more determination.

Rowen's mother snapped her fan shut and began smacking the whimpering Lady Astraea about the head and shoulders.

Rowen bellowed, whisking Lady Astraea to safety behind him as his mother rained slaps of her fan all across his shoulders and chest.

Lady Burchette was relentless. "You. Will. Obey. Your. Mother!" she howled. "Now!"

Rowen leaned down to look his mother in the eye, rebellion still seething deep inside him.

She flicked his nose with the fan and stood balanced on

tiptoe to be nose-to-chin with her greatly taller son. "You will obey me."

"I will—"

"Or you will lose more than *this* supposed family. You will be disowned by your own."

"Now Millie . . ." Rowen's father began but she turned his direction so fast he swallowed the rest of his words and grew so pale it seemed he might in a moment vomit them back up.

She swung back to Rowen, focusing the full force of her glittering gaze on him. "Now, young man. We are leaving."

Rowen looked to his father, but cowed, he was already walking toward the door. He looked round the foyer, but everywhere eyes turned away from him. Catrina waved him in her direction, looking as kind as she ever had.

She mouthed the words, "Come now."

"Rowen!" his mother bellowed.

He blinked, swallowed, and straightened, releasing Lady Astraea. "Yes, Mother."

Chloe snatched Lady Astraea into her arms. "So that's why you carry such a large handbag," she said to Lady Burchette, "you have to fit two pairs of balls in there along with your rouge."

Lady Burchette gasped and whisked her fan open to better behave as a proper lady should at such talk. Then she snapped it shut again and jabbed Rowen in the gut. "Move."

He did, raising his chin as proudly as a young man could when being ordered about by his mother.

"Rowen Albertus," Chloe chided. "Love, you need to grow a pair. No one would bother having you without them—no matter your rank."

Lady Burchette gasped again, poking both her husband and son as she hurried them toward the doors. "I would watch my tongue, were I you," she warned Chloe. "I only need to say a few words and you'll never find work again."

Chloe balled her hands into fists and set them on her hips. "Your threats mean nothing, Burchette. We all know what happens next. Threats and words—kind or unkind— truth or lies—will not shift the path of the juggernaut now rolling."

Lionel, the Astraea butler, yanked the door open and cleared his throat. "The door," he said pointedly to the Bur- chettes. "As it seems you are having difficulty finding it quickly enough for my lady's piece of mind."

"Why thank you, Lionel," Lady Burchette said with an arrogant sniff.

"Oh, dear," Lionel said. "You misunderstood. Not surpris- ing, I would guess . . . My lady is Lady Astraea. She always has been and always shall be. And you have offended her. You must go. Now."

"Why I—"

"Do not say 'Why I never' as if no one has expressed a similar sentiment in which to hie you from their residence," he responded with a snort. "Given your attitude I expect you have been encouraged away from the homes of good people many times."

Lady Burchette took one long spin around to look at the few people who remained—mostly servants. "Catrina!" she snapped. "Come with us, darling, your uncle can join us when he—reappears. But this is no place for a proper lady."

Catrina clicked her way across the floor to join Rowen's family. Rowen let out a loud sigh.

"A *proper* lady?" Chloe snorted. "I daresay it would re- quire a lady of higher standing than you to determine such a thing."

Before they were fully out the door Lionel began to close it on them, much to Lady Burchette's consternation.

The door shut and nothing but the remnants of the Astraea family and their servants remained within walls far too quiet to contain what began as a birthday party for one of the city's most eligible young women.

"Now it is time to clean up this mess," Lionel announced, securing the doors.

Chloe nodded, looking at the youngest of their number. "Laura, escort her ladyship to her chambers. Test the adjoining room's locks and bolt the doors on her side. Cynda will replace you shortly."

Laura's eyes were wide. "Lock his lordship out of her chambers?"

Chloe signaled Laura nearer to her and placed a hand on each of her shoulders. "Men have been known to do horrible things when they suspect a woman of infidelity," she confided. "Lady Astraea may never again be safe with him. We need to wait. To see. And, most importantly, to allow for no unhappy accidents."

Laura nodded, a shade paler than her natural complexion, gathered up her skirts, and hooked her arm around Lady Astraea's to gently pull her in the direction of her private rooms.

Chloe puffed out a breath. "We'll need to release Laura soon. Better all the young ones get out unmarred if possible."

Lionel nodded. "Too late for us," he said with a sad smile.

"True, true," Chloe agreed. "A few last details—too dangerous to overlook—and then we'll do the standard cleanup."

Lionel nodded and Chloe clapped her hands together.

"Sanders." Chloe turned to address a young man with a narrow face and ginger hair. "Gather all the powder."

"Powder?" he asked, eyebrows high on his broad and freckled forehead.

"Gunpowder," she specified. "Remove all bayonets, collect the family swords and sabers, and bring them to the kitchen to be stored. And his lordship's letter opener and penknife. It has a nasty point on it. Scissors as well. Make haste."

He nodded and dashed away to gather all the potentially dangerous implements.

"I will secure all the knives and cutlery . . . and the medicinals."

Lionel caught her by the arm as she turned to go. "How do you know to do all this?"

"I had a household before this one," Chloe said, her voice going low and tragic. She blinked at him, dark eyes damp, and then cleared her throat and dodged away to do whatever she somehow knew needed to be done.

He watched her go without a word, wishing he had said the right thing at the right moment.

Holgate

The knock roused Bran from his reading, and taking the lantern he stumbled to the door of his modest apartments on the tower's thirteenth story. Listening for any sign of trouble (because a summoning at such an hour was highly unusual) the Maker slid open the peephole and peered out at one of the town's watchmen. He was a great beast of a man, tall, broad, and with a wicked scar that turned his every expression to a sneer.

"Mister Maker, sir. Seems we's got a late night delivery of

some import for you," the man said, his rank breath seeping in to sting Bran's eyes.

Bran slammed the peephole shut, squinting. "There is no delivery of such great import that should pull a man from his privacy at this hour. Find me first thing in the morning," he ordered.

As he turned away more knocking sounded. A distinct and rapid rapping. "Sir, good Maker," came the high-pitched voice of Maude, the head servant. What brought her to his door at such an hour raised many questions in his mind. He and she had parted ways weeks ago and he had already seen her enjoying the attentions of another man. "Good Maker," Maude tried again, "I really must insist . . ."

He rubbed his eyes and fiddled with the locks on his door, grumbling his way through each. "Dear God, Maude, what could possibly have been delivered at such an indecent hour and of such great import as to cause you and a watchman to be at my door demanding my attention?"

The door groaned open and he glared at them both with equal vitriol.

One hand tucked behind her back, Maude looked over her shoulder and made a soft cooing noise. The watchman shifted his substantial weight from one foot to another, peering behind Maude's back.

"What?" Bran demanded.

"Have a care, you'll frighten the poor dear . . ."

"The poor—?" He dodged around her, shoving Maude aside.

There was a squeal and a blur of movement as a child dashed behind Maude's skirts to hide again.

"Now, now," Maude soothed. "Come out, lovey. He's not nearly so frightening as he first seems. And he's the Maker—a very important man. Your papá is quite the figure in Holgate."

"Papá—" Bran looked from Maude to the little girl the guardsman nudged forward and back to Maude again. "Impossible."

Maude laughed. "I cannot imagine how you'd dare say *that,* good Maker." She startled him with a bold wink. "Such things have been known to happen to young men sowing their wild oats."

Bran's gaze glued itself once more to the child.

She was small and slender with sallow skin and deep hollows around large green eyes. Shadows nested in her delicate features, winter resting on her heart-shaped face far more than the blush of spring or rosy summer. Curls so pale they rivaled moonlight tumbled down from the top of her head, giving her a halo in the light afforded by the gathering of the three adults' stormlight lanterns.

"How old are you, child?" he asked, his eyes thinning as he thought back over the few lovers he had taken in his loneliest moments.

Her brow creased as her little lips worked to form the words. "Five, sir," she carefully annunciated. "My good mother, God rest her soul, bore the Christian name of Margaret."

Bran blinked. He remembered a Margaret—a Peggy, truly. He had spent eight days that varied in description from being greatly leisurely to filled with intense exercise in her company while his apartments were refurnished after a particularly successful Making of a Hub Witch. "Margaret," he whispered, seeing bits of her reflected in the child. He crouched before the child, bringing the lantern right beside her face. Yes, he saw Peggy in her, no doubt—the shape of the lips, the slight upturn of the tip of her nose, the irrationally lengthy eyelashes that made her eyes a shade darker from their shadows. He snorted.

"And how might you prove she is my get?"

"Your *get*?" Maude asked, watching intently as he again rose to his full height. "She is no man's *get*. She is your *child*. Do you not see yourself in her?"

He looked away.

Maude bent at her waist and now she held the lantern aloft so he might better examine the child. That light bounced off the top of Maude's breasts as well.

Bran swallowed and focused, looking again at the girl.

"Look. Look at the shape of her eyes, Bran," Maude whispered so intimately the watchman raised a heavy eyebrow. "Those are your eyes. Yes, a different color and yes, lined with far longer lashes but . . . they are *your* eyes."

Bran's jaw jutted out, but he looked at her. Hard.

"And here," Maude said, jabbing the girl's ribs so that, startled, she jumped and giggled, little arms wrapping around to protect herself from Maude's fingers as they scurried across her side. "There!" Maude exclaimed. "See your dimples on her cheeks?"

"I have no dimples."

"Oh, you *do*," Maude teased. "When you smile. It's a rare moment, true enough, when the Maker smiles, but I've seen it once or twice."

Bran looked at the watchman. "Take her. For a moment."

The man's face scrunched up, making him even less visually appealing, but he grunted and said, "Come now, li'l dove. We'll walk just a bit down this hall. Not far at all," he promised. "With me."

The child glanced at Maude for consent before following as he bade.

"How can *I* care for a child, Maude? Yes, I can make one, and granted, she appears to be mine, but—" He shook his head and yawned. "What of her mother?"

"Dead, sir. The fever took her. A working girl found her with this little lovey curled at her side, a note bound to her." She dug into one of the pockets inside her skirt and withdrew a scrap of paper. "Here."

His hands shaking, he read it aloud. "Brandon Marshall of House Dregard, father of my dear sweet kitten, Meghan, do raise her well and true. In time she will come to love you greatly and you her."

"The girls could not afford to keep her and they did not trust the poorhouses or the workhouses as many of them had barely survived such themselves."

He nodded, his lips pursed. "As they themselves instead turned to the whorehouses?" he asked with a smirk.

"At least they have some small bit of independence left. But she needs you. A lass needs her papá."

"I have no way to keep her."

"You have fine apartments. A wee scrap of a child needs little room."

"But time. She'll require time."

"She is old enough to assist in your library."

"And when I am in my laboratory? Is she old enough to help in my laboratory or the tower top? To see the things that make me a Maker? Is that what she should see at such a tender age—this *kitten*"—he snapped out the words—"this little *dove*?"

Maude looked away. "You cannot let her go with you there, Bran. Not yet. Not so young. Such things would terrify her. Wound her. But you cannot send her away. I will not allow it."

His eyebrows rose, arching. "You will not *allow* it?"

"Please, Bran. Do the right thing. When you are in the laboratory or the tower top send her to me. Wherever I am. The kitchen, the laundry . . . wherever. A child needs a place where she's looked after. Even if it is a place like this."

"And tonight?"

"Tonight she may sleep in the servants' quarters with me. But tomorrow morning I will need to make a proper place for her here, in her father's apartments. She will require clothing and shoes. Not much, but something. A small allowance for necessities."

Bran nodded, a slow move at first, but a nod nonetheless. "Fine, fine." He glanced around her, down to where the watchman pointed to spots along the hall and talked about the things making Holgate what it was. "Come here, child—Meghan, is it?"

The tiny head turned, curls bobbling. She bounced her way back to them, but slowed her skip to a modest walk as she approached, lowering her gaze, her plump lower lip jutting out as she prepared for rejection. "Yes, sir?"

"*Yes, papá* will serve. You are to stay with Maude tonight and move into my quarters on the morrow. What think you of that?"

"If it please you, sir," she said with a little curtsy.

"It would, Meg. It would please me greatly," he said, though the words fell flat. "But it will be difficult at first. An adjustment for us both."

"Yes, sir—*papá*," she said, raising her eyes to meet his at the correction, a smile pressing dimples into the corners of her mouth once more.

He froze, still as a rabbit catching scent of a wolf, seeing himself there in the twist of her lips and dimples so deep they seemed to cut straight to the bone. "Now go," he whispered, watching how she slipped her tiny hand into Maude's and they trotted away, taking much of the light away with them.

He retreated into his chambers and, closing the door, slid the bolts back into place. A child. He had a child—someone who would go on beyond him and bear some part of him into the future. Someone to carry his name and deeds beyond his eventual demise.

He had his immortality and quite by accident. But she was there. And so very small, so slight and frail and so seemingly ephemeral.

Chapter Five

Then the Lord answered Job out of the whirlwind . . .
—THE BIBLE

Philadelphia

Down the hallway and up one flight of stairs Laura and Lady Astraea went, the only noises the echo of their shoes on the wooden floor, the sound of breathing, and the occasional strangled sob uttered by Lady Astraea.

Arriving at Lady Astraea's door, Laura moved to open it, withdrawing when her ladyship reached out as well. "I did not do it, you know," Lady Astraea said in a strained whisper. "I have never lain with another man. I have never even *imagined* it." She wiped clumsily at tears leaking from her eyes. The small bit of makeup she used to color her cheeks in the European fashion smeared on the heel of her hand and she stood a long minute staring at the lace ringing her delicate sleeve and just barely showing the tender white flesh of her wrist.

"I believe you, milady," Laura assured, pressing down on the door's handle to pop it open. "Here. In we go."

Inside, Laura secured the door, moved the fireplace poker, and checked the connecting door. She turned the key in that one's lock and slid the bolt home.

She set the candles first, eyeing the stormlights with curiosity. She had heard all linked stormlights would extinguish once it was known the family had lost rank. They would be cast into the literal dark as much as their name had been cast into the figurative. While the room now blushed with a cool cast of light, Laura realized she had only ever seen the Astraea rooms illuminated by steady stormlight. The flicker and flare of flame would make everything strange in comparison.

Lady Astraea moved ghostlike across the broad floor to sit on the edge of her bed, fingers smoothing out the small wrinkles in the quilt her mother had helped her make years ago—a quilt that had laid silently in her hope chest until Morgan Astraea came along. She smiled a moment, remembering.

But reality caught her again and she coughed, drawing her arms tight about her shivering body.

"Oh, milady," Laura cooed. "Have no worries. There is a bit of a chill in the night's air. I shall build you a fine fire to warm your body and brighten your spirit. Nothing cheers me so much on a grim day," the girl said, shuffling about the fireplace to set the kindling and find the firestarter, "as a merry fire."

She arranged the tinder and coaxed a fire to life, humming softly as she did. The humming became enunciated, the words growing clear.

No storm that ever strikes
Shall leave me helpless and afraid

And if darkness lingers heavy
I'll be fearless and brave

But if ever I am wary
If ever I am scared
I will listen to the wind
For the answer's always there

The sun burns like an ember
The air is cool and calm
But nothing lasts forever
In this world you must take on

The ground will shake and tremble
As the clouds divide
Rivers flood the land
Lightning parts the sky

When there is no one there to guide you
And no one there to help
Your courage is the key
To freeing yourself

"What is that?" Lady Astraea's question stopped her.

"What, milady?"

"That tune?"

"Ah, it is called 'Reeling.' A play on words, if I am correct. My good father used to sing it to me as he dandled me on his knee. I think I might someday sing it to my own wee one, God grace me with one," she said with a smile.

Laura picked up the song where she had left off, singing,

The sun burns like an ember
The air is cool and calm
But nothing lasts forever
In this world we must take on

The ground will shake and tremble
As the clouds divide
Rivers flood the land
And lightning parts the sky

When there is no one there to guide you
And no one there to help
Your courage is the key
To freeing yourself

"I remember that song. Though singing of storms is . . . unseemly stuff. Lower ranks and Witches only, that." Lady Astraea's eyes narrowed. "How old are you, girl?"

"Seventeen."

"And do you have a fellow?"

Laura blushed. "There is a lad who is courting me."

"Ah, good. Does he treat you well? And you he?"

"Yes, milady. Quite so." The girl took a rush from the metal container hanging on the wall and lit its tip to start the candles. The room shined with both stormlight and flame. Still not comparable to daylight, but fine nonetheless.

Lady Astraea smoothed her skirts. "Good, good. You may be about your business. You may lock me in for safekeeping."

"Oh." Laura blinked. "But . . ."

"I do not require a nanny. I am simply going to occupy

myself here. Read a bit by the fire. Perhaps knit. I will not allow anyone in unless it is Chloe, Cynda, or Lionel."

Laura ducked her head and bent her knees in a curtsy. "Of course, milady. That sounds fine and good to me." She pursed her lips and glanced about the room. "Ah," she said, remembering the poker. "Certainly Chloe would ask me to bring this along . . ."

Lady Astraea nodded. "Of course. Precautions should be taken so that no one does anything rash."

Laura smiled. "Yes, milady." She headed to the door, pausing to address her employer once more. "May I say, milady, it has always been a wondrous treat to serve within your employ. I do so love your family." Again she curtsied, this time slipping out the door and shutting it.

There was a heartbeat before the key clicked into the lock and the tumblers turned and Lady Astraea knew she was safely ensconced inside. She waited until she heard the girl's footsteps retreat down the hallway before she pulled out her yarn and began to knit.

To work on a sweater her husband would likely sooner burn than wear.

She muffled a cry in the mesh of knits and purls and, clearing her throat, pulled back up, straight and proud as ever a woman of the Fifth of the Nine could be. For a moment she sat perfectly still but for the slight rise and fall of her chest and the rapid pulse fluttering along her neck.

Haltingly she continued the same song Laura had begun. "No storm that ever strikes, Shall leave me helpless and afraid, And if darkness lingers heavy, I'll be fearless and brave . . ."

Then, as memories overtook her and she remembered the words, her confidence grew and so did her volume—just loud enough to make the room feel a little less empty.

The stormlights flickered and for a moment Lady Astraea felt a darkness as black as her now-ruined silhouette. "Be brave," she whispered before resuming the song as the light returned.

The stormlights died. For a moment Lady Astraea lost her voice. If the Weather Workers had shared their condemnation and it had reached the Hub then everyone knew. Gossip spread faster than storm clouds.

"When there is no one there to guide you, And no one there to help . . ."

The fire crackled and popped in the fireplace but it seemed so distant—so small in the gathering darkness.

Lady Astraea picked up the song where she had left off and slid the knitting needles free of the sweater she was so close to completing, examining them in the pulsating fire-light. In the adjoining room she heard her husband slam a door. Something shattered against their shared wall. He cursed. And then, cursing again, he added her name into the mix. The tips of the knitting needles glowed, wicked and sharp, and she set the sweater on her lap and knew then what she must do.

"Your courage is the key

To freeing yourself . . ."

Clenching her jaw and gritting her teeth, she did the thing more easily than she had expected. It was true. Nothing was merrier than the light of a fire.

The needles clattered onto the floor and she curled atop her bed, holding her husband's sweater to her chest as she watched the struggling flame go from spark to ember. "Ashes to ashes," she whispered.

The poker was added to the pile of dangerous implements in the kitchen and Chloe looked up, surprised there was one she'd somehow overlooked. Her eyes widened when she saw Laura step away from the pile. "Why are you not with her ladyship?"

The girl shrugged and Chloe grabbed a candle, curling her free fingers in her skirts to hike them above her ankles. She headed toward Lady Astraea's chambers at a jog, the girl close behind.

"She insisted she was fine. Had me lock her inside. Insisted she was going to read and knit."

Pulling her skirts beyond her knees, Chloe doubled her speed, calling over her shoulder, "The key—give me the key!"

Laura raced up to her, handing her the key as they arrived at the door. "Milady?" Chloe shouted, dropping her skirts and thrusting the candle at her companion. "Milady?!"

The key rattled in the lock and she twisted it, shoving the door open with her shoulder and bursting in on the scene.

The fire was naught but glowing embers, one candle out, the other flickering sadly to cast a pall across a small patch of the room—barely catching the butt end of the knitting needles.

Chloe took a deep breath and another step into the room. "Milady?" she asked, her voice catching.

In the darkness something dripped.

The light from the candle crept over the floor and Chloe snatched it back, holding it before her like some magickal wand, color edging shadow back as light reclaimed the bed's edge and the sleek tips of the knitting needles, obscured in a pool of something dark . . . something that leeched from the quilt's hem, dropping onto the floor at a pace far slower than that of Chloe's thudding heart.

One last step forward and the story of the sad and nearly silent scene was made clear.

Laura dodged out of the room and dropped to all fours, gagging in the hall.

"Oh, milady," Chloe whispered, seeing the woman's body, so much like sleeping, but with long gashes down her forearms where she'd opened her own wrists with the knitting needles.

Chloe set the candle on the bedside table and felt for heat, a pulse, some sign of life, as she pulled a ribbon from her lady's hair and, tearing it into two equal strips, bound up her lady's wrists.

It might yet be enough.

If she hurried.

Closing the door behind her, Chloe turned the lock and grabbed Laura by the back of her apron to hoist her to her feet. "Now. You'll do exactly as I say." Her voice cracked again. "You'll clean up this mess. Starting with the mess you just made." She pointed to the weeping pile of vomit that oozed across the hall floor.

Then she had her skirts in her hands again and was running back to Lionel—if for no reason other than to know where he was so she could better avoid him as she did the next dark thing that needed doing. In the service of the Astraea family for five years already, Chloe was not ready to face the rest of her life without them. Not yet. Not quite so soon. She had lost her first family far too early—she would do whatever it took to keep this family together. Her familiarity with the house's layout made it nearly no problem to run in the dark back the way she'd come—*nearly* no problem.

She slammed into him at top speed, the solid mass of his

body enough to throw her onto her rump. "John?" she asked as he reached down for her hand, begging her pardon.

"Yes, Miss Chloe. Is John."

"Perfect. I need you to help me carry something heavy. And we need to make haste."

"I can make haste, Miss Chloe."

"That's what I am counting on. This way. And no questions, you understand?"

She glimpsed just enough of his dark form in the shadows to see his head full of tight salt and pepper curls nod in agreement and once more she hiked up her cumbersome skirts and hurried back to Lady Astraea's chambers.

Rowen stomped his way up the large stairs leading to his family's main porch and would have thrown open the door in a dramatic fashion had not the servants stolen the opportunity by opening the doors quite politely in advance and even bowing to their young master.

It infuriated him even more—the fact he could not throw an appropriately sized tantrum on his family's estate because they were too well taken care of by servants who bent and scraped to his mother's every wish. He turned and watched her hurry up the stairs, her parasol bobbing as she took each step. Ridiculous to carry a parasol at night, but Mother wished not to muss her bonnet in the wet.

"Rowen, be a dear and—" She held out her parasol, its top damp from water still dripping from rooftops.

He took it from her without a word. And seethed a bit more at his automatic reaction.

She cleared her throat and a butler appeared to help her

remove her jacket. "It is simply dreadful out," she said with a disdainful sniffle.

"And the party, madam? How was it?" the butler, a young man only a half-dozen years older than Rowen, asked, glancing at Rowen although he addressed Lady Burchette.

Rowen puffed out a sigh and shook his head.

"Let us never speak of that event—or that family—ever again, Jonathan," Lady Burchette said simply.

The butler's eyebrows shot up, but Rowen turned away, unable to do anything, unwilling to say any more. Rowen stalked away.

"Master Rowen," Jonathan called, "your coat and hat, young sir—"

"Oh, let him be. Poor thing," his mother said. "He nearly ruined his entire life tonight. Over a girl. Can you imagine?"

Jonathan pressed his lips together in a firm line and shook his head *no*. A poor liar, he was not caught because Lady Burchette was uninterested in anything about servants' lives. They lived to *serve*. How important or interesting could their existence possibly be?

Rowen threw his hat to Jonathan.

"Boy," Rowen's father called. "Join me in the study for a drink."

Rowen blew out a sigh, shook his head, blond hair flying, and stomped away. Down the main hallway he went, past the portraits of his ancestors and the picture of his entire family standing together—the picture in which his mother tersely proclaimed Rowen showed too many teeth—men were meant to be stoic, not funny.

He paused before the picture, examining his face perfected in paint. It was not a bad likeness, though his jaw was a bit stronger in reality and the artist had somehow missed the too-obvious dimple in his chin. His upper lip looked oddly long because his mother had insisted the artist paint over his grin.

His father looked suitably stoic. Or cowed. Rowen was never sure which.

But the painter was rumored to be the finest in the city— and one of the best in the entire region. He had quite the reputation and that mattered far more than accuracy. Lady Burchette had even said once Rowen obtained Jordan's promise she would arrange to have her included in a brand-new sitting.

His mother had promised Jordan would be as much a part of their family as Rowen felt he was a part of hers.

And now?

It was all ruined.

He growled out his frustration, his hands snapping forward to grab the picture by its frame and dash it onto the floor where he could better dance on his mother's face. Once she had called Cynthia Astraea her "best of best friends." And yet she had abandoned her—believed the Tester and accepted the worst of all rumors . . .

She had not defended her in her time of need.

His fingers tightened on the frame. Just a small move to lift it off the hook and . . .

"It is a fine portrait."

He jumped, hands clamping down on the picture in surprise and pulling it free from the wall.

Catrina blinked in surprise.

Rowen swallowed a groan. "Would you"—*leave me the hell alone for a while, for once?* He stretched his lips into a smile—"like to see it closer?"

She tilted her head. Weighing the scene with glittering

eyes. "Why yes," she said, stepping over so that she stood tucked up into the curve of his side, her skirts pressing against his hip, her shoulder warm against him. "Oh. Wait," she said, and she ducked under his arm to stand between him and the portrait in his hands.

The change in position was unsettling. Her skirts brushed the front of his trousers and her perfume filled the small space between them. Then she spun in the circle formed by his arms and the huge portrait and managed to press her bodice—*was something that low cut truly the fashion of the day?* he wondered—against his chest. "Remarkable," she whispered, batting her eyelashes, her nose nearly at his chin as she looked up at him from beneath lacy lashes.

She leaned in, stretched up . . .

Rowen belched and she shrieked, engulfed in a scent that surely clashed with the bouquet of her perfume.

Straining his shoulder with the weight of the picture, Rowen's right hand released it to allow Catrina some distance. He turned back to the wall and hung the portrait again. He belched again. "Yes. Nearly as remarkable as the cucumber sandwiches I had at the Astraea estate—they keep"—he belched once more and rapped on his chest with a fist as he turned back to face her—"talking to me."

"Oh, Rowen," Catrina said, pulling her fan free to move the offensive air away. "Whatever would your mother say?"

"She would say, 'Dear heavens, Rowen, have you not yet managed to come to grips that your innards are not capable of appropriately processing cucumbers?'" He shrugged. "I will surely spend more than my fair amount of time in the water closet as a result."

Catrina wrinkled her nose.

"And God help whoever attempts to use it after me—I

can curl your hair without pins or presses," he said, pressing his lips into a firm line and nodding with an expression frighteningly akin to pride.

Catrina fanned faster. "Rowen, that is highly inappropriate talk—*offensive* talk—to share with a lady."

"Then perhaps you'd better go, because I do not feel a desire to be tremendously proper on this eve."

"Oh. I see."

Rowen turned to head down the hall. She had not moved farther, so he determined it was up to him to put greater distance between them. But only a few feet toward his next destination he heard the clatter of her heels as she raced to catch up.

"Perhaps just this once I might be a bit improper, too," she suggested with a wink.

Inwardly he groaned and instead of turning left at the next intersection of hallways, he turned right, pausing at the top of a set of stairs.

"Excellent well," he said, sounding far heartier than the shadows in his eyes proved him to be. "Let's get drunk."

Catrina startled at the suggestion, stepping back from the top of the stairs and eyeing Rowen in disbelief. "Get drunk? *Imbibe?*"

"Imbibe our asses off," he clarified.

Her eyes shot wide open. "Why, Rowen . . . Such language."

"I'm ranked Sixth of the Nine. We imbibe. We smoke. We curse. Jordan understood that."

She opened and closed her fan again and again. "Well, Jordan had reason to understand such behaviors, considering the taint of her blood."

"Do not."

"Do not what?"

"Do not speak that way about Jordan. You know her better than anyone. You were her friend first. You introduced us—"

"And I am so awfully sorry for that, Rowen. I nearly brought you to your ruin because I made a poor choice of a friend."

"No. Do *not* do that. Jordan isn't perfect."

"*Wasn't* perfect," Catrina corrected.

"Why are you putting her in past tense? She's not dead."

"She must be to *us*," Catrina said with a discerning pout. "What is your family's motto?"

"Justice foremost."

"And that is what this is, dear Rowen. Swift and terrible justice, but justice nonetheless. Imagine if she had been allowed to continue unfettered? What a danger to society might she have become? We have enough problems with the Frost Giant lurking about the streets, but a full Weather Witch?"

Blinking at her, he wrapped his fingers around the staircase's broad wooden banister so he wouldn't wrap them around her slender neck. "They are wrong. Jordan is no Weather Witch and they will discover their mistake soon enough and make things right."

"Then how do you explain the storm she summoned—or the sparks the Tester's touch and Test elicited? How, Rowen?"

He shook his head, hair flopping into his eyes again. "I don't know. Yet. Maybe these things happen. Maybe there was another Weather Witch there that they somehow overlooked but it appeared Jordan was the likeliest candidate. Maybe it's really me! Or maybe," he said, leaning down to be on eye level with her, "maybe it's *you.*"

She hopped back from him as quickly as if he'd belched. "Don't be so absolutely ridiculous!"

He descended onto the first step.

"She is gone, Rowen," Catrina insisted. "And we are both

better for it. Now you have a better chance at raising your rank."

He turned and looked at her, his eyes the coolest blue yet. "What do you mean?"

"Be honest with yourself, Rowen. You were pursuing Jordan because you want to step up—not for any other reason. You're a social climber like the rest of us. You never *wanted* Jordan—and why would you—she's as petty as she is pretty—"

He bounded back up the stairs and touched his nose to hers. "Stop now before *I* stop you."

Her mouth opened. And closed wordlessly.

"She is our friend."

"She was a poor substitute for what a real friend should be and you know it," Catrina challenged. "She whined, she worried, she put herself first—even to our detriment. Showcasing herself the way she did! *That* you cannot deny. But now she'll understand what it is to be last. She will be better for being humbled."

Rowen's eyes were mere slits. "If I ever find that you are connected to her family's ruin . . ."

"Rowen! You are insane! Why—"

"It sounds like you have plenty of *why*."

"We both do—and so do most people in this city, if you're honest with yourself. But what could I possibly have done to make a Tester get a wrong reading? The proof is in the pudding."

"Only if Cook makes it with sufficient alcohol," Rowen snapped. "This will be corrected. You'll see. Jordan is innocent." Without another word he stomped his way down the stairs and into the kitchen.

Chapter Six

~~~~

Why fear death? Death is only a beautiful adventure.
—CHARLES FROHMAN

Philadelphia

Chloe scurried around John, patting at him and rearranging the cloth covering the burden he carried. "No, not over your shoulder, cradle her—it. Cradle *it*," she said, adjusting the long thin shape wrapped in blankets and a quilt and held awkwardly in John's arms. "We must be quick."

John nodded, following Chloe's bobbing candle as she moved quickly down the back hallway to the servant's quarters. It was the original stone house that the Astraeas built on the Hill and it had been, at one time, quite the talk of the town with its hundreds of flat field stones arranged and mortared on edge to create a multitude of different patterns and designs—at the house's eastern end an eagle and shield still fit into the upper wall, constructed from the stones' edges. But each generation had different taste and it was not long at all, considering the life span of a well-maintained house, before the Astraeas constructed another house on the Hill overlooking the poorer neighborhoods of the Below and handed the original building over to their ever-growing staff of servants. Then the inevitable happened. The new house was not exactly what a particular generation wanted, but, having no more space for building unless they tore up the gardens and fountains that helped define the estate, they built a home connecting the two previous ones.

The Astraea estate had, at that juncture, become a challenge to the sensibilities of all who loved the simple stoic face and well-balanced proportions of Georgian architecture. If there was anything those of rank could say to belittle the Astraeas, it was that their home was a "unique" construction.

At least that was all they could say to belittle the Astraeas before *tonight*.

It was through that weaving structure that Lady Astraea's most faithful servants carried their ladyship, swaddled in fabric, from her home and chambers into their own with its faintly warped wooden floors. Down one hall and a set of narrow stairs they went by flickering candlelight, casting grotesque shadows all the way.

"Out the back," Chloe whispered, opening the door for John and his burden after giving a quick glance around.

The rain had departed with Jordan and now the sparse lantern light along the streets reflected back in puddles and slick spots on the walkways and bricks that made up the streets in the grander parts of Philadelphia.

Tomorrow all the crystals in the house would be removed and redistributed and the fall from grace would be all but complete for members of the Astraea household. Their last chance was if Jordan couldn't be Made. But that seemed tragically unlikely.

Already cut off from stormlight and stormpower, their choices of transportation were limited. The carriage did not run without sufficient stormpower and neither of them was allowed near the single family horse, a beast kept as a courtesy in the same stable as Burchette kept the city's military-grade steeds. "Old Sir at the Bilibin House been working on a special machine. Looks a mite like a carriage but with a chimney and stove on it."

Chloe spared him a glance. "How does anything that has a chimney and stove on it look like a carriage?"

He snorted. "Has wheels, Miss Chloe. Quite the contraption."

"Ah." She stopped short, staring long and hard at him. "Could we take Old Sir's contraption, you think?"

John laughed. "No, Miss Chloe. I think not. All the thing does now is belch smoke and spin gears—*soon its wheels will spin, too,* Old Sir says. But I don't rightly know. I think all that smoke's poisoned his brain."

"A carriage run by smoke?"

"More rightly steam, Miss. Run by steam. Imagine what such a thing might mean."

Chloe's mind was doing just that—imagining. Imagining the freedom a new power source would bring, a world with no stormlights or stormcells or Weather Witches. Why, steam was produced so easily . . . Lady Burchette could have powered the entire city with the steam rolling out of her ears as she was encouraged to leave the Astraea household! "No use to dwell on such nonsense," she finally said. "Such a thing's certain not to work and dreams and fancies never got people nowhere quick feet couldn't." She looked at Lady Astraea being carried so tightly and raised a finger. "Hold one moment." Hitching the hem of her skirt into her waistband to keep it from sopping up water, she dodged away to the large greenhouse that lorded over the estate's gardens. She returned a few minutes later, grunting as she pushed a wheelbarrow. "Here. Gently now. Place it in here."

John did as he was bade and Chloe arranged her cape over the top of her ladyship's body before they made the bumping descent down the Hill's long slate staircase and into the more frantically paced center of the city and the Below.

The quiet and stiffly proper feel of the Hill on nearly any evening was juxtaposed with the lively bustle that greeted them at its base. People jostled each other on the streets as they jockeyed for position, a steady stream of them heading to the Night Market, scents of fried dough and smoking meats thick and welcome in the close press of flesh.

"We going to the Market, Miss?" John asked, his eyes on the crowd.

Chloe shook her head. "Not tonight," she said. "What I wouldn't give to be there eating delicious foods and watching the wildest of entertainment instead of . . ."

Beside the Night Market's main entrance a cat did a merry jig for a man holding a hoop he lit on fire. The cat gave a shrill cry before bouncing through the burning ring, landing atop a tall hat that it tipped over to collect coins tossed from the clapping crowd.

Chloe's voice picked up again. "Our job is an important one. Come now." She slipped her hand beneath his elbow and urged him to bring the wheelbarrow more quickly, finding a twisting path through the press of people.

Through the mass of humanity they went, weaving a path beneath old Bendicott Bridge, where ragged-looking men around campfires raised haunted faces and watched them scurry past.

"This feels ill to me, Miss," John confided, quickening his pace. "There is darkness here that goes beyond nightfall."

Chloe too lengthened her stride, her jaw tight.

"Who were those men?" John asked, casting a glance over his shoulder.

"Survivors."

"It don't look like that's much surviving going on under that there bridge . . ."

"Survivors of the war."

"This war? The Wildkin War?"

"No, the other war," she corrected softly. "1812. Those men fought to keep us free, John. You saw the one missing his leg?"

"No, ma'am. Saw the one missing his arm, though. And the one with the bandana over an eye."

"Those are our good veterans," she said. "*That* is their fine reward for fighting in our stead so that we might go on serving tea and biscuits for the lords and ladies of the Hill." She paused at a crossroad, rubbing her chin. She looked up one street and down the other. Here the houses were even smaller than in the Below, each only the tiniest bit wider than a single door and stacked so high in shambles of architecture that one might easily imagine an entire block tumbling down like so many dominoes.

"The Burn Quarter," John realized.

"Yes."

The one place the city watchmen, constables, and fire companies had orders to let burn if ever it caught fire. And,

as the fire companies had aligned with the gangs, the likeli-
hood a place would burn while they fought each other was
high. Still, the Burn Quarter was the one place they could
find the particular skill they sought.

A forbidden skill.

"Miss, this be the place of—"

"Hold the course, John. Steady now. What we do is for
the good of our family."

"No good comes from such places," he muttered.

A cat screeched like it was being murdered and Chloe
thought perhaps that was the truth of the thing. She touched
her hip, feeling the little kitchen knife she always carried
nestled in one pocket. Small comfort, that, probably only
good for a poke or two. Only enough to make a thing angry.

Still, small assurance was better than none at all.

She counted the rambling houses with an outstretched
and bobbing finger and paused, pointing to the single house
sporting a fence and gate. The one spot in the awkward
block with a yard, odd though it seemed. "That one."

John swallowed so hard Chloe heard it. Running her fingers along the wheelbarrow's lip, she pressed forward, toward the house . . . seeking some confirmation she had the
right spot.

John found it first. " 'Neath the roof's edge . . . Be that a
skull with stormlight eyes?"

Her answer sounded through the softest of breaths.
"Yes."

"Lord, Lord," John murmured, looking in distress at the
bundle between them, realization slow to dawn. "But . . .
Lord almighty." He scrubbed a hand over his hoary head.
"Miss Chloe, this man . . ." John shook his head. "This man
be a . . ." Still the words eluded him. He groaned. "A bad

sort. Takin' money and grantin' life—and not a life like any of us might reckon is worth livin', neither."

"A person's life is not for me to judge. Not its quality, nor its nature, nor its worthiness of being. Nor is it mine to judge who is good and who is bad," Chloe insisted. "Be it as the Bible charges, *Judge not—*"

"*—lest thee be judged?*" John asked. "Surely I wish not to be the first to cast stones, Miss Chloe, though I daresay I built my house not of glass but on the Rock. Still . . ." He eyed the house, puckering his lips. "I feel safe volunteering that the good Lord may judge me as critically as I might judge this man whose services you wish to contract."

But, although Chloe heard him, she listened to none of his words of warning. Instead her senses focused on the look of the entire place, from its shaggy and overgrown exterior yard to the way the slats in the fence slanted first one way and then the other like a mouthful of broken teeth. "This is home to a Reanimator."

"Is a place without love," John whispered. "Look it. No love for the land—how we 'spect there's love for life here?"

The moon slid out from behind the last remaining clouds and threw a glow about the place.

"Hush," Chloe demanded, slipping past him to undo the gate and enter the yard. Plants snagged in Chloe's skirts as vines crawled from one of the rolling and uneven walkway's sides to its other. Behind her, John hefted the lady and followed.

Chloe tripped over the tilted threshold, her raised fist slamming prematurely onto the door's rough surface and cutting her knuckles.

"Bad omen, that," John said. "Blood calls to blood."

"What does that even mean?" Chloe asked, but the door

opened suddenly and she balked—coming face-to-face with a leering mask. The man who wore it was tall, slim, and graceful.

From the holes designating the mask's eyes, the Reanimator glanced at them both, peering at the shape held in John's big hands. Then he looked up and down the street beyond.

Chloe dug her voice out of the pit of her stomach and asked, "You the Reanimator?"

He snorted as if she'd delivered a surprising smack. "Some call me that. In dark alleys and under bridges and in taverns, I suppose."

"I got your name from none of those—"

He stepped back, hugging the shadows. "My name? You got *my name*?"

Chloe shook her head. "No, good sir—I mean your location. Technically."

His exhale was amplified behind the mask's comically painted lips. "Come in," he said with a slow nod. He waited until they were inside, looked outside once more, and remained silent until the door was shut behind them and latched with two bolts. Only then did he speak again. "Who is it and when did it die?"

John spoke up, anger tinting his voice. "She is—"

But Chloe put a hand on his arm and silenced him. "She is a lady who passed barely an hour ago."

"What lady?"

"Why should it matter?" Chloe pressed. "She is a lady and she is dead—does not time matter in affairs of this sort?"

He squinted at her, his eyes shadowed beneath the mask. "Yes, yes. Time certainly matters. Bring her here," he said, motioning to a table. He immediately reached out to unwrap the body, but Chloe slapped his hand away.

"I apologize," she said, voice wavering. "But she is a *lady*. This much I will do." With reverent and shaking hands she pulled away the first blanket. And then unfolded the second. She glanced at John. "She'd not want anyone to see her this way," she whispered.

He nodded. "Just I never turned my back on our lady afore," he said, thick eyebrows rising. "Never would mean her no disrespect."

"I know, John. Surely she'd know, too. But . . ."

He nodded again and turned his back as, hesitantly, Chloe untucked and unrolled the quilt so her lady's face was once more exposed to the air.

Something small, dark, and furred raced into the room, whining and circling the Reanimator's feet.

John and Chloe jumped.

"Black magick!" John cried, making the sign of the cross.

The thing took flight, landing in the Reanimator's arms and licking the face beneath the mask.

"Not black magick," the Reanimator said with a laugh, stroking a hand down the black beast's back. "Merely my dearest companion—a true vixen."

Her broad, plush tail flipped about like a fine dust brush and with a whimper she hopped back down and slunk back into the shadows. "Although black magick is highly profitable, it is not what I practice," he assured. "There is enough risk with real magick and science—things go wrong and doppelgängers and fetches get born . . ." He shook his head. "Reveal your lady."

Chloe dropped the quilt's edge and retreated, her hand going to her mouth. To see her so still . . . She knew she was dead. She *knew* it. But the shock of seeing death so plainly shadowing her ladyship's features, making her seem sallow, so incomplete . . .

The man wandered around the table, leaning over to examine her more closely. "And precisely how . . . ?"

"Her wrists," Chloe stammered, her hand rubbing at her own wrist, stunned.

"Ah. I see, I see." He shook his head. "No. I *need* to see. Unwrap her fully, please."

Chloe did.

After a long time of him doing seemingly nothing but staring at the ragged tears in her forearms, he untied the ribbons on her wrists and announced, "I can bring her back. I will need to repair some structural damage first." He motioned to her butchered veins. "But it is nothing I haven't managed before. Given a little time and a great deal of luck, I'll have her right as rain." He stuck his hand out. "Hand me her soul."

John's eyes flew wide open and, turning, he stuttered, "H-h-her soul?!"

The man's grinning mask tilted as he appraised his guests. "You do not have her soul?" He looked from one of them to the other and back again, his gaze settling on Chloe.

"How does one even . . . ?" she began, but her voice fell away to nothing.

"Amateurs. The soul or spirit is energy—not unlike that inside your common stormcells and stormlights. When a person dies, especially in a traumatic fashion, their soul wings away because, being power, it is attracted to power, even residual sources and especially tumultuous sources of it. What stormlight was closest to her when she died?"

"They were all dead."

He straightened sharply. "Ah. Lady Astraea."

Chloe clapped her hands over her mouth, eyes wide.

"Word travels fast whenever the Weather Workers arrive. There will be a stormlight near her body's location that will still have the faintest of glows to it. It will shine with a color and hum without the power of the Hub. Bring me that stormlight with the crystal intact and I might revive her to nearly her natural state."

"*Nearly* her natural state?" Chloe asked.

"This is science. And science is an imperfect art. But frequently improving. Hurry now."

Both servants turned toward the door, but Chloe grabbed John. "No. You have your keys. Stay with her. Guard her," she whispered, looking at the strange man. "I'll feel better if you do."

"But." John glanced toward the door and the darkness beyond. "The streets—"

"—were my home before either of my two households took me in," she assured. "I'll be fine."

Yet, hearing the door latch behind her, she drew her arms tight around her body and hurried back toward the Hill and the Astraeas' dark estate crowning its top.

The Road To Holgate

The carriage holding Jordan captive jostled its way across the Hill and meandered down the zigzagging road that descended along properties of decreasing value.

The Councilman perched on the overstuffed leather seat across from Jordan was glaring. "This would all be much easier if you admit that you are what you are," he growled, leaning back until the seat squeaked. He picked at his fingernails and shook his head, making little *tsk-tsk* noises.

"But I am not a Weather Witch," Jordan insisted, rubbing at her cheeks to stop the flow of tears. "I have no affinity with storms—I don't even particularly like them. The only thing I like about a cloudy day is that I do not need to carry a parasol to avoid getting an unsightly tan. Or freckling like some washerwoman."

"You summoned a storm. A large one."

"No. I did not! I have never summoned a storm—I cannot. I am Grounded. Besides, that was not even a large storm considering our weeklies. Magicking a storm is simply *not* within my capabilities *nor* my bloodline."

"Your bloodline is corrupt. Your mother no better than a filthy whore."

"Take that back," she hissed, her manicured fingers curling into claws as her lips twisted in a snarl. "No one speaks of my mother that way. Lady Cynthia Astraea is one of the most noble women to walk this Earth . . ."

"Slut," the Councilman said, lacing his fingers together and peering over them at her with cool detachment in his eyes. "Whore. Two-bit Molly."

A growl grew in Jordan's throat and she leaned across the aisle, eyes bright and sharp. "You stop now or I swear . . ."

The man grabbed a metal bar on the carriage's curving wall, fingers wrapping tight around it as he watched Jordan, a wicked grin on his lips. "You swear you'll do *what*, Miss Astraea? Or shall we give you some other name since Astraea should not belong to a bitch whose mother was nothing but a common coney?"

Shrieking, Jordan lunged across the aisle but the Wardens

flanking her simply held tighter. For a moment she hung in the middle of the aisle, her mouth moving soundlessly as she fought for words to hurl at the Councilman and the cold-eyed Tester at his side. No words came and finally she flopped back into her seat, shaking with sobs as fresh tears seeped free of her eyes.

The folded paper star pressed into her sleeve was a bitter reminder of how far she'd already fallen.

Across the aisle the Tester cocked his head, cooing a single word, his eyes on her hands the whole time. "Interesting."

Jordan sniffled and turned her head to the carriage's barred window, watching her world slip away, lights and familiar sights streaking and blurring to nothing as the last beads of rain raced across the window's glass.

Chapter Seven

For it's always fair weather
When good fellows get together . . .
—RICHARD HOOVEY

Philadelphia

Rowen wandered down the stairs, his fingertips trailing along the low banister as his nose sucked in the familiar scents of the kitchen. Freshly baked bread, sweet biscuits, and stew . . . It was hardly appropriate that he should spend so much time fraternizing with the staff—they were all at least two ranks below him, but Rowen had never cared much for societal norms when it came to friendships. He had grown up with brothers who couldn't be bothered with him and parents who only wanted him to fit a mold. Most of the time he did.

And most of those times willingly.

But there were times as a boy Rowen broke free—disappeared—and had to be hauled back to the house, streaked in mud and laughing like some wild child, clothing torn and hair full of "unmentionable natural objects," as his mother would say. Jonathan was his most frequent accomplice and remained a friend (though that word could never be used around Rowen's mother—it was unseemly having a manservant as a friend). So it was only natural that Rowen headed to a place he knew Jonathan would find him.

A place his harpy of a mother would dare not visit.

He stepped through the kitchen's doorway, his mouth watering and his eyes tearing at the mix of scents. The butter churn sat empty in the corner, the day's butter made so early in the day Rowen preferred to think of that time as night. Between the spices, the meat sizzling as it turned on the spit over the always-smoky fire, and the pungent scent of the small turn dog working the wheel to keep the spit moving, the kitchen featured the richest atmosphere in the entire house.

The cook raised a hand in greeting and returned to chopping vegetables for the next day's meals. The serving girls all smiled in Rowen's direction, a few curtsying. They were all keenly aware that Rowen was untouchable and had become like sisters to him as a result, some older, some younger, all undeniably fond of him and perhaps a bit too protective.

Nancy spun about to greet him, her hair held in a tight bun at the back of her head and yellow as cooked corn, fists on her generous hips, apron covered in flour and grease. "Well if it isn't the hero home again," she joked, her cheeks plumping as she smiled. "Did you show Miss Jordan the trick you've been practicing?"

For a moment the serious set of his face softened. "Yes. I did. I surprised her. Twice."

"Twice was it?" she teased, picking up her rolling pin to jab him in the stomach. "Twice is a respectable number of times to do a thing."

He let out a little *oof,* his expression going boyish and goofy.

"She wanted an encore, did she?" She winked at him, her eyes sparkling.

She needed one, he thought, remembering slipping the pin to her in a sly fashion. His face fell into a more somber expression. "Where's Jonathan?"

"In the wine cellar."

His smile returned for a moment. "Thank you, Nancy." He slid past her, taking the steps at the kitchen's far side down into the cellar. The difference in temperature was remarkable and Rowen snugged his shirt tighter to him and adjusted his waistcoat and cravat. In the wine cellar the smells were as different as the temperature. A chill was ever-present, the moist smell of water on stone overtaking all other sensations. Rowen's boots echoing on the stairs muted the noisy hum of the kitchen at his back.

Jonathan was in the far corner perusing dusty bottles when Rowen found him.

"I think this is the best choice tonight," Jonathan said, holding a bottle out for Rowen's inspection.

Rowen shrugged. "Anything will do."

"Excellent well. I'll fetch us some water."

"Ha." The single syllable fell from Rowen's lips, clearly illustrating his lack of humor at the thought. "Anything but water."

"That is what I feared, young sir," Jonathan muttered, uncorking the bottle with a move that came from good training as a potential sommelier, and a long year of watching Rowen drink in order to make sure Rowen never drank too much.

"Stop with the *young sir,* Jonathan. We are friends and no one is here to judge, are they?"

"No," Jonathan agreed. "There is certainly no one who will disturb us here and certainly not at this hour. I made quite certain your father's nightcap was delivered in advance. The family is well tended." Slowly he poured the drink.

Alcohol was common in the city. Although ale was the norm, many enjoyed wine as well. The other choices were coffee and tea, but the effects of Rowen having too much of either sometimes worried Jonathan more. Rowen on ale was a joking troublemaker, Rowen on wine was calm and sloppy. Rowen on coffee was Rowen as a jittery mess, and tea was not much different. And gathering what he had of Rowen's earlier situation, Jonathan made the very conscious decision that tonight Rowen would be calm and sloppy.

Rowen raised his glass to Jonathan in salute. "You tend to us quite well, friend." Without breathing, he downed the first glass and presented it for a refill.

Jonathan poured a refill and let Rowen talk. And Jonathan poured him another and let him worry and wonder aloud about Jordan's situation—few other than Weather Workers knew what truly became of Weather Witches. By the time they had finished their second bottle (with Jonathan only having half of a single glass) Rowen was a blithering idiot. But he was a calm blithering idiot.

Jonathan helped him up from where he'd slid down against one of the household's untapped casks, brushed him off, and looped his arm over Jonathan's own shoulders to help him back the way he'd come, and then to his chambers. Jonathan opened the door, letting Rowen stumble to the bed where he pulled off his friend and master's boots, hauled the latter third of him onto the bed to better match the arrangement of the already unconscious upper two-thirds, and left him there, pulling the door shut so that he might sleep it off.

It was more difficult sneaking back into the Astraea estate than sneaking out, Chloe realized, standing face-to-face with Lionel and a few additional members of the household staff.

Decidedly *larger* members.

"What are you doing out unescorted on an evening filled with so much family tragedy?" He cast a wicked shadow on the wall behind him, lit only by the candle he held between them.

"There are things that must yet be done that I did not wish to bother you with," Chloe admitted, wringing her hands.

"I fear I see guilt in your actions."

"No. I am guilty of nothing but perhaps caring too much."

"I spoke to the kitcheneers about your previous household."

Chloe stiffened.

"I have put the bits together. I now know the truth."

"No one knows the truth of that," she said, her voice falling away to nothing before she recovered. "This present darkness"—she waved at the thick black pooling around them—"does not compare."

"I'd imagine not. At least not yet. And it is my intention to keep it that way. You will not do to the Astraeas what you did to the Kruses."

Her jaw dropped at the accusation. "I did *nothing* to the Kruses!"

"Both parents and the remaining boy dead . . . only hours after the eldest was taken in for witchery." He stepped forward. "That's why you always wear your hair in such a peculiar fashion—with a cloth binding some of it back—to hide what he did to you in retaliation." He tore the bandana off her head then, sweeping her hair back to reveal the place where a whole ear should have been and showing the stump left after a single sword slice had cut much of it away.

"There is the only proof I need," he muttered, his tone mixing disappointment with disgust. He let her hair drop back down. "Take her."

Rough hands clasped her arms and she panicked at their grip in the darkness, thrashing and flailing her arms.

One thought persisted as she swore her innocence time and again—she had to retrieve Lady Astraea's soul—what good was reanimation if one was doomed to wander soulless? "No!" she screamed, fighting her captors. She pulled, she pushed, she stomped her feet on theirs until they cursed and tried to hold her while dancing away.

"Enough of this," Lionel ordered. She pleaded with her eyes when her voice clawed her throat.

He shook his head, his mouth downturned, and he brought the heavy brass candlestick down on her head and she flopped, limp, into the men's arms.

En Route to Holgate

The world outside Jordan's window whipped past in a series of darkening blurs, drops of water rolling across the glass as air whistled around the carriage and they sped beyond the boundaries of the city's streets. And beyond the city's walls.

Without stormlight the only light came from the moon

and a sprinkling of stars high above. No stormlights meant no houses, and no houses meant they were beyond civilization and, more importantly, it meant Jordan was alone with her captors. Hoping to spot some sort of home or farm she wiggled as close to the window as she could without being anywhere near the Warden seated between her and it. It was not easy to do.

The carriage's clattering wheels threw water up in occasional arcing sprays, surprising those seated inside as much as the four Wraiths clinging to the carriage's corners. Stalwart against both the wind and weather they relished, tails of their long coats snapping against the windows like specters knocking for entrance with barely existent fists, the Wraiths rode.

Jordan curled in on herself, her eyes wide, stomach troubled as she peered out the window. Never had she been so far from home or so out of sorts. Never had she wondered so fiercely what everyone in her household was doing.

Without her.

She screamed, jumping back when the veiled face of a Wraith appeared at the window, peering inside and rapping on the glass. It growled something to the men inside, long gloved fingers moving in a distinct pattern mimicked by the watching Wardens, and turned away, pointing.

The wind tore at the Wraith, its image little more than the silhouette of a filled frock coat and top hat until the wind blew its veil back and Jordan screamed anew. A distended head faced her through the glass, features dented and wrinkled. Wisps of patchy white hair flew wild over ridges above strangely rounded eyes set on either side of a nose with a bridge that was too narrow and a base too flat . . .

It grinned, teeth sharp and thin as a cat's fangs peeking

out from between nearly nonexistent lips. For a moment it struggled with the hat and veil, but giving up it rolled back up and out of her sight, leaving Jordan a sobbing mess.

"There, there," the Tester said, eyebrows aloft as he examined his hands with great interest. "That particular deformity only happens to *some* magickers. Who knows what might happen to *you*?"

Philadelphia

"Time, it is a-wasting," the Reanimator muttered, raising his gore-covered hands before looking at one of the dozen clocks hanging on his wall between narrow shelves lined with hundreds of tiny faceted crystals—each flanked by small labels. "What time did she kill herself? John, was that your name?"

"Yes, sir. I don't entirely know, sir . . . I wasn't there at that moment."

"I'd expect not. She was a good lady, John? Kind?"

"Yes, sir." John rubbed his head, rearranging the wrinkles that crossed his broad, dark brow. "I reckon it was nearly half past nine or ten, sir."

The Reanimator nodded and dipped his hands in a basin of water, rubbing along his arms until the water swirled with the lady's blood. He dried himself on a colorful strip of cloth and reached a hand toward one clock, his finger outstretched to tick off time. "Should your partner not have been back by now, John?"

John nodded slowly, worry etched in the space beneath his eyes. "Shoulda been, yes, sir."

"Well, John, I have good news and I have bad news. The

good news is I still have a little time left to bring your lady back to her nearly normal living state and I've made some necessary repairs to her already."

"And the bad news?"

"I have very little time left and without a soul she'll be nothing but a flesh and blood automaton. Do you know what I mean, John? Have you seen the automatons—those things the government has recently created that look like giant metal and porcelain dolls?"

"I've heard tell of them, but never seen one with my own two eyes. Godless tailed things, folks say."

"Exactly why I'm worried, John. You and I may face a dark decision very shortly. Can you make an important decision, John? Between life and death?"

"I hunt. Make those decisions often."

"Excellent. The procedure takes half an hour; the window through which we can reconnect body and soul only stays open for a few hours before it begins to badly degrade. If your partner doesn't arrive in the next ten minutes, John, we'll either need to condemn Lady Astraea to the death she seemed set on, or you'll need to choose a new soul for her."

The larger man drew back at the idea, pulling into the cloak of the nearest shadow to hide. "Choose a new soul for her ladyship . . ."

"Yes, John, quite so. Well, not exactly a new soul . . . a new-to-her soul."

"A new-to-her soul?" Terror crawled in John's wavering tone.

"Yes." The Reanimator motioned lazily to the multitude of shelves lined with sparkling crystals and strange dolls. "Any of those crystals, I daresay, will serve her well."

"But . . ."

The man adjusted his mask and sighed. "Do not be tiresome, John. Ideally a candidate for reanimation has the soul that once belonged to him or her restored to them. But sometimes life itself is far more important than being exactly who a person was before death. Sometimes the sheer point of existence is of greatest importance. Sometimes *what* a person is is more important than *who* a person is."

"But a person's soul defines—"

The Reanimator stuck a hand in the air between them. "Do not be so simple, John. We are more than the sum of our parts. Yes. A soul makes a significant difference in a person's behavior, but some live on for years without any soul. And, frankly, if you ask me, John"—he leaned forward and John leaned in as well—"some people are born without souls!" He laughed. "A soul is a mere detail in one's life. Like spice in a recipe."

John drew back, his arms across his chest, his stare hard.

"John. This is all very scientific. Her brain chemistry, humors, and cellular memory—"

"Cellular memory?"

He waved a hand impatiently. "Yes. Don't worry about the specifics—as they say—the devil's always in the details."

John eyed the shelves suspiciously. "Seems you maintain a lot of details."

"John, my friend, it's nearly time to make a choice. Life or death."

He blinked. "Miss Chloe believes Miss Jordan would be devastated if'n her mama ain't home when she returns."

"Returns? Weather Witches don't—"

"Miss Jordan's no Witch. Well, no Weather Witch at least." He coughed. "I meant no disrespect, sir."

"I doubt your Miss Jordan would be offended. I doubt,"

he whispered to the corpse on his table, "that Miss Jordan is worried about anything other than saving her own skin right now." He straightened and put his hands behind his back. "Your decision, dear John." He swayed on his feet, a little bob, but a merry movement.

"Life," John said haltingly. "Now I choose a stone?"

"Yes, make a good choice."

He edged toward the shelves, mindful of his mass and the multitude of tiny crystals. Each label stood by its crystal like an elegantly handwritten name card at dinner and John grimaced. "I . . ."

"You what?"

"I don't see so well."

"As long as you're careful you can pick up each card for closer examination." The Reanimator went back to what he was doing.

John stayed perfectly still. "I don't *read* so well," he admitted after a lengthy pause.

"Ah. Then I understand your hesitancy." He stepped to the side of the shelves. "If she was a religious woman, I have a nun who was caught in a compromising position, so to speak. Or . . . a woman who was a gifted hunter . . . a healer . . . a teacher . . . an artist—oh, no, I most certainly wouldn't advise that—they're nothing but trouble . . . Or you can do it the old-fashioned way, John."

"The old-fashioned way?"

"Yes. Stick your hand out over the stones palm down, close your eyes, and try to see which one feels right for her ladyship."

"That sounds simple enough."

"And as Ockham himself would say, oft time the simplest answer is the best."

John nodded and reached out his hand, turning it over as he'd been directed. "I should feel something?"

"Close your eyes," the Reanimator reminded.

John pursed his lips and closed his eyes, slowly dragging his hand through the air inches above the crystals. "I don't know—" He stopped and his brow furrowed. He tilted his head. "Yes," he said. "Something here . . ." He opened his eyes. "This one." He pointed.

The Reanimator plucked a card from the shelf. "Ah. A very good choice."

"What does it say?"

After a moment's hesitation he cleared his throat and read, "Lady Caroline of House Amalthea. A fine and noble lady of good breeding and manners with a kind heart and fine disposition." He slipped the card back onto the shelf and picked up the crystal. "Sounds lovely, yes?"

John nodded. "It sounds much like her ladyship."

"Excellent well. You may stay at this point or you may leave for a bit—it makes no never mind to me." He shrugged. "But the rest might seem a bit gruesome if you are not familiar with the work I do. And I do not intend to shock anyone." He froze a moment before giving a little laugh. "Well, I don't intend to shock *you*." He motioned toward the door. "You may at least wish to turn around again for this part . . ."

John turned obediently toward the door and, in the space of a single heartbeat, the Reanimator had swapped out the crystal's card, stepped back to her ladyship and, carefully drawing back the edge of her bodice's top, he made a slight incision before inserting the crystal John had chosen. "One moment more," he suggested, and, grabbing a small jar from the shelf, popped it open and swabbed a fingertip inside. He smeared the same fingertip across the underside of the incision he'd just made. He pushed the edges of flesh back together, pressing on the small lump he'd created to seal the space shut.

"You may turn about safely now, John." The Reanimator handed the jar of salve to John. He set different stones around her ladyship's body. Reaching beneath the table, he withdrew a container with a wide corked top. Opening it, he daubed a bit of salve smelling of cinnamon on the woman's tongue, saying, "The process is both ceremony and science as much as . . ." He tugged out a copper coin and, opening her mouth, placed it on her tongue. ". . . catalyst and *coin*."

He winked at John and reached toward the ceiling, uncurling a wire tucked among the exposed rafters. He laid it so its end was pinned between her ladyship's tongue and the coin. "Now we wait . . . Have you ever seen examples of my work walking around our fair city before?"

"I seldom leave the Astraea estate. I am kept busy tending the grounds and moving wine casks and—"

"Have you ever seen one of the parties you work so diligently to arrange?"

"Yes. Sometimes I work security. When the Vanmoer family comes to visit—*came* to visit," he corrected. "They will surely return—when things are put to rights."

"Hmm." He paused and glanced at the servant. "When things are put to rights?" The Reanimator nodded and picked up a strand of crystals, which he looped around Lady Astraea's wrist. Another he linked around her throat. One more wrist, both ankles, and he replaced her earrings as well, handing John her original ones. "Well. If and when the Vanmoer family returns for a party you will then surely see an example of one of my finest works," the Reanimator said. He glanced at the nearest clock. "Not long now . . ."

"A member of the Vanmoer family?" John balked.

"Yes," the Reanimator said. "One of their most memorable members, really. They have many excellent reasons not to part from him too soon." The hands ticked closer to a large mark on the clockface and John realized what they waited for. "We very nearly have it . . ."

The Reanimator stepped back. "Now, I must warn you. She will act strange as a result of blood loss and . . . well, being dead, for a few hours. It will take a day or more for her to get her appetite back. It is best most times if you put them into a room, close them up there, and check on them in little ways. If she wonders why she cannot remember certain things, explain that she felt ill and was given a sleeping draught, and memory loss occasionally occurs. I expect your partner can handle the finer points of such subterfuge."

"Surely," John agreed.

The bell in the square sounded and every crystal glowed brighter with the wave of light that poured from the Pulse, and they squinted against the flash.

A spark traveled the length of the wire and connected with Lady Astraea's tongue.

She convulsed.

A long moment passed as both men watched the woman, and the Reanimator reached down to sweep her tongue clean of wire, coin, and most of the jelly-like salve.

She coughed and struggled to speak, her tongue buzzing and thick. "Where am I?" she finally managed. Her hand fluttered to her throat and the Reanimator helped her sit.

Handing her a cup of water he looked at John and nodded as if to say, *This is all perfectly normal.*

She looked over the cup's rim at him as she sipped. "Thank you . . . Now where am I?"

"Asleep, milady. Having the strangest dream of your life. Or of two lifetimes . . ." he muttered.

"Dreaming . . . ?" She cast a worried glance about the room, her eyes widening and narrowing at odd intervals as her gaze fell upon certain strange things cluttering the space. "I daresay this hovel is more nightmare than dream." She paused to lick her lips, eyebrows drawing together. "I feel . . ."

"Woozy? John?"

She nodded and tumbled forward into her servant's ready arms.

"All perfectly normal. She'll sleep now for hours, perhaps a day or two. Certainly long enough to wrap her back up, carry her home, and deposit her in her chambers. Then let your partner do the rest. Presuming *she's* still alive." He shrugged and held out a hand for payment.

John weighed the bag of silver he carried and, handing it over, adjusted his grip on her ladyship to lay her back down and wrap her back up. "Thirty pieces, as requested."

John had the sense that the Reanimator's natural smile matched that of the mask. "Excellent well. Get her home, take good care of her, and keep the crystals near her at all times. Make sure her body servant knows . . . *something* . . . They should not even be removed for bathing."

"I will have to lie," John said.

"Not so much lie as fabricate a newly acceptable truth. Why worry over it, John? Politicians do the same on a daily basis."

John grunted. "I am no great leader of men."

"Neither are most politicians." He waved John and the sleeping Lady Astraea, once again wrapped snugly in cloth, toward the door. "Ah! Do not forget this." He handed the card to John.

John tucked the card carefully into his trouser pocket. "And if there is a problem?"

"I do not stay long in one place. Find me—if you can."

The door slammed shut, bolts sliding home.

John grunted, mumbling to himself and the well-wrapped Lady Astraea, "I am a hunter. I do that on a regular basis."

John set her ladyship into the wheelbarrow and began the return trip up the Hill.

The bumping and backward walk ascending the steps to the Hill was more a struggle than a stroll, what with the drowsing Lady Astraea as his luggage. But, big as he was, he muscled through, keeping well to the shadows, and was un-questioned the whole way home.

En Route to Holgate

The carriage came to a creaking stop at the edge of something that—by the dimly lit, rough-hewn sign—considered itself a town. Jordan sniffed and, looking between the bars on her window, surveyed a swipe of land so dark it blended into the night sky. Two tilting lightposts flanked a walkway and glimmered with stormlights.

An inn slumped behind them, dull and dusty as the road running before it and as worn and weary as Jordan felt. She squinted, focusing. Nothing about it seemed at the correct angle, its door sunken into a threshold that had been dug out to compensate. The few windows lining the front wall were bowed and looked ready to pop under the sagging weight of the walls.

"It's not much," the Councilman admitted with a shake of his head, his tone nearly apologetic, "but"—he sneered at Jordan around his next words—"but it's far more than a Weather Witch deserves." His fingers enclosed her arm and he pulled her forward. "And it's far better than you'll have until you're truly and rightly Made."

Jordan's eyebrows rose. "I'm no Witch," Jordan protested. "I cannot be Made. When you see *that* . . . When you all realize that—"

He yanked her around to face him, drawing her close. "When we all see that you can't be Made, that the Tester was wrong? What do you think will happen then, Jordan of the House Astraea, who once ranked Fifth of the Nine?"

"You will be—" But she froze, seeing something in the pinched features of his face that made bitterness and amusement bedfellows.

"—sorry?" he whispered, his nose brushing past hers, his breath washing over her face until all she smelled was remnants of the food he'd last devoured. "You think we'll be sorry? You think everything will go back to how it was, before House Astraea fell?" He gave her arm a firm shake and again began to drag her forward. "There is no going back, so you had better hope you *can* be Made. Because to have chosen you wrongly would bring shame to the Council. And the Council is not fond of shame. You have heard of the scandal surrounding past Councilman Braga?"

She swallowed. "Yes. The scandal broke and he disappeared. Ran from the shame."

The Tester even laughed, saying, "Is that what they say up on the Hill? That old Braga ran away?" He laughed again, shaking all the way from his head to his gut at the idea. "He might have tried to run. Briefly." He looked introspective, as if caught in the grip of memory. "But from what I saw of his corpse, he didn't get far."

Jordan sucked in a deep breath. "They *murdered* him?"

The Councilman spoke up. "It seems so harsh when you say it that way. *Murdered.* We like to think of it as *removing an obstacle to continued political success.* A high-ranking Witch that cannot be Made . . . Now *that* is quite an obstacle. *If* you catch my meaning."

Jordan looked down at the mismatched slabs of slate making up the awkward walkway and forced her feet forward.

She was not a Witch, so she would die.

And if she was a Witch . . .

She looked at the sky, wondering how many Conductors powered airships right now, how many were in service to the Council, making sure the upper ranks' wine and silks and slippers arrived on time. Were the Weather Witches truly *Conductors*—did they have any control in their lives or were they glorified slaves?

She was shoved into the tavern's dim interior. The room fell silent, its few occupants setting down their food or drink to stare unabashedly at the strangers. Once again the center of attention, flanked as she was by Wardens and Wraiths, Jordan swept one hand down her rich gold skirting and frowned—it was already beginning to show wear even though the metallic embroidery still sparkled in the lantern light.

Tipping her chin up with pride, she set her lips into her most practiced pout.

The Councilman shoved her into the gloved hands of a Wraith.

Jordan shivered, trying to look beyond the dark veil that

hid a face full of horrors under the brim of a fashionable hat.

"We require three rooms," Councilman Stevenson ordered the man behind the bar. "The Wardens will precede us to Holgate."

Dismissed, the Wardens stepped outside. A vicious wind rose up, shaking the building, and Jordan pulled free of her captor long enough to push her cheek to the nearest window and watch the Wardens be whisked into the sky and fly away, their bodies nearly swallowed up by the clouds they called.

The barkeep glanced at them, set down the tankard he was toweling out with the cleanest bit of his apron, and called, "Sersha!"

A mouse of a girl slipped out of the kitchen and glanced from him to them.

"Three rooms," he instructed.

She nodded. "Come along."

They passed through the main hall and into a narrow hallway that opened only for stairs and a slender ground-level door.

"Up we go," the girl encouraged, beginning her ascent after lifting her skirts high enough to flash the entire group with her pale ankles and calves.

The move was not lost on the Wraiths, Councilman, or Tester. The stairs cracked and popped beneath them and Jordan clutched the worn railing with nervous fingers as she lifted the hem of her own dress—only far enough she wouldn't die tripping over it. Not above her ankles.

Never above her ankles. And certainly not high enough to show her calves.

Even a young lady accused of witchery had to maintain some sense of decorum.

Dust danced in flurrying designs across the warped floorboards as the girl led them to the second floor and Jordan wasn't sure whether to be dismayed or delighted. Few visitors meant the place had less patrons of an ill-reputed variety, which Jordan hoped meant things were less worn.

Sersha paused before a door and pushed it open. A spider scrambled off a web the door broke, tumbling to the ground and scurrying away as Jordan bolted backward and bumped into a Wraith.

Its snarl jolted her forward and she stomped on the spider herself—the crunch of its exoskeleton audible beneath her shoe. She shuddered.

Seeing the door open and the girl light the shabby space with her lantern did nothing to alleviate Jordan's trembling. Dust motes spiraled down in the musty-smelling room. "There's no"—she looked over the small space quickly—"no window."

"You do not need a window and we do not need to worry about your possible escape," Councilman Stevenson said. He pointed. "Go. Sleep if you can. Wraiths will wait outside your door, so do not even imagine an escape."

He pushed her forward and slammed the door, locking her in.

She heard them move down the hall, leaving her with the muffled sounds of Sersha explaining the rooms, the click of doors closing, and the scraping and settling noises of stools or chairs being positioned outside her door.

And occupied.

A few minutes passed before her stomach settled enough for her to realize she was hungry. She had *watched* Rowen eat at the party and now her stomach rumbled deep beneath the many layers of her clothing.

Seated on the edge of the bed, it groaned beneath even her weight, ropes stretching and rubbing beneath the lumpy thing that served as mattress. There was no pillow and the quilt left for her was moth-eaten. She rose and turned, for a long moment staring at the bed.

It took her a while to realize she was waiting for someone to appear and fix things: the bed, the room . . .

Her life . . .

No one did.

Resigned, Jordan pulled the quilt free and shook the thing out, coughing on the dust that tickled her nose and lodged in her throat.

At least the dust was no longer on the bed.

A soft sound escaped her throat—not quite a whimper, but not far from it either.

The paper star from her party made her arm itch and, reaching up to pull it free of her sleeve, her fingers encountered the gift Rowen had given her. She flushed at the memory of his kiss. Quite the distraction! Her fingertips explored the gift: it was cold. Made of metal. And . . .

She fumbled with the lace it was hidden in, trying to work it free enough that she could finally see it. There, pinned to her sleeve, was a domed and detailed brass heart.

She ran her finger over its shining surface and smiled despite everything. Bringing it as close to her face as her flexibility and fashion allowed, she examined it closely. Along the edge was an elegant engraving. A script of some sort. She squinted to bring it better into focus.

Be brave.

She eased onto the bed, hands clenched so tight her knuckles whitened in her lap. There was nothing to do but sleep and be hungry. And brave. Only she couldn't imagine sleeping.

It wasn't so much the here as the *now* that kept exhaustion from taking her. Her nerves jangled from being stolen from her household and the journey in the carriage thus far had done nothing to quell them.

She glanced toward the door. The Wraiths waited just beyond it, wicked teeth and haunted features veiled beneath high hats . . . *That* could happen to Witches, and something similar made the Wardens?

She shuddered.

A knock at the door made her straighten and it opened. The girl, Sersha, entered holding a bowl of something and a dark chunk of bread resting on its top. The scent was unlike anything Jordan had smelled before—spicy and pungent. Although her mind urged caution, her stomach rumbled in anticipation.

The girl was nearly to her when she tripped, the bowl flying from her hands and falling with a clatter and a loud, wet *splot* onto the grimy floor. Sersha's face drew into an expression of terror as she scrambled to right things, scooping up the ruined food with both bread and bowl. She muttered apologies and, kneeling, held the mess out to Jordan.

"I—I cannot . . ."

"Please, lady," Sersha whispered. "I cannot ask for more . . ."

"I cannot eat that . . . It is . . ." Her lips puckered. "The reason for the one nearly clean spot on this floor."

The girl bit her lower lip, but nodded. Rising, she backed up all the way to the door, knocked to be released, and disappeared down the hall.

Jordan's stomach clenched, panicking with hunger, and she rubbed it. Bending awkwardly forward, she slowly unlaced the silk ribbons wrapped around her ankles and took off her shoes. They were pretty pointed little things made for those brief moments during a dance when a dress's hem might lift ever so slightly and reveal footwear.

They were designed for fashion, not comfort.

Without a knock, the girl appeared again, surprising Jordan with a fresh bowl of food. The barkeep followed close behind. "Show me how you managed to dump an entire bowl," he demanded, eyes different sizes in his head as he seethed.

Sersha walked toward Jordan, limbs stiff, eyes wide.

"There is no lump in the floor," he muttered. "No board so swollen . . ."

Sersha was, once again, nearly to Jordan.

"No bloody reason to *trip*." Reaching out he cuffed her across the cheek and she stumbled, ducking her head tight to her body, and handed over the bowl, arms trembling so hard the bowl shook in her hands.

Jordan grabbed it and glared at the man.

He pulled back his hand again.

Sersha's arms flew up to protect her and Jordan shouted, "Stop!"

He blinked at her, stunned, his arm still raised, fingers curled in a fist as he pivoted toward Jordan. "Stop or *what?*"

She glanced at the bowl in her hands. She could threaten him with a bowl of—whatever it was . . .

"See, that's how it always is. A demand and nothing to follow it up." He whipped back around to the girl.

"No," Jordan said, startled by her own voice. Be brave. She clambered to her feet, setting the bowl aside. "Dare not hit her again. She had an accident." Challenge flared in her eyes.

"I will discipline my daughter as I see fit."

"Do not."

"Maybe I should discipline the both of you . . ."

Jordan's voice rose. "If you raise a hand against either of us, I will *destroy* you."

"*Destroy* me?"

"Everything that is yours, I will sweep away. From the first shingle of this tavern's shambling rooftop to its last board and cornerstone. I will not rest until nothing of yours remains—I will scrub out even the *memory* of you," she added, her voice fading into a soft tone all at once gentle and fierce. "Do not touch her."

His eyes narrowed, weighing her resolve. His hand lowered, fingers unfurled, and he backed toward the door, seeing something in her.

He left, followed quickly by the girl, and Jordan's knees had the good grace not to weaken until the door shut again. She sat down heavily on the bed, barely keeping the bowl upright.

When she recovered, she sat up and scooped a few mouthfuls of the stew onto her bread and tried to eat without thinking.

Without tasting.

The girl returned too soon, but Jordan relinquished the bowl and remainders to her.

"Next time," the girl said, "do not help."

"Why not?"

"Because I would never help *you*, Witch," the girl snapped. She spun on her heel, striding out of the room with more attitude than Jordan usually mustered for a proper social outing.

Jordan flopped back onto the noisy bed and closed her eyes, fingertips wrapped round the heart as she let exhaustion claim her. All around her the night melted away into something less grim for a time.

Chapter Eight

Poor naked wretches, wheresoe'er you are,
That bide the pelting of this pitiless storm . . .
—WILLIAM SHAKESPEARE

Philadelphia

In a room usually reserved for Council business, Chloe was fielding enough questions to wear down anyone ever accused of doing anything. She sat behind a small table, and a row of dour-looking men sat in opposition behind a long table. Watchmen and constables stood at the door and across the Hill she was fairly certain more watchmen searched her quarters and others' for evidence. If they were searching thoroughly they might find the worst thing of all—the truth about Lady Astraea.

Her fingers tapped the little table's surface. It was better this way. If they found her ladyship and ended it all—again— it would be better than letting her wander soulless.

"Explain to us the loss of your ear."

Chloe sighed and focused on constructing an appropriate answer. "My previous lordship, Lord Kruse, found my service to be lacking and my ears to be too readily available to receive gossip. And so he removed one. With his saber. It was a memorable lesson."

"And after the loss of your ear, what did you do?"

"I certainly didn't listen at doors anymore. And I no longer desired pairs of earrings."

"You make light of the obvious doubt cast upon your character?"

"No, sir, certainly not, sir. I am most grievously offended by the aspersions being cast. But I recognize my station and am quite aware of my innocence."

"Three people—people from your previous household—one where you ran the kitchen—are dead."

Chloe nodded. "And if I could identify their killer you would have a fierce fight keeping me from doing him harm."

"Bold words from a woman who abandoned a fallen household and now finds herself in another household facing ruin."

"The Council has ruined us already with the accusation of witchery and Harboring—with mere words. Such little things to bring down such a great family."

"The Tester found a Weather Witch. There was nothing to be done but bring her in."

"Bring her in and bring the rest of them down."

"Show some respect," one Councilman ordered.

"How can I when I am given none?"

"Respect must be earned."

"I have earned it. For eight years I worked for the Kruse family. I baked for them, cooked for them, cleaned and straightened accounts for them. I was more than a kitchen girl or body servant—I was a nanny to the children, a friend to the lady. I was *family*. And when they came and proclaimed the boy a Weather Witch—I *wept* for them. I died inside—all for the love of him and my adopted family."

"Then why did you kill them?"

"I did not kill them—I *loved* them!"

"The morning after Marion Alan Kruse was taken in for magicking, they were dead. And you were gone."

"So was the rest of the staff. We were horrified—finding them like that . . . their bellies distended, tongues swollen and black . . ." Her eyes squeezed shut and she clenched the small table until her dark fingers whitened.

"It must have been dreadful to face the results of your actions."

"How did my actions cause such a tragedy?"

"Through the leaves with which you flavored the biscuits."

"What?" She straightened, her face going blank for a moment. "We used nothing toxic in the cooking."

"Then how did they wind up in the biscuits? The biscuits you had none of?"

"I don't . . . The staff seldom ate with family—and almost never the same food."

"But they were like your *family,* you said. It seems unlikely your family would not allow you to sup with them."

"It was well known. Ask anyone."

"We would if there were anyone left to ask. But it seems you all ran as fast as cockroaches when a stormlight flares. So where did you obtain the leaves used in the biscuits?"

Then her jaw dropped.

He rounded on her. "Ah, so you *do* remember now, do you?"

"Harold. He wanted to help. We went into the garden to

pick mint. *Mint.*" She looked at him, her eyes damp. "It was mint."

"Mint doesn't kill."

"We didn't kill them. It was *mint.*"

"Did you pick it yourself?"

She shook her head. "No. I let Harold . . ."

"You allowed a child of four years of age to gather herbs for your cooking?"

"Yes. He had gone with me several times before . . . It was mint."

"It was negligence. What you and the child thought to be mint was a toxic plant—the same that killed your master and his family shortly after he sliced off your ear and the family fell to ruin. The timing is suspicious."

"I would never . . ."

"Would you blame the child?"

"No," she gasped. "Of course not."

"Then accept the blame yourself."

She deflated, slumping over the table, head cradled in her arms. She sobbed. Ever so softly.

Even from the sidewalk outside the Astraea estate John saw lights on in the rooms along the upper floor where Lady Astraea's chambers were. Watchmen stood in stiff pairs flanking the main doors, men dressed in dark trousers and long, crisp gray coats with silver piping and fancy epaulets on their broad shoulders. These were Council watchmen.

Dangerous men searching for something.

John shifted the bundle in his arms, the wheelbarrow leaning in the shadow of the estate's wall. He considered his options. Getting past the watchmen carrying the lady might not be impossible . . . but the odds were far from being in his favor.

He felt the faint beat of her heart and the rhythmic rise and fall of her chest as she breathed. This was his household's lady, as defenseless as ever a woman could be. He would not openly risk her. Especially not after they'd come so far.

He clung to the shadows lining the property's tall wall, only the occasional glimmer of light bouncing off his high cheeks and wide forehead telling of his passing. He halted at the back of the main house and looked up, examining its back wall.

A trellis ran along most of the wall, old rose canes and ivy warring to reach the rooftop first. Stepping forward, he grabbed the wooden trellis. He shook it, testing its strength.

"Apologies, milady," he muttered. He adjusted Lady Astraea's body so she hung across his chest, shoulder, and back like a sack of grain, and, his hands ignoring the prick of the rose thorns, he began the arduous task of hauling them both toward the open shutters marking her windows.

He was puffing out breath by the time he reached her windows. He crossed one last section of trellis and placed his hands on the edge of the nearest windowsill. Slowly he angled over so his head was just above the window ledge and he could glimpse the room's interior.

Her bed lay freshly made, the wood floor before it shining in the moonlight seeping in. A few candles still burned— brightly—fresh, considering the amount of time that had passed. So someone had been inside.

Cynda or Laura?

Or Chloe?

John wondered only briefly, knowing it made little difference. He would slip her ladyship into her bed, make his way outside the room, and find one or all of the girls.

With a final glance to assure himself no one watched, he braced his feet, bent his knees to squeeze them into the spaces between the trellis's narrow wooden slats, and lifted her ladyship off his shoulder, resting her on the window's broad ledge, one steadying hand on her waist.

Another slide and a step and he was directly before the window, climbing up to rest one knee on the cold stone sill. With a grunt, he got his hands onto the thick wood and iron shutters and hoisted the rest of his bulk up, struggling to not be indecently near her ladyship's prone form. It was difficult, maintaining appropriate decorum during a rescue.

He slid past her and dropped his feet to the floor before scooping her up. Crossing the floor to her bed, he laid her down and freed her from the quilts and blankets.

She was nearly as quiet as the statues gracing the cemeteries near the middle of the Hill—where the elegant people were buried, if they couldn't afford a proper tomb or a Bone Shrining. He shivered at the thought of being Bone Shrined—to have the flesh stripped from your bones so your bony bits could be strung up as chandeliers or stacked as walls or doors in your chosen church, where you could forever watch your fellow parishioners and descendants . . .

His thoughts straying, he stepped away, backing to the door and opening it. He slid into the blessedly dark hall and locked the door before making his way to find either Cynda or Laura.

Or best yet, Chloe.

John found both Laura and Cynda seated outside on a stone bench in the gardens, huddled together over the remnants of one of his lordship's cigarettes. He should have asked how they came by it, he knew he should, but the way they hung so close together, wary eyes on the house, words soft and sad, he no longer cared.

They startled when they saw him approaching and there was a brief fumble as Cynda tried to hide the smoking thing.

John put his hand out, shaking his head.

They lowered their eyes and Cynda presented the cigarette to him. He hesitated, watching them, before raising it to his lips and sucking down one long breath. He coughed a moment and the girls shared a giggle as he passed it back to them. "S'been a long time," he muttered. He turned to look at the house, too, at the trellis he'd clambered over and the veranda Miss Jordan and her friends had been entertained on not many hours before. "We have a problem," he said, looking over his shoulder at Laura.

She snatched the cigarette from Cynda and, eyes wide and wild, placed it to her lips. She nodded.

"You both had best know 'bout it."

Laura shook her head and ducked when Cynda tried to reclaim their stolen prize. From around the cigarette she said, "Cynda's got herself a job offer. She'll be leaving tomorrow."

"Where?"

"The Bertrams," Cynda said.

John appraised Cynda with a long, slow look. The girl had nice features, long curling blond hair, and an easy smile that was never far from her generous lips. She was not the most efficient household servant but most understood that what

Lord Bertram wished for in household servants had less to do with efficiency and more to do with easy attitudes. "If that is what you wish . . ."

Cynda pouted. "Yes, John. 'Tis. To be cared for in a household free of magicking and witchery is what I wish."

"Then you had best step away from us now before we begin our conversation," he warned. "I would not wish to entangle you in family matters."

She recoiled as if she'd taken the verbal slap physically. Rising from the bench, she snapped her fingers, reclaimed the cigarette, and stalked a distance off, strides so long her skirt swished angrily.

John glanced at the bench and Laura scooted as far over on it as possible so he might sit down and still no one could remark on the closeness of their proximity.

"It's my fault," she whispered. "I should not have . . ." She closed her eyes tight and swallowed hard. "And now Chloe has been taken by the Council . . ."

John's lips thinned, pressed so hard together. "Is no one person's fault. She did not have to do such a thing."

"I think such a thing is only done when a person feels there is nothing else a person can do." Laura shook her head. "They have Chloe. Say she's the one murdered the Kruses."

John pulled away so fast he nearly fell off the bench's back. "Chloe could not hurt anyone."

"Still. They took her and have her locked away. They mean to try her for the Kruses. And maybe this. Somehow."

"They cannot . . ."

But the look she gave him said what he did not wish to admit. They most certainly could try her for both. If they wanted a scapegoat they could certainly find her guilty of both—and a dozen other things she had nothing to do with.

Attaching a string of known crimes to a single low-ranking person was the easiest way to keep the crime rate appearing manageable.

John sighed. "You must know things about Lady As-traea," he said. "Things her body servant would be privy to." He looked at the space between them—the foot and a half of bench—and he scooted closer to her, closing the gap.

She gave a snort of disapproval, saying, "This is highly improper . . ."

"These are not the times for proper behavior, Miss Laura. These are the times when we must correct things that have gone horribly wrong best we can and trust the other knows our motivation."

She pressed her lips together now, too, nodding slowly.

John leaned forward to whisper all he knew about Lady Astraea's strange new condition, hoping her new body servant would prove loyal.

Holgate

Bran woke in the middle of the night, the sound of his own scream filling his ears. He clutched the covers, his body shaking and damp with the sweat drying all across it.

A wind rattled his shutters and he went to them, crossing the cold floor in bare feet as fast as he could. He tugged the shutters tight and latched them at one more spot before straightening, his face full of wonder.

He picked the small journal off his bedside table and flipped through it to the day's date. He had scheduled no wind. The water in the pitcher he used for washing sloshed as if shaken.

His shutters shook again in defiance. He closed the journal and stepped back to the window. Was an intruder outside on his balcony? Did someone mean to finally murder him in his sleep? Tiptoeing to his fireplace's mantel, he took down his father's sword. Another relic from the war that might yet serve him well. He unsheathed it and only jumped a little when the shutters rattled again.

Sliding up to the shutters, he unlatched them and pressed forward to gain the advantage on his attacker. He threw them wide open with a shout. But no one was there. The air was still, the humble balcony empty except for the pineapple plant Maude had obtained for him that he'd forgotten to water.

Blustering into existence again, the wind tore at him, twisting and biting its way around his body and blowing past his head with such force and such a chill that all his hair stood on end and bumps rose on his arms.

Then it was over and there was no wind, no breeze.

The cruel, chill air was gone and the night was once more still and warm, but with a touch more dampness—and darkness—than before.

Bran tugged the shutters tight and, leaning the sword beside his bedside table, slid into bed and drew the covers up as tight as he used to when his father stormed around in a drunken rage to forget his son's very existence—that Bran's birth had ruined everything that was good in his father's life. Somehow the cold, unwanted wind reminded Bran of the aspects of his father few knew, aspects he'd rather forget.

Jordan woke to a pounding on her door. She tumbled out of bed in the dark, trying to tighten her dress's back but getting caught up in a struggle. Had she been of lower rank she might have cursed, but saying such words only showed a lack of a more elegant vocabulary.

And class, she remembered. It showed a definite lack of class. Although she was on her way to wherever they took Weather Witches and most of an evening's travel from home, still she was a day closer to proving her innocence and helping put to rights an entire system that had somehow broken down.

Lord Stevenson threw open her door and (obviously having no concern for decorum) stepped inside, holding a lantern before him. A bit of light streamed in from the hallway's distant window and Jordan struggled to wrap her mind around the time. She barely had a chance to snatch up her shawl before he raised his voice to her.

"Hurry, Witch," he snapped. "We have places to be today so we may Gather more of your kind."

"More of my kind?"

"More Witches. They are bringing in their newest Gatherings from all up and down the East Coast. And I will come along at least as far as Holgate. To make sure you arrive safely." He grabbed her shoulder as she was slipping on her shoes and shoved her forward so that she hopped to maintain balance. Her shoes' silk ribbons trailed in the dust and she stopped to lift her skirts and tie the laces, saying, "Transport us *all*? But the carriage—"

He shoved her against the wall long enough to bend over her shoes and rip the ribbons free. Then he resumed prodding and pushing her down the hall and the stairs, across the main hall, and finally out into the sunlight.

Her golden gown sparkling in the morning's first light, she realized there would be no more carriage rides until she cleared her name.

Behind the carriage and its horses stood a wagon with heavy-boned horses all its own. They were harnessed tightly to their wheeled burden, their hooves broad and black, legs and necks thick with cords of muscle.

The wagon reminded her of one she had seen the day Rowen sneaked her into the Below for an incoming circus they would otherwise have not been allowed to attend. There had been wagons much like this one in the long line pulling into Philadelphia. Heavy-framed on wide wooden-spoked and steel-tired wheels, the wagon's body was framed with long metal bars creating a cage.

Her brain slowed at the thought, realizing how easily she'd moved from caged animals in her birthday's menagerie to caged people. "You mean to put us in there? Like animals?"

"You are Witches," Stevenson reminded. "Oh. Oh, you really don't know, do you? You are no longer afforded any special treatment. You no longer rank." He looked at her and wiped at the tip of his nose. "Though I daresay you will *smell* rank at the journey's end."

She stared at him, stunned.

"It sometimes amazes me," he admitted, "considering your education and money, how ignorant your rank can be.

"Load the girl," he ordered a Wraith, shoving her forward one more time.

Hissing, the Wraith closed its hand on her, hauling her along toward the back of the wagon and the door with its bulky antiquated lock.

She scrambled up three slanting steps and fell into the cage, landing on fresh straw spread across the wagon's bottom. Straw. Like she was livestock! The door clanged shut, and the wagon rattled as the lock snapped closed and the wagon lurched forward, rocking from side to side nearly as much as it crawled ahead.

Jordan tried standing, holding the bars for support, but the jerking and jostling of the wagon over uneven roads pitched her to her knees again and again. Finally she sat, adjusted her skirts so she was as ladylike as could be given such circumstances, and leaned her back on the bars to watch the countryside pass by.

Through forests thick with wildlife that scurried, flew, and sang from the treetops and across cleared swaths of land where small clusters of houses gathered together and called themselves villages they went, the wagon groaning and Jordan becoming increasingly sore. The road narrowed as they climbed into strange foothills. At rare moments Jordan glimpsed water miles away and far below, sparkling like a bed of shifting sapphires.

She scooted to the other side of the wagon, clutched the bars, and pressed her face against them to get a better view. The water was so wide! She had never been allowed to view such a large body of water. Her father said seeing such places (especially the sea) did strange things to a man or a woman— gave them what he called "the longing," a desire for adventure aboard ship.

Jordan snorted and sat back, her eyes searching for water between the stocky hills. She crossed her arms. Her father was odd about some things. She felt no longing. Yes, she might admit a fascination with such a large body of water but she had heard enough tales of the Merrow to have no desire to board any ship—not even the aptly named Cutter, its hull bristling with blades for slicing waterborne enemies to ribbons. No. She had no longing to be on any ship. Or in any wagon.

She peered out from under the wagon's roof. No. Not even an airship gliding through the sky and cutting through clouds or stealing thunder for its newly rumored thermo-acoustic engine could tempt her aboard. No. Certainly not. She was Grounded and would stay that way.

On horseback now, the Councilman dropped back to ride beside the wagon. Jordan tipped her chin up and looked away in defiance. She would prove she was no Witch. She would forgive them the indignities they had served her and might even be so gracious as to not mention it again in public.

Stevenson pressed his horse close to the wagon and smiled. "It won't be long now," he assured. "And you'll be with your own kind. All will be *right as rain*," he said, his tone mocking.

But beneath his slick smile she remembered the threat. If she could not be Made she would be made to disappear. And there was only one way to do that.

Murder.

Chapter Nine

~~~~

I am he that walks with the tender and growing night ...
—WALT WHITMAN

Philadelphia

The young man no longer stuck to the shadows, no longer waited until nightfall to work his magick—or *mischief,* as those Grounded would claim. He was tall and broad of shoulder with dark hair and gray eyes and a coolness about him that made people think of first frosts and snowfalls. And with good reason.

Because Marion Kruse was a coldhearted young man.

Truth be told, he wanted nothing more than to return to a simpler time. A time he didn't wander the roads and towns doing small things to amuse himself and set others to wondering. He wanted nothing more than to be back at his mother's feet, reading books about pirates and scoundrels that made her laugh and tell him and his brother to never grow up to be wicked—that goodness was its own reward. He wanted nothing more than to grow fat on Chloe's generously proportioned biscuits and call her "nanny" again. Nothing more than to go fox hunting with his father and friends (even that frustrating pretty boy Rowen Burchette) and dance with an attractive girl.

He wanted nothing more than to go back to before he'd been Made.

But Marion had been taught that going back was nigh unto impossible.

For a few years after his escape he had drifted through the forests and along strange roadways, meeting people and learning more about them than he'd ever known before. Too often knowing more meant respecting them less. But over the years he kept drifting closer and closer to his home city of Philadelphia. Not intentionally, but one night he looked up at the stars and realized they were nearly in the exact position as those he'd watched from his bedchamber on the Hill.

He paused on the sidewalk by a window box filled with begonias. They were his mother's favorite. So he moved on, glancing at the sky and the airships hanging there, big glass-bottomed airboats fat as fruit in fall. He lifted his face to better view the shadowy bellies of the ships overhead and wondered how many were infested with pirates—or respected captains with a pirate's worldview. The airships were modern ones with wings, rudders, and a large balloon keeping them aloft even when their Weather Witch of a Conductor could not. They were the stuff of myths and legends.

Like his kind had been once.

Funny how magick and myth became reality so readily. He grunted, looking back at the begonias.

He wouldn't harm them.

But roses . . .

There were bushes of them in the next yard, bold blossoms so big they nodded on thorny canes. Nearly perfect,
blooms wide to drink in summer's sun. The gate and delicately crafted wrought-iron fence separating these roses
from the ones inside looked familiar. He'd been here before.

Funny how your feet led you back to the places your
heart longed for most.

This was her house. Her estate. These roses? The pride of
her family—pictured proudly on the Vanmoer family crest.
Her family?

Ruined his.

Her family was the reason, even after all this time, he
dared not go home. Not that his family was where they used
to be—but he dreamed someday to find them again. To track
them down. To be their prodigal son.

But knowing such a move might ruin whatever they had
raised themselves back up to he had never asked after them.
Never tried to find them. Never sent them word he was free.
It was the same reason he had hesitated outside the city's
gate, reconsidering. The same reason he had halted at the
base of the Hill.

But sometimes you couldn't help but be led back around.
Sometimes destiny called so cruelly you dared not disobey.
So he had climbed the Hill. Had found this house. And, as
destiny seemed to dictate, he would make her family suffer.

In small, quiet ways.

At least at first.

He bent to sniff the bouncing blossoms, touching the
stem of just one. Because all it took was one when your heart
was full of ice.

Then he was on his way again, ambling merrily along,
before anyone noticed anything was amiss. By the time they

shouted, seeing how the rose petals blackened, dropping, and how the cane frosted, darkened, and twisted in on itself, deadening all the way to its knobby heart—by then he was gone.

En Route to Holgate

Wagons holding sweaty-looking occupants were already parked when Jordan's transportation pulled alongside them, and came to a snorting stop. Their wagons were smaller, their occupants less well-dressed, and their horses more worn from what Jordan supposed had been longer journeys.

The Councilman and Tester walked over to a small crowd of agitated and mean-looking men. Voices raised and Jordan pressed her face to the bars again, hoping to hear something of importance. The crowd grew more animated, arms flailing and pointing to the wagons before motioning down the hill toward something just beyond her sight.

Then she saw the guns.

Men stood beside the wagons, muskets and rifles at their sides. Some carried the weapons, switching them from one hand to another and always—*always*—looking down the hill to something beyond.

The Tester and Councilman nodded, the Councilman growling out, "Hurry now! And you"—he pointed to one of the strangers—"you tell Johnson I'll lynch him myself if this goes wrong. It stinks of treason, him arranging us all to meet so near to water and him being noticeably absent. He needs to remember where his loyalty lies now!" The wagons began to unload, guns on the would-be Witches as much as the mystery downhill. Jordan's door opened and she bounded toward the exit but was met by others being escorted in. "But . . ."

"You will travel together now," Stevenson reported, sweat heavy on his brow.

Watching his eyes she realized that although he spoke to her, he, too, watched what everyone else watched. Another wagon opened, and more Witches were loaded in with Jordan. No, she corrected herself. Not more Witches, more *prisoners,* Jordan thought. Maybe some of them were as she was.

Mistaken.

Two more wagons—these carrying a few sad-eyed prisoners—and the door clanged shut, the lock turned, and the Councilman took the key.

"And your name," a boy asked her, his gaze raking across her dress and now less than perfect hair, "what did they used to call you?"

"The same thing they will call me when this misunderstanding is all cleared up. *Lady.*"

She barely flinched when the wagon's inhabitants fell into fits of laughter around her. Turning her back on them, she pressed her face to the bars, steeling herself to the idea that she would not bother knowing any of them as she would be plucked from their questionable ranks soon enough.

Then she heard it—they all heard it—a noise that made the hairs on her arms raise and set her teeth on edge. A thin, trilling wail accompanied by soft, wet sounds like a child in oversized boots sloshing through puddles. The men with guns lined up, backs to the wagons. The drivers held the reins of their horses tight but still the beasts stomped and cried, tugging at their bits and bridles until their mouths foamed and bled.

"Get into your wagons and carriages and away," the Councilman commanded. "This is no place to make a stand— not with so much water . . ." He abandoned them all— handing his horse's reins to another rider, and, leaping into the carriage, he knocked so hard on its ceiling to signal the driver that they all heard.

"Johnson's doomed us all!" someone shouted as the other men scrambled to follow suit, climbing onto the wagons or into the carriages.

Horses bolted, carts jolting away as steeds panicked. Jordan and the other prisoners saw them then as their wagon bounced forward and away—a long line of wet and glimmering speckled shapes, hunched and slithering over the hill toward the retreating wagons.

They moved like fish forced onto land, even their awkward motions made with inherent grace, an alien fluidity that Jordan had only seen basely mimicked by dancing prima ballerinas. They flopped forward, heads covered in spines and long, limp green-and-blue things that shimmered and looked like weeds that grew out of their domed skulls. They pulled themselves onward with broad hands and webbed fingers, thick bodies ending in a long, winding tail rather than a pair of legs and feet. But what caught Jordan's attention most were their mouths . . .

Huge hinged jaws removed any chance the beasts might be considered beautiful and were lined with rows of needle-sharp teeth—so many teeth, in fact, the creatures seemed incapable of closing their mouths. Thin, rubbery lips could never stretch far enough to obscure such razor-filled mouths.

Jordan only realized as they raced away that her position in the packed and standing-room-only wagon had changed. Instead of pressing close to the bars to better witness the attacking Merrow, she pushed as far as she could into her fellow prisoners—decorum and all things proper forgotten in the face of horror.

Their wagon was ahead of a few others, and, wide-eyed, they watched as the Merrow paused in their slick progress to coil onto their tails and then—

They launched. Bodies sailed through the air like the school of exotic fish swam in the Mayor's much-lusted-after aquarium. They were all at once silver and blue and green, flashing like the ocean's sapphire waves and landing on the closest horses.

One horse reared up and struck out, squealing, forelegs flying. But the Merrow were everywhere—a swarm of flesh and teeth, burrowing wide mouths into horseflesh. Screaming, a horse bucked and broke free of harness and traces even as the carriage's driver fired his gun and reloaded. Men on the same wagon fired a volley, their guns cracking out their reports' noise as both bullet and ball left barrels and the sweet scent of black powder filled the air.

The escaping horse went down on its knees and Jordan turned away when blood fountained up from it, but turned back (morbid curiosity winning against fear) in time to see more Merrow launch themselves.

This time at the men.

Those deaths were faster than the horses'. Not cleaner, not gentler, but faster. Bones cracked and heads came free of bodies and Jordan discovered another use for the bucket in the wagon's corner when she emptied the sparse contents of her stomach into it. She rose again, watching as the bloodshed disappeared from sight, their wagon's rioting horses calming as they gained greater distance from the threat. Soon the horses slowed to a jog, their sweat a lather so thick it dropped to the road in clumps like freshly whipped meringue.

The awkward caravan paused a few miles farther down the road, pulling to a stop at a broad crossroads. The Councilman and Tester exited their coach and the group reconvened. There were no more worried looks although the men were clearly shaken and filled their sentences with curses. A few fierce words were exchanged and everyone remounted, the wagons going their separate ways. Jordan settled as best she could among the crowd of bodies, wondering how soon—if ever—they'd feel safe again.

Holgate

"You come from a proud tradition," Bran said, tucking his hands behind his back and leaning forward to better look at the little girl. Her eyes wandered the space, her gaze bouncing from item to item and drinking each in almost as often and fully as she drank up the water he kept handy. "You've gotten dehydrated," he said. "I thought Maude would take better care of you."

"She took excellent care of me, Mister—papá," the child corrected, rolling the horn cup between her hands. "She is sweet. My mother—God rest her soul—would have liked her."

Bran paused and nodded agreement. "Yes. I feel certain she would have. Here." He took the cup and set it on his desk's slanting surface. "This is my main library. Here there are three rules you must follow: listen, obey, and never, never open the door to the laboratory. It is here that you will help me do the gentle parts of what Making means."

"What are the gentle parts?"

"Research. You will fetch me books and learn to read and tidy up as we work," Bran said.

"And the not so gentle parts of Making?" she asked, her eyes so big and bright his heart thumped oddly.

"There are parts of my job that are—"

"Too hard for me?"

"Too hard for you to *see*," he clarified. "It is not an easy thing I do."

"Is it hard for *you*?" she asked, her voice soft as rainsong.

He straightened, twisting his fingers together before him. "It used to be," he finally said, his voice matching hers in gentleness. "Yes. It used to be nearly impossible." But he smacked his hands together and she gave a little hop. "But. We both come from a proud tradition," he assured her, perhaps more to assure himself than the blond little sprite before him. Why did the words trouble him so much now?

They were hardly a lie . . .

His father had said the same words every day that Bran could remember. And, if nothing else good might be said of his father, it could always be said he was honest.

Brutally so.

Philadelphia

Rowen couldn't remember a time without Jordan. It was strange knowing there was no Jordan to call upon, no Jordan to joke with, no Jordan to frustrate to the point he swore steam would pour from her ears . . .

No Jordan to confound.

And no Jordan to court.

He played with his hair a bit more, focusing in the mirror with fierce determination deep-set in his brow as he ran his brush through it again. He paused, staring at "fierce determination" reflected back at him, and he snorted. Such an expression would give him wrinkles prematurely. And although wrinkles on a man were a distinguishing mark of character (whereas on a woman they were simply ugly) Rowen did not care to add any character to his face until he was at least forty. Or fifty if he was fortunate. So he relaxed every muscle in his face and stared slack jawed into the mirror.

"Young sir." Jonathan's voice startled him from the other side of his door. "You have a visitor, young sir."

Rowen opened the door and arched an eyebrow. Thinking better of the wrinkle that too would eventually bring, he slid his eyebrow back into place and stared flatly at Jonathan. "Who is it at this hour?"

Jonathan smirked. "At this hour? It is nigh unto one in the afternoon, sir."

Rowen grinned. "Well, that explains why I am so famished." He reached out and smacked Jonathan on the back. "And just who is here visiting me?"

"Lady Catrina of House Hollindale."

"Sweet Jesus. What a way to ruin a man's appetite." He dropped his arm from around Jonathan and rubbed at his brow. "Why is Catrina here?"

"It seems your good mother sent for her."

"Of course." He groaned.

"Your good mother has a stake in a successful match being made of you," Jonathan pointed out. "If you rise, she will be better taken care of in her advancing age."

"I am well aware of my mother's grasping nature," Rowen assured. "And quite unimpressed with it."

"Catrina may be a bit of a reach."

Rowen snorted. "Perhaps according to rank, but . . ."

"Understood, young sir. She does seem to be quite smitten with you. I daresay she has been for some years."

They walked down the hallway side by side, Rowen shaking his head. "It matters not one whit. Not any of it."

"Because you are in love with Lady Jordan?"

Rowen stopped dead and, turning, stared at him. "I am not in love with Jordan."

"Right, right," Jonathan said. "My mistake."

"You could send her away."

"Would you wish me to? Your lady mother would be incensed."

Rowen sighed. "No, no. But do bring us some sandwiches from the kitchen, please. With cucumber aplenty."

"But, sir . . . Cucumber and you . . ."

Rowen's smile slipped to one side of his face. "Agree as much as Catrina and I do."

That day Lady Astraea slept soundly. She did not cry out, she did not die, she showed no sign of fever—if anything, she showed so little sign of life Laura was puzzled about the true nature of her existence. As far as Laura could tell her ladyship had not even rolled or moved in bed since John first placed her there the night before.

Laura gently removed the pillow from beneath her ladyship's head, fluffed it, and reset it. Then she moved around the room dusting and adjusting the positions of things so it did not seem so absolutely unlived in. She returned to her lady's side and carefully unwrapped the bandages on her arms, laying the skin bare to the air's caress. It was odd knowing how little time had passed and yet how healed the flesh was already.

Laura applied the salve to her arms and rewrapped them. It was not impossible that if she slept a few more days and the salve continued its miraculous work her wounds would be completely closed—perhaps even to the point no mark remained.

That evening found Rowen on a table, arms wrapped around Kenneth Lorrington and Chadwick Skellish, two of his like-ranked fellows, while belting out a song few of them remembered when sober and Rowen only recalled when drunk off his ass. But drunk off his ass he was and his friends didn't mind because at least Rowen was moving forward—in a sodden and weaving sort of way, but still it was forward. Never had "The Apparition of a Dandy" been so boldly sung and the regular crowd knew, if Rowen stayed on, he'd follow it up with "All for Me Grog."

Rowen released his friends, watching them waver a moment beside him, and then swung his arms wildly, the crowd in the tavern joining in on the chorus as the bartender clanked an empty tankard on the bar in time to the song. They roared at the end and Rowen swept them a bow and tumbled off the table and into the surprised arms of several men and their ladies.

Well, not so much ladies as *wenches,* Rowen reassessed, tearing his eyes away from their overly displayed décolletage as he apologized for his clumsiness. The women grinned at him, one running a hand over his stubbly cheek

and saying through a laugh and a haze of ale-scented breath,
"You can tumble into me any time, love."

"Men tumble into you too easily, you sly thing," her companion teased. She placed a finger in Rowen's dimple and
smiled, wiggling her eyebrows at him. "You should come
pay us a visit later this evening . . ."

Kenneth hopped off the table and, swinging an arm over
Rowen's shoulders, belched in his ear. "Emphasis on the
pay," he said with a laugh.

The women tittered but denied nothing and Rowen,
swinging around to seek a new source of fun, knocked into
the back of a well-dressed man who responded with a string
of well-used curses.

"Apologies, good sir," Rowen said, realizing the man's
drink had spilled across his front.

"Apologies?" the other countered. They locked gazes.
"Apologies!" The man grinned, lips twisting like snakes, and
he said, "You cannot begin to apologize to the likes of someone like me, Rowen Burchette. Not anymore."

Rowen cocked his head. "What mean you?"

"I mean, boy, that you are so low of station now—having
nearly become engaged to that whore's offspring—that nothing you say comes close to correcting the dishonor your
mere presence brings to a room."

"So low of station—" Chadwick rounded on the man, but
Rowen thrust his hand between them and focused as keenly
as one in his cups might on the narrow-faced man before
him.

"Whore's offspring?" he asked as if he'd gone hard of
hearing. Rowen blinked and Chadwick stepped back, recognizing the look on his friend's face.

"You heard me, lout."

Rowen merely blinked again, but Chadwick and Kenneth noted the faint lowering of his brow and the way his jaw jutted forward—the slightest bit more pronounced.

"Jordan Astraea is the result of a whorish pairing. Until her the Astraea clan had been clean of magick's taint and now—they have produced a Weather Witch? Morgan Astraea's heritage is clean yet he is ruined because of a woman's indiscretion. And *your* trollop—"

Rowen seemed to swell in size, casting a larger shadow across the man.

Kenneth stepped back, spreading his arms wide to signal the crowd back, too.

"Trollop?" Rowen spit the word out in two sharp bites.

The man snorted. "So was it fun, I wonder—spending time with a Weather Witch? *Cavorting?* I've heard they burn like wildfire in the bedroo—"

The crack of Rowen's fist into the man's jaw stopped his talking. And caused him to fly back half a pace. He fell against the table Rowen had so recently danced his way across. Rowen rubbed his knuckles and glared at the other man.

His opponent was rubbing his jaw, his eyes huge as he found his balance and stood once more, shocked. His friends patted his shoulders, brushed off his back and whispered words of—Rowen couldn't make them out as the blood pulsed in his ears—were they advising him to back down or encouraging him forward? Rowen didn't care. Insults rolled through his head like they were connected in one continuous string.

"Breathe, Rowen, breathe," Chadwick said, watching the other man spread his feet into a fighter's stance and tap the place where his sword would have normally hung.

"You," Rowen said with a grunt. "Take back what you said about Jordan. Now."

"I will not," the other said with an impertinent shake of his head. "I never apologize for speaking the truth."

Chadwick dug in his heels and held on as Rowen lugged him forward.

Rowen was a bull preparing to charge, shoulders hunched, a mean gleam lighting his eyes. All he saw was the man before him.

"Rowen, Rowennnn," Chadwick warned.

"Then I demand satisfaction." Rowen ground out the words, his nose nearly pressed to the other man's.

The stranger scoffed. "So you received no such satisfaction from Jordan Astraea?" He laughed.

Chadwick shook his head. There was a fine line between bold action and stupidity. And this man enjoyed bouncing straight across it.

The man retorted, "You must be the only one she didn't satisfy from what I've heard—"

And then Chadwick was flying forward, unable to keep Rowen's arm back, and the man tumbled to the ground again, legs flying out from beneath him with the impact. "I demand satisfaction," Rowen growled.

The man's nose streamed blood. "A duel?" He coughed, spraying Rowen's shirt with red.

"Yes," Rowen agreed. "A duel."

Kenneth wedged his way between the two, trying to catch Rowen's eye—and force some small scrap of sense into him again. "Illegal, Rowen—duels were outlawed . . ."

Rowen looked at him just long enough that Kenneth stepped back, clasping his hands behind him and rocking on his feet. "Jordan Astraea is innocent of witchery."

The other snorted. "I am Lord Edward and I will give you your duel," he growled.

"To first blood," Rowen said.

"Oh no," Lord Edward stated. "*Á l'outrance.* To the death. I will put the ending date on your tombstone, you great ass."

Rowen snarled, "Commenting on how great my ass is will not make me spare you—I have heard it before from far prettier mouths. I will see you on the morrow at Watkin's Glen. Be prepared, for I will be!"

En Route to Holgate

Jordan was sore from the bounce of constant travel along the roads unwinding like a tangle of yarn from Philadelphia's careful grid work of streets. That night there was no tavern or inn and they rested as well as they could, curling atop each other in an awkward, shifting, and snoring mass of humanity. Rain clouds dampened the skies and a sad drizzle filled the air, soaking anyone too near the wagon's edges. Clothing grew wet and stained with rust from the bars. A light came on in the carriage and the Tester appeared, snarling at the *squish* of mud beneath his boots.

"Who is responsible for this?" he demanded. "Which one of you brought a storm without permission? Do you not understand the consequences of such things? Our country thrives due to a uniquely maintained balance. Crops have the correct amount of water and all have the proper ratio of sun." He peered into the cage, watching the prisoners shift as the light stung their eyes. "There is a way we do things.

A way we maintain a proper balance. Now. Speak up. Who is magicking this rain?"

They were silent—cowed with fear.

He dragged the lantern across the bars, making a rhythmic clanging as he paced the area, watching them. Silent, they watched him in turn with frightened eyes. "Fine," he finally said. "The truth will out. I will know the culprit tomorrow and I will need no Test—nor further questions to find my answer. That is *my* magick," he muttered as he disappeared once more into the carriage.

Chapter Ten

I will make you brooches and toys for your delight
Of birdsong at morning and starshine at night.
—ROBERT LOUIS STEVENSON

Holgate

"And here we are," Maude whispered, taking Meg's hand. She reached up and knocked on the Maker's door. "Tonight, and from now on, you will sleep in your papá's chambers and be the proper daughter of the Maker."

Meg looked up at her with wide and worshipful eyes.

Maude pulled something out of the pocket hidden in her skirts and held it before Meg, shaking the soft body of a stuffed doll. Meg's eyes shot rounder and she grabbed the doll with both hands before squeezing it to her chest. Holding it straight out before her, she examined it with a cocked head. "Who . . . *what* is it?" she asked, looking at its long flopping ears and obvious arms and legs.

Maude bent down and gave it a little shake. "Well, what does it look like?"

Shiny horn buttons made its eyes and nose glint big and

black. Its mouth was stitched into a permanent smile. But stitching also designated fingers and toes—five on each hand and foot.

"Like someone . . . and a bunny. Oh!" Meg gave a little hop. "Somebunny," she dubbed it.

"Excellent well," Maude said, taking it back for a moment. "Here," she instructed, "give its hand a wee squeeze."

Meg nodded and obeyed.

There was a whirring noise and its legs shuffled, its arms rising and falling in a rhythm that mimicked walking. A voice forced through its frozen expression, fuzzily saying, "A place for all."

Meg stared at it, her tiny rosebud of a mouth hanging agape. "It is lovely!"

"See, it has a clockwork within it," Maude explained.

"Where is the key to wind it?" Meg asked, turning the doll around.

"There's no key, silly bear," Maude said with a giggle. "It's powered by crystal."

"Stormpowered? Like the automatons that guard the Council?"

"Well, not nearly so impressive as all that, but similar."

"It is wonderful."

"I got it for you through an amazing trader I know—"

"And just how well do you know this amazing trader?" Bran asked. The door stood open. Neither of the girls knew how long he'd stood there, watching and listening.

"Well enough to warrant a fair price on goods."

"So he provides goods." He gently picked up the toy to better view it. "And you—provide *services*?"

"Ha!" She laughed before remembering herself and

straightening. She smoothed her skirts and tugged at her hair. "No. I most certainly do not."

He nodded, watching her face the whole time. "It is a remarkable dolly."

Maude cleared her throat and led Meg around her father and to the side room just off his sleeping chamber. It was not much to speak of, but not much was still plenty if you came from nothing. Maude had placed a small bed in it and a trunk for clothing. "Not far to go from bed to clothes," she said with a smile. "And it is a large space for a tiny sprite."

Meg climbed onto the bed, smiling, before her gaze returned to the doll Somebunny. "That's my little lady." Maude shuffled backward out of the doorway and looked at Bran. "Good Maker, sir, it is time for our evening ritual."

He looked at her blankly.

"Dear little Miss Meggie is ready to slip into her evening clothes and be told a story."

"Oh. Then do go right ahead." He motioned her toward the child.

"No, sir. Well, not entirely *no,* but I am only going to change her and wash her face and hands and then the story is for *you* to tell."

"I . . ." Bran looked from the one to the other of them.

Maude smiled. "Give us a few minutes?"

Bran nodded, moving as quickly away as he could, busying himself straightening the odds and ends scattered throughout his room.

In only a few minutes Maude called him back. Meg was seated on the edge of her bed in a linen chemise that served as a nightgown, her hair loose and glossy from being freshly brushed. Tiny hands were folded in her lap.

"Good sir Maker, please seat yourself on the bed's edge and regale your daughter with a delightful tale."

He sat. His hands clenched in his lap like a schoolboy readying for a scolding. "A delightful tale?"

Maude nodded encouragement.

"And if I know none?"

Maude blinked. "Any tale that might not frighten a wee one will do."

He closed his eyes, pondering. "And if I know none?"

"Just tell one your mother or father told you."

"They told me no tales."

Maude's mouth slid closed, lips pursing. "Then something read to you?"

He shook his head.

"And you yourself—in neither of your libraries have—"

Again he shook his head.

"I see," she murmured. "Then I guess the task falls to me."

Bran made to rise but Maude lifted her hand and, surprising them all, stopped him.

"The task may fall to me tonight, but she is your sweet daughter tonight, tomorrow night, and forever, and so the task will be passed along." She sat on Meg's other side, spread her skirt so it lay neatly, and said, "Have you heard the tale of the Wise Little Fool?"

Meg shook her head.

"Well, little dove, tonight you shall!" And with that she leaped into an exciting tale of adventure that required wild gesticulations, funny voices, and one brief song. At the end, all three were smiling and Meg looked somehow healthier.

There were hugs from both adults and a quick peck on the forehead from Maude as she tucked the child in.

"Might I have a cup of water?" Meg asked as they prepared to leave her in the dark.

"Oh," Maude said, looking at Bran. "I suppose one cup won't hurt." She bustled away, filled a cup from Bran's personal pitcher, and returned with the requested drink.

Meg gulped it down. Immediately. "Might I have another?"

Bran took the cup and refilled it. This one the child set on the floor at her bedside. She smiled at them both and laid back, snuggling her head into the pillow.

"You'll need to brush those tangles out in the morning," Maude whispered as she passed him by and headed for the main door to his chambers.

"Wait," he said, stopping her by placing his hand upon the door.

Her eyebrows rose.

He lowered his hand. "Thank you."

"Don't thank me yet," she said. "The first night in a new place is most often the hardest. Good luck. To you both." Then she opened the door and ducked outside to leave him wondering.

En Route to Holgate

"Which one is it?" the Tester asked, a grin twisting his features. "Who has been begging for water?" From behind the bars of the wagon the prisoners all stared at him, licking their lips. "Bring me a canteen," he commanded a Wraith. "Here!" He shook it so the sloshing of liquid was unmistakable.

A dark-haired boy lunged forward, his eyes caught on the canteen, arms shooting between the bars.

The Wraiths clamped down on his wrists, holding him pinned.

"You, is it?" the Tester asked. "You are the one who called last night's storm and disrupted the balance?"

Most of the wagon's inhabitants looked at the Tester blankly. A few looked away.

"Know this. If you are thirsty it is for one of two reasons. Either you have been without water for too long or you are Drawing Down. And it is only through Drawing Down that you can call a storm, or Light Up. That is why it is so easy to find your kind. You are as thirsty for drink as we are thirsty for your power." He looked at the Wraiths. "Whip him so that all might see the price of disobedience."

They hauled him out, kicking and shrieking.

The Tester looked at the prisoners coolly, saying, "There shall be no storms, there shall be no weather of any variety unless we command it."

Then they tore off the boy's shirt and whipped him until his skin was raised and red with welts.

Holgate

It was the sound that woke him. Bran sat bolt upright, the covers falling back as the chill caught him, kissing all the way along his neck. He tugged at his nightshirt's collar and sat there in the dark, catching his breath and wondering why it didn't feel like he'd screamed at all.

He ran a shaking hand along his throat but felt no lingering hoarseness. So he listened, the night heavy and deep in his ringing ears. When the shriek came again he launched out of his bed, covers flying, and vaulted toward Meg's room, catching the waiting lantern in his hand as he flew past his nightstand.

The light from the lantern was harsh, washing out the scene before him and casting the child in an eerie glow. Seated in the center of her bed, her eyes were screwed tight against some unmentionable horror, eyelashes quivering as her entire body trembled. She screamed again, covered in a sheen of sweat and caught in a cruel nightmare's snare. He leaped across her bed and pulled her into his arms to wake her, but hopped back, Meg clutched to him, as he shifted his weight from foot to foot.

His feet were damp.

As was her entire nightgown.

He glanced down at the horn cup beside her bed. Turned on its side, there was not even a drop of liquid remaining within. Carefully he held her out before him, feeling her slick arms slide in his grasp. Tightening his grip, he gave her a little shake as her mouth opened in another cry. "Meg!"

Her eyes flew open and she gasped like someone too long beneath water. "Papá?"

"What happened?" he asked, setting her on the edge of her bed—one of the few spots yet dry. "Did you"—he glanced at her wet gown—"wet yourself?"

"I . . ." She looked down, mystified. "I was frightened . . ." She shivered, the cold and the damp combining to wreak havoc on her tender skin. Her flesh turned to goose pimples and she rubbed her arms furiously, her tiny brow knitted.

"Well. You most certainly cannot stay like that," he muttered, setting the lantern on the floor and opening the chest at the foot of her bed. He rummaged through things, shifting one thin stack of clothing and then another. The chest held the remnants of her mother's things and any worldly possessions not already on her back. There was nearly nothing to speak of between it all.

"Here," he said, tugging free an old chemise with a drawstring neckline. It was far too big for a child of her size and would pool around her feet if she stood, but at least it was dry. "Take that off," he said, "and put this on."

Timidly she set her feet on the ground and he turned away until she said, "I am well."

He turned and looked at her, the chemise's neckline slipping down to expose one petite shoulder, and the ridiculous way she hiked the hem up so she wouldn't trip over its startling length. He could not help but smile. "I am going to send for Maude," he explained. "You may stay here while I do, or you may come along."

She wiggled awkwardly forward, but followed him as he left her room and crossed the main bit of his to where a horn hung by a crank and flywheel. The Maker spun the crank so the flywheel hummed and a small crystal lit and blinked. He leaned toward the horn. "Yes. Servants' quarters."

There was a hum and the sound of someone speaking in the distance.

"Yes. Maude."

A pause and then there was more noise, as if someone spoke to him from far, far away.

"Are you speaking to her now?" Meg asked, stepping closer, her eyes on the horn.

The Maker wrinkled his forehead and nodded. "Yes," he said into the horn. "We need you now. And fresh linens. And a nightgown if you have one to spare."

A sound like tinny laughter drifted out of the horn.

"No, of course I understand you don't have one to spare. Just come. Quickly, please." He grabbed the handle as it spun free and pulled it to a grating stop. The stormcell's crystal blinked off and the strange hum ceased.

The room was heavy with silence as they stood there staring at each other.

"Do you remember what you were dreaming?"

She shook her head, damp curls clinging to her forehead.

Bran reached out a tentative hand and slid a few locks back from her heart-shaped face. "Are you certain? Try and remember. Anything. It might help."

She puffed out her cheeks and blew out a deep breath. "Water," she finally said, screwing her face tight in thought. "I remember water."

The shutters rattled so hard the water in Bran's washing bowl rippled and they both jumped.

Bran laughed, setting a hand on her shoulder. But the sound felt false in his ears and he was certain she saw the way his gaze shot, telltale, to both the shuttered window and bowl.

But she giggled and they stood together for the minutes it took Maude to dash up the stairs, linens in hand.

She was breathless at his door and bent over to suck in air after taking a quick look at Meg to reassure herself that nothing was broken so badly it might not yet be mended. She clutched the linens to her chest and rallied. Rising she said, "She is wet?"

"Yes. She was."

Meg looked away.

"It's the water," Maude said with a frown.

Meg's head snapped up, but Maude was already walking toward her room, muttering about having given a child with

a pea-sized bladder just enough water right before bed that
any dream would wring it back out of her. "It's not your
fault, little dove," she assured as she stripped the bed and
tossed the wet sheets on the floor. "Oh." She paused, seeing
the broad stretch of wet on the mattress. "It seems quite
wet." She glanced at Bran, but his expression revealed nothing. She folded an old blanket she'd brought along and
spread it over the wet area before placing a sheet over it.

Maude patted it. "Much better. Now. Let's get you out of
that before you trip and kill yourself."

Bran snorted. "She needed to be dry. Warm."

"No disrespect intended." She smiled at him and, twirling
the child around, stripped and redressed her faster than Bran
could leave the room. "Come, Meggie," she said. "Scoot in."

The little girl crawled across the now lumpier bed and
settled in. Maude pulled the covers straight up to her chin,
seeing her wiggle happily beneath them. "There's a good
lass," she said, and swept the last of her darkly sticky curls
away from her face before leaning over to give her another
soft kiss. Maude turned and Meg's hand snapped out to grab
her wrist.

"Sing me a song?" she asked, her eyes imploring.

Bran leaned in the doorway, watching the scene play out.

Maude glanced at him. "Who could ever say no to such a
face?" She sat at the bed's side and, taking Meg's little hand
in her own much larger one, splayed out her tiny fingers and
began to sing "Rise Gentle Moon." Her face lifted as the song
carried her happily along and she raised her eyes to the ceiling. She blinked, one note strangling in her throat before she
caught the tune and continued.

But it was too late. Bran was looking where she had
looked.

"What?" he asked as soon as the song ended and she stood and readjusted Meg's covers.

"A spider. I thought I saw a spider," Maude said. "I hate the furry-legged bastards." She brushed past him and snagged his arm, leading him out of the room quickly.

"Spiders bother you that much, do they?" he asked as they neared his door.

"Yes. Wretched beasts."

He nodded. "I was wondering . . ."

"She should sleep straight through the night now. But no more water before bedtime."

"No. Not about that."

"Oh. What then?"

"Are you still seeing the baker's son?"

She looked down. "You are the one that ended what was between us."

"But what if I wanted to begin things anew?" he asked, reaching a hand toward her face.

She stepped back faster than either of them expected, her back bumping up against the door. "No," she said, the word a frantic puff of air. "No." She looked back toward Meg's room—the dark spot from which soft snoring much like the purr of an oversized barn cat sounded. "She needs stability. And we"—her eyebrows slid closer together—"are anything but stable when we're together. We're like powder and match."

"That merely means explosive," he insisted, taking a step forward again.

"No." She ducked beneath his arm. "We *are* explosive," she conceded. "Dangerous. A combination that flaring can both wound and maim." Before he could say another word she ducked out his door and dashed into the darkness of the hall.

Chapter Eleven

No one conquers who doesn't fight.
—GABRIEL BIEL

Philadelphia

The pounding on the door of Rowen's chamber was only rivaled by the pounding in his head. "God," he groaned, pulling the pillow tighter over his forehead and pressing it against his ears so hard his head echoed with the throbbing of his pulse.

"Rowen!"

He recognized the voice and rolled out a groan again. *Catrina*. What was Catrina doing at his door this early . . . ? He peered out from under the pillow, eyes squinted against a surprisingly large amount of sunlight. "Wha—" He vaulted up in bed, the covers falling back and off of him, and grabbed the bedpost as he knelt on the mattress swaying. "Damn it . . ."

The pounding changed to a nearly-too-polite knock. "Young Master Rowen, it seems you are running behind by a bit today, young sir." Jonathan. "You do have . . ." There was a pause, a sigh, and muttering between Jonathan and Catrina. "You do have a rather imperative previously scheduled engagement, young sir . . ."

"What time is it?" He released the pillow and let go of the bedpost long enough to press the heels of his hands into his eye sockets and growl. "What day is it . . . ?"

"Open the door for me!" Catrina demanded.

"Young lady, that is quite unseemly . . . I daresay he is in a state of undress . . ."

There was the noise of a scuffle, a few words exchanged between the two outside that caused Rowen's eyebrows to rise in surprise.

A key turned in the lock and the door swung open, Catrina lunging in with Jonathan right on her heels, grasping for the key and settling for her wrist instead. She thrashed against him for a moment, but froze when she spotted Rowen on his bed. In only his loose-fitting nightshirt.

Catrina had the good graces to blush.

Jonathan took advantage of the moment and wrested the key from her hand, holding it high in victory.

Rowen glared at them both and pulled the quilt around him.

It was not nearly fast enough that Catrina failed to notice the strength in his bare legs or the slight bit of hair on his chest, just viewable between the open laces at his neckline.

"What the devil are both of you doing here?" Rowen demanded, following the question up quickly with, "Jonathan, trousers, please?"

"Yes, milord, of course, milord."

"Did you truly drink that much that you do not remember

what occurred last night?" Catrina asked. "Everyone knows of it!"

Rowen drew back, worry plain on his face. "What occurred last night . . . between *us*?" He swallowed hard.

Catrina blushed. Harder. "No, no. Of course not . . . Do you not recall your challenge?"

Rowen looked at Jonathan askance but took the buckskin breeches he offered and, clearing his throat and pointing with his chin, instructed Catrina to turn her back on him. As soon as she was facing his armoire, he dropped the quilt long enough to pull on his pants and tuck in his shirt.

Then he paled, remembering. "The duel."

"Yes!" Catrina spun around, disappointed. At seeing him nearly dressed or at the fact he'd challenged a man to a duel? "You could send Jonathan with an explanation that you were quite in your cups when you threw down the gauntlet, and that with the return of daylight your senses also returned and you realize now that Lord Edward was right. This is precisely why duels occur most oft in daylight—so you might sleep off stupidity. They would surely be lenient if you admitted being so horrendously wrong due to the evils of alcohol . . ."

"But I was not completely soused. Not until after they left."

Jonathan grumbled something as he put away Rowen's nightclothes.

Catrina wrinkled her nose. "True, but they do not know that. So you just say—"

"So you would make me a liar twice over? I was not drunk. And not wrong."

"Rowen. You made a bad decision. In the heat of an argument. You tried to protect someone's honor—someone whose honor was not hers to give—all because of some time you spent with Jordan in the past. You were wrong to do so. Many times over."

He glanced at her and then at the window and the light flooding in. "What time is it?"

"The bell in the main square rang out eight just moments ago," Jonathan said.

"Just enough time," Rowen muttered.

"Yes," Catrina agreed. "If you write the note and send Jonathan—"

Rowen fixed his gaze on her. "Just enough time to make it to Watkin's Glen," he corrected. "Are my sword and pistol ready?"

"Wh—"

Jonathan nodded. "Yes, sir."

"You can't be serious!" Catrina shouted. "I will—I will . . ." Her eyes widened, realizing what the most potent threat was. "Tell your mother."

Rowen sighed. "Do so. My head is already pounding, my fate already sealed. I am no marksman. Tell her so she might at least scream something akin to a good-bye to me—as it will surely not be a farewell that passes from her lips."

"Why . . . I . . ."

"Do not, Catrina. Do not bring additional drama to me in this, the last hour I will likely spend on this Earth. Let me at least do what I said I would. Let me at least be enough of a man to be true to my word."

"Rowen . . ." she protested weakly.

He addressed Jonathan. "Will you do me the honor of standing as my second?"

"It is not even legal . . ."

Jonathan ignored her, nodding. "Of course, young sir. 'Twould be my honor."

"And if the moment comes—you will be man enough to end my agony?"

"I pray that is not necessary, sir."

Rowen shrugged. "We shall see."

"He will be implicated in murder," Catrina insisted. "Rowen. If you will not think of yourself, then at least think of Jonathan; he will be an accomplice if you succeed, a victim of lawlessness if you fail."

Rowen nodded. "Wise words, Catrina." He stepped to his nightstand and pulled something out of the drawer. Holding it in his fist, he crossed to Jonathan and took his hand, placing the thing in his palm instead. "Regardless of the outcome once the deed is done, you must take a horse—"

Jonathan retrieved his friend's sword and pistol from their usual places and set them on the bed.

"Good God, you'll be stealing horses from the militia stalls to do this, too?" Catrina howled, her voice reed-thin.

Rowen's eyes widened briefly and returned to their normal appearance. "Regardless of the outcome you must take a horse and leave. Get as far away from the city as you can. Go and pack your things now," he suggested, and Jonathan turned on his heel and left, walking quickly back to the servants' quarters to obey what might very well be the last request his young lord would make of him.

"Rowen, you cannot do this," Catrina said.

"You mean to say: Rowen, you cannot *succeed* at this. That much I know. Do you not realize what I have lost already? I had a friend in Jordan. Not a perfect friend, but a suitable one. A match for me. A friend I was beginning to court. Do you know how few men of any station can say they were fortunate enough to wed a woman they were friends with first? Look at my parents. Most days they barely make it through without throttling each other. There is no love lost between them because there was never any *love* between them."

"You can find love elsewhere. If you just look," Catrina said.

"I do not want to look. And, frankly, I do not care that much for love—if it comes, it comes. But compatibility . . ." He shook his head. "I had that. Jordan may not have loved me, but she knew me. She understood me."

"I know you, too . . ." She reached out a hand and he shook it off.

"No. Not like she did. I cannot explain it. But I had something that was growing—something that was good . . ."

"And that—what you *had*—is worth dying for? *That*—the past—is worth ending your life?" She grabbed his sleeve. "Do not die for something that no longer exists—do not die for the sake of memory or of what might have been. Live for what might yet be. Write the damnable letter! There is still a way out."

He pulled back from her, hearing the rip of fabric as the seam on his shirtsleeve gave way. "Dammit. As if the day could not get worse . . ." He pushed past her, brushing the hair back from his eyes and examining the sword lying beautiful and still in its scabbard. His finger traced the length of the metal and leather case hesitantly, pausing on the weapon's crossguard before he snared the hilt in his hand and yanked it free. "A pretty thing, is it not?" he asked, looking across the blade at her. "I have never truly fought someone with one. I fence, yes. What man doesn't? But truly fight?" He shoved it back into its scabbard so that it clicked, metal meeting metal. "Perhaps we will not even come to blows with swords . . . Perhaps it will end before that . . ." He set the sword down and opened the wooden case that held his pistol, powder, patch, and ball.

"You must stop thinking that way," Catrina insisted. "You must think of the act itself. Of aiming. Of firing. Of ending a man."

"A highly unlikely outcome," Rowen muttered.

"It is possible. Hold that thought in your head. Kill him so that you might yet live."

"Say I do. Then what? I win, I'm a murderer. I lose, I'm a dead man. I asked for first blood."

"Write the blasted letter!"

He snorted and raised his chin. "My penmanship is god-awful. No one should be subjected to reading what I write." He attached the scabbard to his belt and, picking up the gun case, thrust it into her arms. "Let us do this thing. Now."

"No," she said flatly, refusing to hold the case. "I am not giving up so easily. I am telling your mother." She turned on her heel and strode out of his room.

"As if the day could not get worse," he said through a grimace, steeling himself for the next fight of his day.

Lady Burchette was waiting at the door for her son, hands on her hips like a scullery maid, Catrina standing right beside her, chin tipped up in what surely approximated victory.

"My coat and hat, Jonathan," Rowen said.

Jonathan obliged.

"Just where do you think you are going, young man?" his mother shrilled.

"Most likely to my death, but I daresay it will be far more peaceful than this household." He slipped on his coat and took a moment to appreciate her stunned silence.

"You cannot," she finally croaked. "I will not let you . . ." Her face was turning red.

"Mother. You cannot stop me," he said.

"I most certainly can!" She turned to Jonathan. "Stop him!"

Jonathan choked a little at the command. He clicked his heels together and gave a gracious bow, but rising from it, he said, "Dear lady, your good son is three inches taller than I and a half stone heavier. I daresay if he wishes to go somewhere I am not the man to stop him."

Rowen gave him a small bow of acknowledgment. "I do tend to agree. Although, if Mother insists, we could at least give her a good show . . ." Rowen bent his knees, widened his stance, and put his arms out at his sides in a braced position, a sharp smile on his lips.

The square's bell struck the quarter hour.

"As much as I agree regarding the value of a good show, I fear if we pause too long we will miss your date with destiny. And quite possibly muss your outfit. Or your hair."

Rowen straightened suddenly at that thought. "I do intend to look my best. Less to be done in burying me."

Lady Burchette stomped her foot. "Stop this madness at once."

Rowen paused, the sly expression slipping off his face for a moment.

"I have no choice. I said I would do this thing. My word is attached to this—my oath—my value as a man."

"You were drunk," Catrina snapped.

"Shut your mouth, Catrina," Rowen advised, his tone a low rumble.

She did, and he briefly marveled at the fact.

"Mother," Rowen continued. "I am a man. This is one of the things that matters to a man such as myself. You must respect my decision." He turned back to the door.

"You are *mine*," his mother snapped. "I love you," she whispered.

Rowen stopped dead at her words. He turned back to her. "It is for that reason that I must go. Because I am your son and I represent our shared name." He watched her for a moment, and then a strange expression crossed his face and he bounded over to her and laid a kiss on her forehead before settling his hat on his head and pushing the door open.

The bold stride Rowen had adopted to leave his family home became a sliding creep as soon as he and Jonathan had stepped off of the Burchette estate. Together they moved quickly and quietly in any of the areas the morning light flowed across and then slunk through the remaining shadows on their way to the stables.

They paused beneath the shade of a tree and Jonathan raised one finger to his lips before leaving Rowen to walk toward the large sliding double doors that opened on parade days and the smaller worker's doorway.

Jonathan looked about and, spying no one to raise questions about his presence at the stables, tried the door.

It opened easily and, startled, Jonathan flashed a grin over his shoulder at Rowen. He disappeared inside a moment, and then stuck his head and one arm back out just enough to signal his young lord.

Rowen hurried across the yard and slipped into the darkness of the unlit stables. He rubbed his nose at the pungent smells of warm horseflesh, hay, and straw. His father might be in charge of the military stables in Philadelphia and Rowen might be a fine horseman, but neither meant he spent much time in the stables themselves. That was the place for grooms and staff.

Jonathan took him by the elbow and leaned in close to whisper, "I see no grooms. The place seems deserted for now."

"Excellent," Rowen said, his eyes adjusting to the dark. He tripped over the corner of something. His eyes adjusting *mostly* to the dark . . . "Let's look at our options." His arms still loaded with his personal gear and saddlebags, he tried adjusting it all to turn on the lantern he took off the wall.

It was a frustrating, fumbling minute in the dark.

"You should take my old coat," a voice said, and Rowen and Jonathan jumped at the noise.

Light oozed out of a strangely pierced pattern as a tin lantern glowed to life. Gregor Burchette sat on a hay bale, watching his son and faithful servant of more than a decade prepare to steal the horses under his care.

"Father," Rowen mumbled. He shifted his weight from foot to foot.

Burchette nodded. "Rumor spreads faster than western wildfire. And you, dear son, are predictable." He grunted and patted a bundle at his side. "The coat's old and far less than the spectacular fashions you're accustomed to, boy, but it served me well in the militia and, if I reckon right, where you're going you'll be needing something serviceable far more than something fashionable." He rose with a groan and tossed the bundle to Rowen, who caught it awkwardly, balancing his own scant supplies and light.

Jonathan made a *tsk*-ing noise and helped relieve Rowen of his burdens.

"You know . . ."

"That you've come to steal horses for the ride to your ill-advised duel?" The corner of Burchette's lips dug deep into his chubby jowl and pushed his cheek nearer his eyebrow on the left side of his face. "Of course. Do I support the potential ruination of our family's good name because you are in love with Jordan Astraea?"

Rowen began to sputter, "I am not in—"

But his father gave a look and Gregor raised his hand for silence. "Save your protests for the day you try to explain these actions to some low-born girl you finally marry."

Rowen's eyes went wide and his cheeks puffed out.

Still his father talked on. "Love is a strange thing. Often not recognized until it is far too late. And for you, dear boy, it is far too late."

"I do not love Jordan!"

"Of course not. It is not as if you've been lost in your cups each night since she was taken."

"It is not as if I haven't been drunk before," Rowen said.

"Not so frequently, nor so solidly," his father pointed out. "And smelling of the cheapest smoke that has ever assaulted my nostrils . . ."

"It was all that's been offered."

"Then buy your own if you must. And you have not shaved. You look the villain's role."

Rowen rubbed the stubble shadowing his jaw so the move was audible. "I am about to steal two military-grade horses and do my damnedest to kill a man. Certainly not the actions of a hero."

"I'm afraid you are due to learn that heroism is all a matter of perspective, dear boy. The winner writes the story in the end." Burchette slapped his hands together and the nearest horse snorted. "Well, have at it, why don't you? Which two are you intent on stealing?"

Rowen swallowed hard, seeing the look in his father's narrowed eyes. He straightened his back and strode to the first stall. Giving the horse a quick look, he said, "This one will do."

The old man snorted. "I daresay you're wrong. Copper develops a soft left hind frog after a three-mile gallop. He'll lame up on you if he's pushed much beyond that. And you need a firm and fast five miles between you and the trouble you'll be making here today."

Rowen clenched his jaw and stepped to another stall. He glanced at the horse inside, holding his stormlight high, and then stepped away.

Gregor grunted approval.

The third stall held a tall bronze-backed steed. The horse arched his neck and shook his mane out at Rowen, his nostrils flaring as he stomped a broad black hoof.

Rowen stepped away.

"No," his father said sharply. "Bold choices require bold companions to back them. Ransom is a bit of a handful, but he'll be more than sufficient for your needs."

"Ransom . . . ?" Rowen adjusted the height of his stormlight to better see the nameplate hung on the stall's door.

The horse snorted in response.

"As in *King's Ransom*?"

"The same."

"Do you want me dead, Father? This is Stevenson's prize stallion."

"There's a reason for that. Ransom's a damn fine beast."

Gregor shrugged. "Why go halfways about something? Commit fully to your actions. Doing a thing halfways only ever gets you halfways to your goal."

Rowen swallowed. "Jonathan . . . ?"

His father spoke again. The man barely breathed without riding the air out of his mouth with some thought he obviously had to share. "No. Saddle him yourself. You do this thing and you might as well be riding to war. But you will have no army behind you and little to speak of in the way of family, either. You know how your brothers are. If you are going to do this thing, then take all the steps yourself. Steal him, saddle him, own him as you do the choice you make here and now."

Rowen stared at him.

The stallion shook his head and whinnied.

"Or will you write the letter?" Burchette asked, his voice soft and low. He took a step toward his youngest son. "Will you undo this thing before it goes too far?"

Rowen's fingers twitched on the lantern's handle.

"Will you write the letter, man down, and ask for Catrina's promise as your mother desires? Will you, by this"—he thrust out his bearded chin toward Ransom's stall door— "*inaction* prove you are correct about *not* loving Jordan?"

Rowen's eyes widened. He stretched his head back on his neck and rolled his shoulders. "I. Do. Not. Love. Jordan. But I did set this duel. And you have said many times that a man is only as good as his word."

"No, I have not." He snorted. "I most certainly have not said *that*."

Rowen's eyebrows lowered and a small crease appeared between them before he blinked and banished it away.

"Well. Someone did. Repeatedly. And I must agree with who-ever it was and act accordingly."

With that he strode to the tack wall and tugged down the bridle and reins, slapped them across a saddle, and grabbed a blanket. He picked it all up, looked at his father, nodded curtly, and slid into the stall with Ransom.

There was far less fighting than any of them expected, although Rowen strung some choice words together. In a smart six minutes, Rowen led Ransom from his stall. And only had a few bruises as a result. He looked at Jonathan. "Can you . . . ?"

"Choose and saddle my own horse?"

Rowen's nod was a slow move.

"Of course. Unless," Jonathan said, turning to Burchette, "his lordship would like to recommend a suitable steed to me . . ."

"Of course. You have been a faithful servant and a friend to my youngest son. Take Silver. He'll serve you well. Here," he added, heading to the tack wall. "I will gladly assist you."

Rowen let a groan escape his lips and rolled his eyes. "Thank you ever so much, Father. Do not assist *me* in the slightest in the saddling of the devil you recommend I ride, but *do* help the help . . ."

Gregor rounded on his son, his eyes sharp, saddle in his arms. "You have been babied far too long. As my youngest everyone has provided you with everything you might ever want for and—I daresay—a bit more. But you have chosen a path of your own. Finally. Now grow into it. Grow up and do things yourself." He turned with a huff and bustled into the stall ahead of Jonathan.

Jonathan looked at Rowen and shrugged, his eyes wide. "Sir, I must ask . . ."

"Speak your mind, Jonathan."

"Where are the regular grooms and attendants today? Usually there are at least two young men here standing guard . . ."

"Oh. That. Yes. It was quite unfortunate. Some sudden confusion with the schedule occurred. Quite suddenly, in fact. It would seem they all have the belief they have the day off."

"Ah," Jonathan said, giving Rowen a glance just before he stepped inside the stall himself. "Yes. How unfortunate."

With both Ransom and Silver saddled, they made their way from the barn and out into the widening light of day. "At a trot?" Rowen asked over his shoulder to Jonathan.

"I do believe we must at least go at a trot, young sir. Unless you intend us to only be taken in for horse theft and not for the additional charge of attempted murder . . ."

"I think it is time to indulge in Father's advice. What was it he said?" Rowen asked, tipping his head up. Sunlight streaked across his rough cheek and made the stubble glow like molten gold. "Why go halfways about something?" He grinned at Jonathan.

"He also has been known to say that a day spent reading indoors is the finest way to pass one's time. Are you certain you wouldn't yet choose that over the other?"

Rowen winked and pushed his heels into Ransom's sides, sending him shooting forward with a snort.

Chapter Twelve

—✦—

The ice was here, the ice was there,
The ice was all around.
—SAMUEL TAYLOR COLERIDGE

Philadelphia

The boy waved the newspaper like someone swatting flies.
"Frost Giant strikes again!" he shouted. "House Vanmoer's
roses die just outside their estate gates! When will the madness end? Read more in today's *Gazette!*"

The dark-haired man shuffled over to the boy and looked
down his nose at him. "Here," he said, pulling out some
coins. "I'll take a copy."

The boy snatched his money and thrust a folded paper
into his chest, shouting his sales pitch all the while.

"Do they know what this Frost Giant fellow looks like?"
Marion asked, unfolding the paper and giving it a shake to
straighten it out better.

The kid shrugged. "No idea. I think he's a myth, meself,"
he confided. "The government trying to stir things up and
distract us from the real issues—it being an election year

and all. Get your copy here! Know the news before your friends! Be the one with all the answers!"

"Ah. I had forgotten. An election year . . ."

The kid scrunched up his face. "Yeah . . . what rock have you been living under?"

"No rock. Why would the government do that? Make trouble that makes news?"

"So they can pin it on some poor Ninth Classer, clear the books of yet another crime, and better prove the incumbents deserve reelection."

Marion nodded sagely. "An intriguing idea."

"It's not just an idea—it happens all the time. Just open your eyes."

Marion grumbled assent. "Pity about the roses."

"Really?" The boy blinked at him. "Lady Vanmoer's one hard-nosed bitch, you ask me. Never tips for delivery, never has a polite word for anyone. I wish they'd gotten her prize roses, too. The ones inside the gate."

Marion straightened a little.

"The Festival of Flowers is coming up shortly. It would be a bitter pill to swallow if the repeat grand champion can't even enter . . ."

"Ironic, yes," Marion agreed, refolding his paper to tuck beneath his arm. "Here," he said, withdrawing another coin to give to the boy. "A tip from someone completely unlike Lady Vanmoer."

The boy grinned and pocketed the tip gladly. "See, you're the type who should be leading this country of ours—you're a right good chap, you are!"

Marion just ducked his head and, lengthening his stride, sought out the quiet of a public seat in the park to be alone with his newspaper. And his thoughts.

A leader of the country? He very nearly laughed at the idea.

Very nearly.

Holgate

There was a thickness to the atmosphere—a particular way the air clung to a body in Holgate. Moisture rested like dew, sparkling on the worn and rounded stones of the compound's outer wall and dripping in wandering streaks into moss and spongy grasses growing along the wall's base.

A black slime had begun to film over the stonework of the main bridge and water hissed along the wagon's wheels as they made their way over the narrowest part of the lake by which Holgate sat.

The Tester sat atop the carriage with the driver, his head moving from side to side as he examined the compound he had ventured out from only a few days before. Even the Wraiths clinging to the carriage's corners straightened as the horses whisked them underneath the arching entranceway.

Within the walled sanctuary of Holgate they removed their hats and Jordan jumped, seeing the way the light gleamed along their ragged-looking heads and made the remaining wisps of silver hair glimmer. They never bothered to tug their hats back into place. In Holgate there was no flinch, no fear.

The Wraiths were home.

The carriage came to a stop in a courtyard of sorts, modest storefronts and houses running parallel to the wall's interior and then hopping narrow streets and alleyways to form blocks of businesses and residences. It was far smaller a space than Philadelphia's Hill, Jordan noted, and cramped, but it was also an area someone could easily get lost in.

Ahead of them the Wraiths leaped from their perches on the carriage's corners and pulled wide the carriage doors for the Councilman. A step slid out from the carriage's belly and the Councilman, Lord Stevenson, descended onto the cobblestone street. He tugged out a handkerchief and held it to his nose as the Tester climbed down from beside the driver.

"Do you smell it?" he asked the taller man.

The Tester nodded. "Someone is Drawing Down without repercussions and making the walls weep."

"I can very nearly wring water from my handkerchief just by exposing it to the air," Stevenson complained. "And the lake. The lake is low."

The Tester nodded slowly, turning to look at the impos-ing building in the compound's center with its broad walls and sweeping height.

Jordan counted a miraculous sixteen stories, including a tower that threatened to punch a hole in the sky pulling up high above even those.

"I'd rather the lake be low," the Tester said with a wary look back the way they had come, "than overflow and min-gle with a high storm surge. We would be at their mercy . . ." He signaled to the gatekeeper and he signaled to another man who released a large handle on a spinning mechanism. There was an awful grating of metal skimming stone as a portcullis was lowered to lock them all inside Holgate.

Stevenson smiled. "The Merrow would never make it

this far up. And the other Wildkin are so disorganized as to pose no threat," he said with a laugh. "We are as safe as we can be—"

"—locked in a compound with nearly a hundred angry prisoners we've allowed to be tortured," the Tester added.

Stevenson blanched. "Not tortured. Made. We have the Wraiths. Wardens. And the town watch. And the Maker."

"The Maker would only buy us time if we tossed him to the magickers he's Made. They'd rip him apart."

"At least we know he serves multiple purposes . . ." Stevenson glanced about and shouted to one of the watchmen. "You there! Escort those to be Made to Processing."

A large man shuffled forward, propped his rifle against the nearest wall, and removed the sword from his belt. "Now, none of you's gonna try 'en give me any trouble, right? Y'hear?"

The occupants of the wagon nodded dully, grunting as they watched the Tester hand the key to the watchman. Only a few minutes within Holgate's walls and already they were damp and dreary, more ragged than their time on the roads had made them.

They faced the main building as the key turned in the lock. Over his shoulder he said, "Tether them. I want no trouble." Two other watchmen stepped up and nearly stepped back when the Wraiths came forward to assist. "I'll root out this new trouble," the Tester muttered. "I'll have no bread of mine soggy, no toast points limp with damp . . ."

Stevenson nodded. "An odd set of priorities you have, but understandable. Do you think it's one freshly Made?"

"Does it matter?" the Tester asked. "It's a Witch that is testing its bounds. I'll have none of it."

"I did not expect—"

"—so many people, young sir?" Jonathan asked, eyeing the crowd that had gathered on the edge of the meadow. "You are quite the curiosity. You have always been more focused on friends than fighting."

A touch of fog still crawled along their ankles, swirling away to create a far stranger atmosphere than Rowen had hoped for.

"I do have a reputation for throwing parties more frequently than punches . . ."

Men raised their arms when they saw him—and a few aimed rude gestures in his direction, too. "Seems like a nearly fair mix," Rowen muttered, pushing his heels in the horse's sides to urge it forward onto the site of the duel.

Edward stood across the meadow with a few of his closest followers, watching Rowen and Jonathan ride in. He nodded sharply at his fellow duelist, his eyes sharp and hard as flint.

"He wants to kill me," Rowen noted, returning the nod.

"I daresay that is the goal of this particular exercise, sir."

"Thank you, Jonathan, very reassuring. May we yet recall I suggested *first blood*?"

"Sir. Do remember that shooting a man is a reasonably simple act merely requiring a steady hand, a clear eye, and—in most cases—some premeditation. You are quite capable in this regard. You are also no slouch with a sword. I have seen you fence quite well."

"You have also seen me fence quite poorly."

Jonathan cleared his throat. "This too is true. But I feel that today your skill and luck will meet and yield the opportunity you so need. Be steady, be strong. Be brave. And kill the obnoxious prick for what he said about Miss Jordan's parentage and morality."

Rowen blinked at him and nodded, smiling grimly. "I shall endeavor to do just that."

Rowen slid from his saddle and grabbed both sets of reins as Jonathan dismounted more carefully, his hands quickly going to the saddlebags. He withdrew the pistol box and looked at Rowen, his eyes bright. "We will wait until the last moment possible to load. The air is quite sticky and we do not want a misfire."

Kenneth appeared, a bit worse for wear as a result of the wildness of the night before. "I shall wish you good luck and sharp aim now, Rowen," he said, reaching out to shake his friend's hand. He paused, though, switching something from one hand to the other.

Rowen raised an eyebrow.

"Oh. Yes. I have been asked to hold the money," Kenneth explained.

"The money?"

"Yes." Kenneth cleared his throat and looked away a moment. "Yes, it seems this is quite the event to place a wager on."

"Indeed?"

Kenneth nodded.

"And how are the odds?" Rowen asked, the words coming slowly.

"Nearly equal," Kenneth assured.

"Nearly?"

Kenneth's gaze flicked to Rowen's and then away again. "A few more betting against you than for you, but that is how these things go . . ." Before Rowen could say another word Kenneth flung up his hand and, waving to someone across the meadow whom Rowen had not seen wave first, jogged away.

Jonathan was beside him. "They are betting on you," he said.

"And betting against me," Rowen added.

"Do not worry about your naysayers—or your supporters. Now is not the time for worry at all," Jonathan said, brushing Rowen's shoulders as if he were brushing them clean before a grand entrance to a ball.

Rowen took the pistol, a grave look on his face. "Remember what I asked. If I need to be finished—"

"I will not hesitate if the time comes," Jonathan assured.

"Excellent." Rowen walked to the meadow's center, boots rustling through the small blue flowers. "Forget-me-nots," he muttered. The dew slicked his boots, bringing them to a gloss so high the sun sparked across their detailing and glittered across his belt and buckle. The scabbard whispered against his hip, flashing like an automaton's tail, flicking back and forth with each stride he took.

He paused before his opponent, his pistol's muzzle in the air, and they both weighed each other: their manner and motivation, the sharpness of their eyes and attitudes.

A third man joined them, by his outfit a judge of one of the outlying circuit courts. "I am Lord Michaelson. I will tell you when to stop, when to turn, and when to shoot. And if there is a need, I will tell you when to switch to sabers." He glanced at them both solemnly. "I will be the sole determiner of the match's outcome and my word will be taken as law. Are we quite clear?"

"Quite," Rowen agreed.

"As clear as a stormlight crystal," Lord Edward added.

"Then turn your backs to each other and prepare to pace off. You will stride in time to my count. You will go to a distance of ten paces and await the command to turn and fire. At that point, turn, take aim, and discharge your weapon." He paused briefly before saying, "You may pace off."

They measured the distance stride by stride and when Rowen heard the count of ten, he stopped in the dewy grass and waited for the next command.

"You may turn and—"

BOOM!

Rowen felt the ball cut past him, his hair stirring in its wake as he brought down his pistol's muzzle and fired. The blast rocked the pistol in his hand and he stood, silent and awash in the blowback of gunpowder and spark, stunned as the other man dropped to the ground.

Rowen stared, his jaw hanging loose, as men scrambled to kneel or crouch beside his fallen opponent. Rowen was already stumbling back as the judge crossed the distance to Lord Edward, leaned over, and reached out a tentative hand to touch the fallen man's neck.

Jonathan was beside Rowen. "Sir, it is time to depart." He took Rowen's hand in his to gently remove the pistol from his grasp.

Rowen nodded dully as the judge rose and announced, "We have a victor—Rowen Burchette."

And then Rowen and Jonathan ran to the horses, mounting and speeding away from the scene of the crime—for crime was what it was even in the meadow just beyond the city limits—their lives ruined and nothing but a black mark and whatever was in their stuffed saddlebags to their names.

Holgate

Bran set down his pen, hearing someone again knocking at his door. Standing by the corner of his desk, Meg peered up at him from beneath a tumble of platinum curls, pausing as she rearranged his loose papers. Recognizing one particular sheet, he fought the impulse to snatch it away, recalling that Meggie could not yet read and that was the main reason she was allowed to shuffle her way through his often grim writings. Once she began to make out his scrawling words she would be kept from this task as well. And likely still be too young to help amidst the horrors of the laboratory and tower top . . .

The pounding came once more, this time followed by an insistent voice saying, "Good Maker . . . The boys, they say . . . Please come to the door, good sir."

He pushed back his chair and reached forward to pat Meggie's head. "Let them lie," he instructed with a glance to the remaining papers. "Relax for a moment," he added. He watched as she ambled obediently away before he opened the peephole in his door and found himself face-to-face with the gigantic watchman from the other evening.

The man looked down, eyes shifting and shining with nerves. "There's another something here for you, good Maker. Something the boys say wants to be in your keeping. I say, leave it lie, but they tell me it won't. Not still at least. Never have seen the like of it, they say . . ."

The door groaned open and Bran saw a burlap bag hanging at arm's length from the man's boulder-sized fist.

"Won't stay in the ground, they say." The bag trembled in his huge outstretched hand, his knuckles clenched and white. *"Ashes to ashes and dust to dust* for all but this one, it seems. But mind, sir, is clean as such things can be. White as snow. Picked to perfection as if it lay in the desert a solid year. Though seems to me it's been not yet a month . . . It's not natural."

"Quit your muttering and hand the blasted thing to me."

"Aye, sir—as you wish, sir." He ducked his head and thrust the bag into Bran's chest, backing away hurriedly and only nodding a brief bow before he spun on his heel and loped down the hallway.

Bran stepped back into the library, hands wrapped round the thing in the bag. It was not heavy—maybe the weight of a bowl, with a dome like a bowl's bottom . . . Not large, either, he realized, locking the door back and striding to his desk.

He set the bag down on the slanting face of his desk, catching it as it tried to roll away. Hands resting on either side of the thing in the bag, he shifted the fabric away from what it contained, revealing the white curve of bone.

His hands dropped away from it as the fabric settled and he realized what the object was that had set the burly guard to trembling.

Empty eye sockets peered at him from a child's hollow skull.

Sybil.

The water in the horn cup on his desk rippled and splashed and Bran was torn between the small horror in his hands and the weird way of the nearest water.

The sound of small feet on the wooden floor stirred Bran to action and he jerked the burlap back over the impossibly clean skull, tucking the bag's ends away to hide the cruel proof of his most recent failure.

Philadelphia

Chloe stood before the Council, her head raised, her hands clasped before her, a chain hanging between the manacles connecting her wrists. The bandana that usually kept her hair from her face had never been returned once they all had examined the absence of her ear. In some places they had begun identifying people by printing their fingers—or so she had heard. But here some ideas came into existence more slowly and some—much faster. As the Council members shuffled their papers, she took a moment to marvel at the hall she stood in.

A mosaic floor showing the subjugation of the natives was underfoot. "Suitably so," one Councilman was rumored to have said when the mural was nearing completion. She shifted, trying to move her feet off the image of a native whose face was being pressed into the dirt by the foot of a colonist declaring, "A Place for All."

But her movement attracted attention and there was a whirring and popping noise as two tall automatons took a heavy-footed step forward. They watched her, glass eyes sparkling and yet somehow still dead. She focused her attention on one of them, noting how between the joints of the heavy white flesh that seemed so much like porcelain she could glimpse the clockwork underneath. Gears hummed, wheels and belts shifting and moving to make each giant doll appear a clumsy mimicry of life. In the center of their bare and genderless chests was a single shining crystal. A stormcell.

She glanced from the stormcell of the nearest to its vacant eyes. The last burst of power a Weather Witch had was said to fall into such things, infusing them with eternal light.

Just as the Reanimator had mentioned Lady Astraea's soul being trapped in whichever stormlight's crystal was nearest her body at the moment of her death.

What was that like, she wondered, to be trapped for all eternity in crystal? Did you remember things? Could you see the outside world? Or were you simply a power source to be siphoned by automatons and stormlights? Did you, at death, become nothing but someone else's battery?

Perhaps there was no Heaven or Hell, she mused. Only a crystal cage.

Or . . . Her eyes saw a twinkle of light—like a sudden spark—flare in the crystal of the nearest automaton. Or perhaps that *was* Hell . . .

She shuddered.

The men at the Council's long table were staring at her, Lord Stevenson still noticeably absent, as was her own Lord Astraea. "Are you quite well?" one asked, though from his tone she knew he did not care—he was merely speaking the words. Following proper societal protocol.

She hated that. Especially bound as she was. Innocent as she was. Punish her for any wrong she had done and punish her appropriately—that was well and good. But this?

"No," she said, her voice carrying to fill the room. "I feel quite ill. About these proceedings and the way such things might damage a woman's reputation."

"Well," he said, picking up one sheet of paper and holding it to a light for better inspection. "You need not suffer such indignities for long."

Chloe let out a breath she felt she'd been holding for days, her eyes wide and thankful, her hands clasped in victory now instead of prayer.

"You, Chloe Erendell, previously of both House Kruse and Astraea, have been found guilty."

The word shot through her like the burn of a bullet and she reeled, stumbling backward. "Guilty?" she whispered, disbelief hanging from her lips with the most horrifying word she had ever heard applied to herself.

"Guilty of manslaughter, three cases on behalf of the Kruses, and guilty of inciting a Weather Witch–related incident on behalf of the Astraeas."

"It is not . . ." She was staring straight ahead but seeing nothing. "Not . . . possible . . ." The words sounded as soft as her head felt. Her brain had become a pudding in her skull, thick, useless, and overcooked.

"The penalty for such crimes is death."

She fell to her knees and bent at her waist, her cheek to the cold, hard floor as water poured from her eyes. "I did nothing . . ."

But the Councilman continued. "We sentence you, Chloe Erendell, to be hanged by the neck until dead on Wednesday hence. May God have mercy on your soul." He snapped down the gavel. "This Council and court is hereby adjourned."

The automatons moved in, awkward hands curling under her arms, their broad tails counterbalancing as they hauled her back to her unsteady feet.

There, in a puddle of her tears, was the native crushed beneath the other man's boot. They had been cheek to cheek and eye to eye. Her sobbing renewed as they half hauled and half pushed her back to the most narrow of the Council's hallways and down the winding staircase full of tilting stone stairs until they came to the cell where she would wait out the last bit of her life.

In dampness.

And darkness.

The door clanged shut behind her and, falling into the straw she curled there, knees to her quivering chin, her eyes leaking in treachery.

Her left hand reached up and touched the ragged remnant of her ear and for the first time in her entire lifetime, Chloe Erendell knew hate and wished some way to escape.

Holgate

When Meggie was deeply asleep in her small room for a well-deserved afternoon nap Bran determined to bury Sybil's skull himself. Back in the burlap bag, Sybil's skull felt far heavier in his hands than it had when the bear of a watchman delivered it the night before. He trudged to the spot on the slope where he'd left her body not so very long ago. The earth was still torn up, a pile of lifeless dirt, marking the place they had buried her.

The ground grew moist here, as if a swamp had crept up the hill to saturate the area. That was good. Soft soil was heavier but easier to move. He set the bag down atop the recently disrupted dirt, determined to leave the skull out of view for as long as possible. He found a shovel leaning against Holgate's imposing outer wall and set to work, his feet straddling the hole he dug. For every bit of earth his shovel's blade moved, his feet sank in equal increments, boots squishing into the wet substrate.

Something moved in the muck threatening to suck his boots free of him and Bran watched as earthworms wriggled along the sides of his feet, pulling free of the muck to crawl up and over his boot tops. He tried to step back, tried to tug his feet loose, but they were only sucked farther down as more worms roiled out of their loamy kingdom, sparkling wetly in the sun.

"Ugh!" He snatched up the bag and shook it into the hole, the child's ivory skull quickly devoured by darkness.

The worms ceased their palsied movement, slipping away into unseen capillaries in the ground as suddenly as they had come.

Bran managed to step back from the small pit he'd dug, his feet no longer mired. He plunged the shovel's blade in the discarded lump of dirt, ready to bury Sybil's skull as much as he was ready to bury the failure of her death. But as he swung the shovel back across the pit to dump the dirt, he heard something moving in the dark maw he'd dug. A noise like a thousand anxious fingers sifting through the muck rose to his ears and he set down the shovel, leaning forward to peer into the shadowy recess.

Eyes wide and mouth agape, Bran Marshall of House Dregard stared in morbid wonder as a twisting mound of earthworms, maggots, grubs, and centipedes writhed and rose together from the hollow, the skull on the living hill's crest.

Not far down the slope the cattails rustled, giving voice to the jawless specter. "They commmmme . . ."

The undulating hill stilled a moment.

As did Bran's heart.

The earth trembled and the hill erupted, launching the skull into the air—and into Bran's arms. He held it before him a moment, the jawless thing still somehow managing to grin in death in a way he'd never seen the child do in life. His vision spiraled into nothing and he collapsed.

He woke to one of the local men leaning on the shovel and staring down at him, the man's tongue working along the inside of his lips in thought. He popped his lips together and nodded at Bran before revealing a mouth devoid of most teeth to say, "It's a bitch burying that thing. Poor Wendall ruined his pants twice trying. Determined bastard, he is. Best be taking it along with you, master Maker. Seems to wish to watch over you."

The man reached down a hand and helped Bran regain his feet. "Watch over me?"

The man released him and shrugged. "Or scare the piss out of you at random intervals," he offered, lips smacking as he sucked on one of his remaining teeth. "Far be it from me to speculate on the designs of the dead." Taking the shovel with him he strode away, whistling a merry tune.

With shaking hands, Bran slipped the skull back into the bag and hurried to his laboratory, where he cleared a space in his shadow box–style shelves and nestled the skull as far back in it as he could.

Chapter Thirteen

What dreadful hot weather we have!
It keeps me in a continual state of inelegance.
—JANE AUSTEN

Holgate

"Move them along," Stevenson commanded, gazing at the sky. Unloading the wagon, chaining the prisoners, and moving the horses was taking far longer than normal. "It seems as if our good Maker is in the process of bridling a Weather Witch and I'd rather not be caught outside in the rain."

Jordan followed his eyes up, as did a dozen other prisoners. On the tallest tower on the largest building in the walled compound was a snapping banner and, near it, a longer metal pole. The pole plunged into the sky, gashing open its gut, a circle of thickening clouds seeking to close the wound. Invisible fingers tugged dark cotton filaments from the sky and pulled them together to be spun into something stronger, wisps clumping together to build imposing thunderheads.

"Move them along," the Councilman demanded again.

But they were all rooted in place, as dull as trees, transfixed, by what was going on in the sky and on the tower top far above them.

"Damn it all," Stevenson muttered, sprinting unceremoniously for cover.

The scent came first—the odd taste of moisture and metal that filled a nose with the promise of rain. The drops sprinkled down, a drizzle at first, then fattening, falling faster until the rain was a blinding sheet cloaking the observers in a dark, wet wall that only relented when lightning sparked in the sky, snaring the metal pole. The bolt wrapped it, blinding them as thunder joined in and rattled their bones with a *crack* so loud they jumped and huddled together.

Then it was over, the last wave of rain fell in a soaking solid line and the air cleared, the clouds dissipating until nothing remained except a remarkably cerulean blue.

"Now!" the Councilman shouted from his spot in the hulking building's doorway. "Move them *now*, you idiots!"

The Wraiths shoved them forward, snarling and threatening, their lips pressed close to their captives' ears, their teeth bared like fangs.

The prisoners pressed forward, a wet wave of flesh, all knees, elbows, anger, and fear. They were herded through a broad doorway and down a hallway that ended suddenly at a wall. The Councilman rounded on the group of them, pushing them back from the hall's end, angrily waving his hands.

A Wraith stepped forward and stomped once, twice— three times.

A heavy wooden door with iron cross bracings and a thick inset iron ring lay flush in the floor. There was a rattle from the ceiling above them, and, looking up, Jordan noticed the entire section of wall and ceiling was ribbed with iron strips. A hefty metal hook descended slowly

from a hole in the ceiling, suspended by a fat black chain
that lowered one clanking link at a time. The Wraith grabbed
the hook and, lifting the ring in the door, connected the
two and stomped on the door once more before sliding
aside.

The chain went taut with a groan and the door opened, a
hungering mechanical maw. Inside only the faintest hint of
light split the deep darkness, broad steps beginning at the
doorway's edge.

The Wraith gave a short and keening cry.

"Down," the Councilman commanded, and they were
jostled forward, descending clumsily into a darkness so per-
vasive it had its own unique scent. Somewhere between the
rich smell of forest loam and freshly sprouting fungi and the
thickest plume of sewer steam Jordan had ever accidentally
walked through was the residence of this particular place's
scent. The prisoners gagged at first, gathering at the bottom
of the stairs, and then choked down the scent, their lungs
struggling to accept it as breathable air.

Stevenson peered out at them from behind a mask, the
noise of his breathing amplified through a strange filter that
gave him even more of the appearance of being some variety of wild hog. "This way," he said, and they followed, eyes
and noses streaming against the overpowering stench of
earth and filth and, above it all, overripe humanity.

Even the Wraiths wore masks there, the backs of their
deformed and nearly bald heads pinched into straps to keep
the mask's front snug to ill-formed faces.

The prisoners walked between them, subdued as sheep,
led down a wide aisle flanked on either side with heavy
doors bearing wide hinges and barred windows at eye level.
Jordan stretched up on her feet as they passed one by, trying

to catch a glimpse of what lay inside, but she saw only darkness and the barest hint of movement.

"These are the Reckoning Tanks," the Councilman's voice
hissed out as he motioned the Tester forward to explain.

"You will be kept here until the Maker calls you for Reckoning."

"Reckoning?" someone asked. The simple act of raising a
one-word question sent him into a fit of coughing.

The Tester smiled, his mask fogging. "Yes. The Reckoning is the first step in being Made."

"And," Jordan spoke up, giving a little cough and pawing
at her nose, "if it is discovered we cannot be Made? That
this is all"—she choked down another cough—"a horrible
mistake?"

The Councilman and Tester looked at each other and
turned away, ignoring her. "Load them," the Councilman
commanded, and the Wraiths grabbed them one at a time
and, opening the doors, shoved them each into their own
Tank.

Jordan pitched forward into the dark cell, her hands
stretched before her and the only thing that stopped her
from colliding face-first with the stone wall marking the
Tank's far end. She struggled to catch her breath, but her
body still rebelled against the heady scent of her polluted
environment.

She straightened up, tried to smooth out her skirts by
feel, and stretched her arms out at her sides. Her fingers
brushed two walls. The place was the very definition of
small. In the inky black she hesitantly reached around in
hopes of discovering some bench or stool. But, after circum-
navigating the grim space, she was back to where she had
started with no appropriate seat on which to sit.

She stood until her feet ached and then, with a ragged sigh, she sank to her knees to wait for the Weather Workers to realize they'd been wrong all along and that she should be set free immediately.

The place wasn't so bad, she thought, her fingers finding the heart on her sleeve, when you knew you wouldn't need to suffer such indignities for long.

On the Road from Philadelphia

If there was one thing Rowen could say for his father, it was that the man was a fine judge of horseflesh. When he had suggested King's Ransom for Rowen's escape, he had surely made the best choice.

They rocketed down the main trail away from the meadow where he'd just murdered a man, their backs to the city, Ransom leading by a good few lengths with Silver stretching his long glossy legs to close the distance.

Hooves beat out a rapid rhythm as they raced toward safety, the only thing beating faster their panicked hearts. They had sprinted a solid mile when Silver finally caught Ransom and Jonathan pointed to an opening in the brambles at the trail's side. "There," he shouted, "follow me!" Silver slipped around Ransom and shoved his way into the winding deer path, brush slapping his haunches.

Rowen forced Ransom up beside Silver so he could speak rather than shout over the thundering of horses' hooves. "Where are we heading?"

"I believe it is prudent to stay off the main path and far from the road," Jonathan said. "We will keep the city to our back and the arc of the sun's path ahead of us and I believe we will find the cottage of my second cousin before nightfall."

"And water?" Rowen asked, looking down at the lather that made his horse smell pungent. "Will we need to cross water before we get there?"

Jonathan nodded slowly. "Undoubtedly so. And the horses will require some to drink. As will we when we empty our canteens."

Rowen nodded solemnly. "How far upstream from briny water are we?" he asked and, if Jonathan had wondered why he was worried about water, he had no doubt now.

"We will need to be prepared for Merrow and their allies, good sir," he said. "Keep your sword and pistol at the ready."

Philadelphia

Marion shifted his feet off the stacked stone fence he had claimed for sitting, refolded the newspaper across his lap, and rolled his lips together in thought. He had avoided asking after his family for years now, determined not to bring trouble to them if he could avoid it. But something wriggled in the back of his mind, insisting it was time to return to the family who had loved him and Harbored him and lost everything because of those things.

Now he would have to ask about them to track them, although he was relatively certain they would not be found on the Hill anymore. He stood and stretched, rolling the paper to fit beneath his arm again, and walked to the edge of the park. Here it butted against the steep side of the Astraea's

estate, a narrow rock wall the only thing holding most of
the properties back from falling headlong into the Below.
From here one could see nearly all the rest of the city tumbling down the Hill and filling the space between the tightly
woven edge of the Below and the high sea walls that kept
more than the water at bay. The wealth, too, rolled down the
city's Hill, dissipating as it went. Where he stood was the
apex of power—the homes of families who had come from
money and power in the Old World but were mostly younger
brothers of far too healthy male siblings. Dissatisfied by the
standards of primogeniture, they sought out a new land
where second and third sons might rule.

The wealthiest took what they wanted most. Land high
up. Defensible and with a ready view. They locked down
the things they could not control like magick among the
masses and worked to eradicate such offensive traits. The
ones that followed settled the Hill below the slopes occupied by the First Families and the Ranks that came to de-
note their stations filled the slope in nearly perfect descending
order until the last bits of society, the dregs, took the least
defensible spots nearest the water's edge. They were the
workers on which the walls were built. They were the butch-
ers, bakers, and candlestick makers. The musicians, arti-
sans, crafters, and clockmakers, the ones who maintained
the sewers and guarded against Merrow. They were all re-
placeable. And they knew it.

Still, it was better than what most had left behind. "The
War across the Water," as the Americans now called it, was
the most treacherous sort of war: a magickal one.

He would ask no questions about his family's whereabouts until he reached the Below, and he would take the
long way down. Past the Vanmoer estate. It seemed there

were more roses that needed some of his particular form of attention.

Holgate

In the dark of her Reckoning Tank, Jordan Astraea held two words in her head: be brave. It was these two words that kept her from crying out when something rustled in the straw beside her. It was those two words that kept her from screaming when something scurried across the top of her right foot.

Be brave.

She clutched the pin hidden in her sleeve and willed herself to follow its engraved instructions, simple as they were.

Whereas most of her fellow prisoners were dragged from their Tanks needing to be pushed and prodded to bring them before the Maker for the Reckoning, Jordan Astraea walked proudly (if not a bit stiffly, worn as she was from travel) all the way down the remaining dank hall, up the stairs at its far side, and all the way to him as a proper lady should when faced with the knowledge that someone's comeuppance was due.

The room was large and filled from floor to ceiling with books, their shelves sporting stormlight lanterns so there was no spot wanting light.

With no introduction, the first instructions came. "Remove her accessories."

The Wardens made quick work of it, taking her shawl, plucking her bracelets and even the fan off her hip.

The man giving orders looked up from behind a desk where he tallied the objects she'd come in with. "Gloves, too," he reminded a moment before the Wardens peeled them off her arms. "Leave the necklace."

Jordan would have worried about the proceedings were she not certain everything would be handed back (in a most apologetic manner) momentarily. Besides, she still had her butterfly wing necklace, the paper star, and Rowen's heart to remind her of who she was.

The man behind the desk could not have been more than a dozen years her senior. Golden-haired, he had barely looked up from where he was scrawling notes in a journal when Jordan had entered the room flanked by two Wardens. She gathered her wits, gave a disdainful little sniff and a rattle of the leather manacles and metal links connecting them that they'd again placed her in for her appearance.

A towheaded little girl appeared from behind him, sipping from a cup, a stuffed toy with long ears tucked in the crook of her elbow. She blinked at Jordan. And then she smiled.

"Go on," the man urged the child. "I need to return to my work."

The child looked back at him. "Is she a—a—abom . . . ?"

"*Abomination?*" Bran said, matter-of-factly. "Yes, little love, she is, so steer clear."

The child's eyes grew wide and she obeyed, giving Jordan and her Wardens wide berth.

Bran looked up at Jordan then, brow wrinkling. "Name?"
Be brave.

"It doesn't matter, as you will not need to enter it in whatever that book of yours is," she assured. "I am no Weather Witch. I cannot be Made."

Bran drew in a deep breath and tapped his pen against the inkwell's lip. "Name?"

"Are you deaf or daft?" Jordan retorted. "I am no Witch. I cannot be Made. You must set this horrible situation to rights before we have a problem."

Bran's eyebrows rose on his forehead and his mouth turned up at its very ends. But his expression hardened. "Do you know how many times I hear that on a Reckoning Day?" he asked, stepping around his desk to better make clear that he was the dominant force in the room. The pen still in his hand dripped once on his boot, leaving a mark like a black teardrop. He was unfazed. "Cooperate and things will go easier on you."

"But—"

"No," he said with a shake of his head. "Hold her."

The Wardens clamped their hands around her arms and dragged her closer to him.

"Name," he repeated.

She opened her mouth to refuse him again, but saw something spark in his eyes and thought better of it. "Jordan of House Astraea," she whispered.

He stepped back around and brought his journal forward. "City?"

She again tried to protest and was again shut down by a look from his sharp golden eyes. "Philadelphia," she replied.

"Excellent well. And"—he dipped the nib of his pen into the ink and tapped it off again—"when did you first discover your affinity for weather and storms?"

"I have no affinity for either," she said, her tone sharp.

He shook his head. "Why do they never simply admit to the fact?" he asked the Wardens.

They remained mute as was their nature.

"If you only admitted to being what you are we could move along with the process. And it would go ever so much more gently."

"But I have no . . ."

Putting on a pair of gloves, he slid open a drawer in his desk and withdrew a long needle. "No worries about infection. It is freshly cleaned and as sterile as anything in Holgate gets." He walked back to where she stood, pinned in place by the cruel grips of the Wardens, their fingers looped into the links binding the manacles and pressed into her flesh. "Now tell me what I need to know or I Reckon we'll get it out of you the hard way."

"No," she whispered, struggling. "I can't . . . I'm not . . ."

"Jordan of House Astraea, ranked Fifth of the Nine, your rank is forfeit, your life is ours, our pleasure your duty, and that duty a great one." He grabbed her right hand and turned it over so that her palm was face up. It trembled like a frightened animal, independent of Jordan's will. "Say the words," he urged.

But her brows arched over the delicate bridge of her nose and she shook her head as tears welled up at the edges of her eyes.

He sighed and dug the needle into the tip of her finger until she screamed. Sparks flared all along the beautiful embroidery of her dress, and danced across her bare skin as she screamed again.

"Thank you," Bran whispered, tugging the needle free. He held the journal open before her. "Please sign."

Whimpering, she asked, "A pen?"

He chuckled and grabbed her bleeding finger. "Not necessary. Sign with your internal ink, please."

Quivering, she signed his book in blood.

"You may take the Witch away."

And although she had walked proudly to her Reckoning,

Jordan of House Astraea, Fifth of the Nine, had to be dragged most of the way back to her Tank.

The moment they dumped her inside and slammed her door shut, she plunged her bleeding fingertip into her mouth. Tears ran down her face and filled her mouth so that around her white and perfect teeth the tastes of saltwater and blood mingled.

Such a seemingly small pain, and yet it was as if something within her had died.

Philadelphia

The stormcells glittered along Lady Astraea's neckline, like three dozen stars strung together. Laura swallowed hard, watching the way her ladyship reached a trembling hand toward the fine collar of crystals. "Why do I not remember this necklace?" Lady Astraea asked the servant girl, her eyes catching on her reflection. "And these bracelets . . . truly, is one on each wrist a necessity? It seems quite garish. Especially over long gloves . . ." She reached for the clasp of one to undo it, but Laura's hand was on her own, the girl's voice thin but insistent.

"Milady, it is quite in keeping with the style in France. I do recall you mentioning having read so in one of the more popular journals before you ordered your own," Laura assured. "I believe you said the style now is all a matter of balance of design. Which, I may only presume, is why even your shoes are thusly adorned."

Lady Astraea raised her skirts modestly and stuck out

the toe of one shoe for examination. "That seems quite wasteful. Who will ever see my shoes? I have not once danced a dance so immodest as to show off my feet and certainly never"—she blew out a little puff of air—"my ankles, for heaven's sake."

"Perhaps milady might yet find something about which to kick up her heels," Laura suggested, carefully adjusting the smaller crystals threaded throughout her ladyship's hair.

"I truly doubt I will have much of anything to celebrate now that my daughter is stolen and my good name is sullied."

"They might yet make amends," Laura whispered.

Lady Astraea snorted at the idea. "The Council? Make amends? You are so very young, dear, aren't you?"

Laura blushed. "If by young you mean naïve . . . I suppose so, milady. But I have discovered much to assuage my naïveté in just these past few days. And much of it is far less than I ever wished to discover."

"Life is full of disappointments," Lady Astraea agreed, rubbing slowly at her gloved wrists. "But it is still life—still something we are expected to muddle through."

Laura winked at her. "Why muddle through when you might dance through it instead?"

"Who has ever made a life for themselves by dancing through their existence? Oh." She waved a hand at herself. "I must sit down. I do not feel quite . . . myself."

Holgate

He pulled out his journal and let the pages flop open to the day's date, the cover's brass-tipped corners tapping against his desk as the book's spine settled and flattened. The Tanks were nearly full again, even though there would be the inevitable shuffle from the Reckoning Tanks to the Making Tanks. Still, there was never anything quite like a full house . . .

Not far from his feet Meg played with the doll she called Somebunny.

Bran scoured the day's pages, his finger skimming over his notes as he searched for the information he felt certain he had overlooked.

Received Today for Reckoning:

1 female...17.....Philadelphia....House Astraea....Jordan

2 males..5 and 18..German Towne.....House Merridale.... Patrick and Hussong

1 female......12.....Amity........House Jerard..........Sophia

1 male...23......New Baltimore.....House Ravendale.....Christian

7 males and females...4 through 9...Boston and Surrounding.... Houses Martin, Arran, O'Connor, Sampson, Smith, Fenstermacher, and Andreia

His finger went back to the page's top and he paused at one name in particular. Astraea. Why did that name seem so very familiar? He rose and stepped to one of the library's many bookshelves, bumping his fingers across each spine as he read their titles aloud.

"Ah." He stopped, pulled one out and opened it. The interior was lined with marbleized paper and the spine was trimmed in gilt design and lettering. *"The Hill Families of*

Philadelphia." He paged through it carefully until he found the Astraea entry. Walking back to his seat, he sat and propped his heels on the edge of his desk and leaned back, beginning to read.

The Astraea Family

The Astraeas trace a long and distinguished history of landholdings and titles back to the Old World and at the time of the Cleansing boarded a ship to the New World not due to political or religious reasons as many did but rather for the good of economic and territorial expansion. Having holdings in India where they own several hundred acres of tea plantations, and sugar cane plantations in the West Indies, the only thing the Astraeas lack is a suitable number of male heirs, the last generation yielding only Morgan Astraea, the only direct male family survivor of the Fever that swept the region. Losing his mother, his father, his elder brother, and one of his three sisters, Morgan became a risk-taker in business, and, at nineteen, swept up many entrepreneurial opportunities that the deaths of others left behind (expanding local holdings so they included two taverns, a clockmaker's shop, a modiste's shop, a haberdashery, two tea houses, and rumored holdings in the Below).

Morgan married Cynthia Wallsingham, the youngest daughter of Albertus Wallsingham (holder of the Wallsingham estates) after a three-year courtship, rumor being that he waited so long to see that her elder sisters bore children readily. Cynthia bore him three children nearly one on top of the other and all of them girls. The three, Morgana, Loretta, and Jordan, were taught the skills required of young ladies of standing including flirting and courting, embroidery and needlepoint, dance, music, and polite conversation. Morgana married up, Loretta married laterally, and Jordan, as of this edition, has yet to come of age.

The Astraea Holdings

Theirs is one of the oldest and grandest houses on the Hill. Three and three-quarters stories high and an architect's nightmare, the house ambles across three acres, the original structure being built of fieldstone in a seemingly haphazard fashion, long flat stones jigsawed together in herringbone patterns creating a busy-ness of design that was at once striking and enough of an oddity that the last generation of Astraeas decided—rather than living in a stone spectacle—that section of the estate would house their growing multitude of servants. As a result, the servants are one of the best housed in all of Philadelphia, that too being a distinguishing oddity—and a costly one.

The interior of the house includes such luxuries as · dumbwaiters, summoning bells, running water, decorative molding, wainscoting and chair rails, the first elevator in the New World, stormlighting—

At the mention of stormlighting Bran snorted. "Not anymore; one can be certain they have been reduced to using candles now."

—proper paint, and wallpapers and boasts multiple water closets, a warming kitchen, true kitchen, parlor, sitting room, living room, den, dining room, and six spacious bedrooms.

They were rich. Powerful. They had a nice house and a grand estate. That was not enough for them to be of note in Bran's head, and certainly not in his book. He tapped the open pages, thinking. When he was a boy he had spent time in Philadelphia. Might he have heard of the Astraeas then or met them? Something was definitely prodding him.

He stood, stretched again, returned that book to its shelf, and sought out another smaller and more worn tome. He had always kept journals—it was one of the more peculiar things about his nature and one of the things his father had hated most about his bookish son.

"You will never discover the real world if you always have your nose tucked twixt the pages of a book," he'd told him.

But the world his father spoke of discovering was not one Bran had wanted to partake of. He had not wanted to be a party to war. He had no desire to meet painted women when he was only twelve and hear unsavory stories of his mother's death when he was far younger. He had been a boy in love with his imagination and, according to his father, frivolous pursuits.

But he had not been allowed to remain frivolous for long.

When had it been? His twelfth year they stayed in Philadelphia. He flipped through the journal, pausing twice to stroke his fingers along a sketch of a bird and a boyish doodle of a turtle. His journals were once alive with such things and he'd spent many a day flat on his stomach observing the mysterious realms of ants and salamanders and spiders. Worlds within worlds fascinated him.

Then.

Before he became a Maker.

He found an entry from the fourteenth of August.

There are many children in Philadelphia now, some live here
year round and some only come in for the spring and summer
festivals. Today I was introduced to the Hill families
Burchette, Hollindale, and Astraea.

He paused and reread the names. Aha! That at least made
sense as to why the name struck a chord with him.

We had a merry afternoon playing hide and seek and Ring
Around the Rosie although I, being much their elder, was
required to watch them more than participate with them. All
was well until two of the little girls got into an argument.
There was screaming, yelling, crying, and hair pulling, and
then the strangest thing happened—a thing I dare not tell my
father due to the tender age of the children and my father's less
than tender nature. In the midst of the fighting an unscheduled
wind blew up and whipped 'bout us until we tumbled to the
ground, I sheltering the children with my own mortal coil. The
wind died down and the screaming and fighting abated. I was
mystified. They might have been terrified if only they knew
enough to wonder about what I now wonder about.

Had that been it, then? He had met Jordan Astraea when
they were both children and been a witness to her odd affinity even then? Or was there something else?

The library's shutters rattled. Meggie's head snapped up
and she clutched Somebunny to her.

Bran stood, patted Meggie's soft curls, and returned that
book as well to his shelf.

Returning to his desk, he spun sharply around, seeing
someone reflected in his lantern's glass. No one was there. A
chill raced over him and for a moment he was as chilled as

he'd been trying to put Sybil's skull to rest. He shook himself.

He was a man of science. Such things were easily explained away if one only sought the truth.

Again at his desk, he opened a shallow drawer and moved a few things out of it. With a quick look to Meg to be certain she was occupied, he slid open the drawer's false bottom and pulled another journal free. Turning to a blank page, he wrote the day's date and began his daily entry with, *"All things do come full circle and there is, in fact, no escape from the past."*

Chapter Fourteen

———✳———

Society is no comfort
To one not sociable.
—WILLIAM SHAKESPEARE

On the Road from Philadelphia

Rowen was stiff and dusty from the road when the cottage Jonathan promised came into view. With renewed energy he gave a little push with his heels into Ransom's sides and the horse picked up the pace, Silver's head bobbing along at his hip.

Jonathan pulled Silver ahead of Rowen once more and only pulled the horse to a stop when they were as close to the cottage as they could get.

Herbs and flowers rioted across a modest fenced yard around which a few sheep wandered, grazing. They looked up at the horses with mild interest and then returned to clipping down any greenery on the wild side of the fence. Rowen and Jonathan looped their horses' reins round one of the fence's posts and Jonathan lifted the small bolt that kept a wooden gate shut and slipped into the yard to knock on the door.

"Do we know how near the closest water is?" Rowen asked, his back to the fence and his eyes on the woods and the meadow both.

"Far enough it'd be a struggle for them to get this far inland," Jonathan said. He knocked on the door but the answering shout came from around back.

A broad man sporting an equally broad hat came around the cottage and gave them both a long, appraising look before he laughed and shouted, "Jonathan! Well, I had no idea you would so soon take me up on my offer to revisit my home. What has it been? Merely two years?"

"Three, Frederick, three," Jonathan replied, smiling.

"Too long either way. What a pleasant surprise." He reached over and surprised Jonathan with a bear hug before signaling Rowen to join them inside the yard.

"The horses?" Rowen asked, his eyes roaming.

"They will be quite fine as long as they do not run away. I will fetch them each a bucket of water in a moment. First, though, come inside, both of you."

The door shut behind them and introductions were accomplished with the efficiency of men on the run.

"One of the Burchettes?"

Rowen nodded. "The youngest of Gregor's sons."

"Hmph!" Frederick said. "That's quite a coup for someone like me to host someone like you."

"Well," Jonathan said slowly, "it might cause a coup if you tell anyone, as we are on the run from the law."

"Oh."

Some people might have reached for a chair, given such news, and Jonathan was quite certain that some of high social standing would have swooned at the mention. But not

Frederick. He said, "Well do tell," and stoked the fire in his small stove to start the water for a proper cup of tea.

Over tea in the small but generously decorated cottage that stood between the woods and the meadow, Rowen Burchette, Sixth of the Nine, and Jonathan Smithson, his manservant and faithful friend, related their tale to Jonathan's second cousin, who nodded and asked, "Might I use your adventure as inspiration for a story I am writing? Ah, yes," Frederick said with a wink as he tipped the teapot to refill his own cup. "I fear you have found yourself in the company of the lowest of the low: an author!" He laughed then, and Rowen glanced to Jonathan for some clue as to how to react.

Jonathan was smiling. "Will you publish our adventures yourself then?" he suggested, playing along.

"Do what Poe did recently? Self-publish?" He shook his head and grinned. "No, cousin, I want to be remembered!"

"So you're still writing for the penny dreadfuls?"

Frederick let out an exasperated groan. "I wish they'd stop calling them that, but it does garner the public's attention. So much about writing is marketing nowadays. But I must say that *dreadful* is not the most accurate description of them if you are writing for them. The publishing world is like anything else: not nearly so awful if it pays you." He took a long sip of his tea and said from the side of his cup, "So may I fictionalize and immortalize you two in prose as bold young adventuring heroes, one golden-haired and one dark?"

The pair exchanged a glance and, shrugging, agreed.

"Excellent!" Frederick raised his tea cup, saying, "A toast to tea—the great social lubricant!"

"What of wine?" Rowan asked, raising his cup.

"We'll have no whining here," Frederick said, laughing.

"Then include in our toast *ale* for what ails you . . . ?" Rowen returned with a grin.

Jonathan shook his head and, raising his cup, tapped it to the others. "A toast to adventures that end happily and authors who write their characters with kindness!"

"Hear, hear!" they agreed, and for a brief while it seemed they were men starting a grand adventure, not men on the run from the law. In that way it was far easier to settle in for the night—imagining what lay ahead rather than all that had been left behind.

Holgate

The whirring of gears woke him as much as the feel of something tightening around his neck like a noose. Breath burning in his throat, Bran clawed at his attacker, fingers slipping past its grasp. He got a grip on it, prying at fingers so strong they felt like this midnight marauder had a skeleton of steel. His tongue managed a curse when his hand started to bleed, cut. Fabric ripped and he heard a creak and snap of metal. Finally freed, he threw his attacker—much lighter than he imagined!—threw him so far he heard the body slam against the far wall and slip down to land limp on the floor, the humming of parts louder, a gear grinding against another. He flipped the switch on the nearest stormlight and held it before him partly for the sake of illumination and partly because it had enough weight to serve as a defensive weapon.

From the other room a small voice sounded, still thick with sleep.

"Go back to sleep, Meggie," Bran urged.

"Papá?" she whispered. "Somebunny?" The ropes supporting her mattress creaked and Bran recognized the sound of small feet approaching.

He swung the lantern, letting the light cascade across her form briefly before, as she rubbed her eyes clear of sleep, he raised the light to illuminate the thing that had attacked him as he slept.

The thing that was always with his daughter and a gift from his ex-lover.

"Somebunny?" Meggie whispered.

They stared at the broken doll, its movements jerky and faltering as its voice growled out the most haunting rendition of the country's motto that Bran had ever heard.

"A place for all, a place for all, a plaaaa—"

"What did you do to her?" Meggie cried, reaching for the doll.

But Bran snatched it up first, turned his back to his sobbing daughter, and ripped the mechanical spine from its soft fabric body, knocking free the glowing soul stone wedged in its grinding, cog-encircled heart. Dropping the doll to the floor, Bran ignored the gasp of his daughter and stomped his way to the horn that hung on the wall by the crank, crystal, and flywheel.

A sleep-deprived Maude was talking to him soon over the contraption and she was at his apartment door shortly thereafter, a look of horror on her face.

But, instead of coddling him and the cut on his hand that he had hastily bandaged, she went first to Meggie, and, pulling her into her lap, freed the limp doll from her arms. "Hush now, princess, hush," she soothed. "We'll fix her up all right and good—never you fear." She wrapped the child and doll in her arms, giving both a reassuring squeeze. Maude spared Bran a look that softened immediately.

The metal skeleton was still on the floor where he'd dropped it and their gazes both fell to it.

"I didn't realize it was an automaton," Bran murmured.

"It was just a toy. A doll. Harmless."

"Powered by a soul stone." Bran flexed his bandaged hand. "The trader you got it from, the one who gave you such a good deal, did he ask who the doll was for?"

Her mouth moved, the single word working its way out slowly. "Yes."

"Did you not think that odd?" He stared at the doll, avoiding the troubled eyes of his daughter.

"I thought he was being curious. Friendly."

"Who did you say the doll was for?"

"The Maker's daughter."

Bran nodded. "I'll need his name, of course."

"Of course," she agreed.

He crouched before Meggie, but she twisted away, unwilling to give him the satisfaction of looking in her face. He groaned and glanced at Maude for help. She simply nodded encouragement.

"We'll have Somebunny fixed up with proper springs and gears, fine mechanics, a right good windup toy for my child. Or no mechanics at all. Either choice is safer than a doll powered by a soul stone."

Meggie wiped her nose with her sleeve and looked up at her father. She held Somebunny tighter, bits of flax stuffing falling to the floor. There was fire in Meggie's eyes, balanced with a touch of fear.

"Come now, my sweet," Maude coaxed, scooting the child off her lap so she could stand up. "In we go. I'll get Some-bunny fixed up right as rain."

Bran stopped her. "Right as rain? Try again, please."

Maude swallowed. "Good as new," she corrected herself, her voice soft.

"Much better."

Even inside her new prison cell amidst the Making Tanks, Jordan's world remained dark, dank, dripping, and grim, the sun only slowly crawling its way over the eastern hills. The tower's stones bit into her back now that she'd discarded her boned corset, but still she leaned against the wall, pressed into it to feel something as she watched a swatch of sky change colors between the bars on her small single window. The stars slowly winked out as the black of night was infused with colors that reminded her of a bruise lightening as it healed.

She tugged at the leather manacle on her wrist, running a finger along its edge and wiggling it partway under the itching thing. She shifted and her tether's chain rustled in the straw. How recently had she been offended by having straw for sitting and sleeping? And yet now she was thankful the straw here was cleaner than that in the Reckoning Tanks. Grabbing a piece of straw from the bedding that littered her floor, she slipped it between the flesh of her wrist and the bulk of the cuff and wiggled it around, finally sighing, her head rolling back on her neck when its tip connected with whatever itched her. A look of fierce focus crossed her face as she dug the straw underneath the cuff, moving it back and forth frantically, her tongue sticking out the corner of her mouth in a most unladylike fashion.

She froze, realizing, and, slipping her tongue back to its proper place behind her teeth, slowly withdrew the straw and set it aside. She patted the cuff with her right hand, rubbing it like she might polish a very large and unsightly bracelet. Flaring her fingers out, she noted the tiny notches in her previously perfect nails. And the dirt beneath them. She set to work, slipping a nail from one hand beneath a nail on the other and working with fierce determination to worry each finger clean again. The itching of the straw was relentless, bits of the stuff getting caught in her stockings so she finally tugged them off, leaving them by her shoes. Satisfied, she smoothed her skirt over her legs, tugging its hem down so that it almost covered her ankles as it should, even with her knees drawn up nearly to her chin.

And where was Rowen, she wondered. Was he sleeping off a headache from another party she'd missed? Was he readying for a hunt with his friends? Or was today a day he would find his way to the gentleman's club and talk politics and sip wine? Could she even see Philadelphia from her spot in the tower?

She sighed. Did it really matter where Rowen was anymore? Surely if her whereabouts didn't matter to him, his shouldn't matter to her. Besides, now she'd been accused of witchery he outranked her. She was untouchable, utterly unwanted. It should not surprise her that Rowen would not ride to her rescue—he had better things to do now that she was out of play. He was a highly eligible bachelor in search of a rank-raising woman and she no longer fit that description.

Still she stood at the window, her fingers wrapped around the bars, her face pressed between them, feeling the heart on her sleeve, and she wondered.

The sound of metal scraping along metal grated in her ears and Jordan said, "What is that?"

A voice growled out from just on the other side of her wall and she scrambled away from it, her metal links rattling between her wrists. "Morning bell."

Jordan spun when another voice, this one thin and high and most definitely of the female persuasion asked, *"Bell?"* with as much embittered irony as Jordan had ever heard packed into such a small word.

She went to her knees, briefly mindful of the straw and dust grinding beneath the golden fabric of her dress, but her curiosity won out and she pressed close to the wall, searching the dim area with probing fingers.

"We calls it the morning bell," the female voice at her back explained, "as 'tis kinder than what it truly is. Gots to find a bit of kindness somewheres, you know?"

Footsteps echoed in the hall running between the Tanks, and Jordan tried to focus. Heavy boots . . . two pairs.

"And what's the morning bell for?" Jordan's fingertips swept an opening and she pressed her face close to the seam between floor and wall where a small hole was—just the width and length of a single stone.

Jordan squinted into the blackness of the hole, pressing close to it. "Is it for breakfast?"

Laughter echoed harshly in her ears. "Ain't she just the optimist?"

"Optimist? Fresh meat is all she is."

"Do we not get breakfast, then?"

"Not all of us."

"And not anything most'd dare to qualify as worthy of breaking your fast."

"So what is it then—this *morning bell?*"

A door clanged open and there was shouting, the sound of an argument and the noise of a scuffle.

The noise became so loud, the words so fierce, Jordan shrank in against herself, her eyes wide.

"*Breakfast* she asks us," the voice from the hole directly before her said with a wistful tone that twisted in on itself and became a grim snicker. "It's certainly not that. The Maker—he calls it *exercise*. Count yourself lucky if you never experience it firsthand."

Philadelphia

"The Kruse family?" the old man asked, looking up from a spot where he leaned against a large planter. He squinted up at Marion, keeping the much taller man in a position to best block the rising sun. "You mean old Francis Kruse, his wife Sarah, and his boys?"

Marion nodded. If there was one thing he'd learned from his travels it was that if you wanted the most complete story about anything, you found the oldest man nearby to ask.

"You must not be following the ways of our world, son," the man said. "You know their eldest—a lad by the name of Marion was found to be a Witch? They were Harboring." He shook his head sadly and leaned forward to rest his chin on his gnarled hands as they gripped the top of his cane. "Pity. Nice folks. Handsome family. Still astounds me that things are as they are. Imagine what possibilities our world has if

only the Maker, the Witches, Wardens, Wraiths, and Reani-
mators joined forces . . ."

Marion cleared his throat, determined to steer the old
man from such fancies and back to the conversation at
hand. "I heard about the eldest," Marion said, careful to keep
his voice steady and his tone relaxed.

"Then you know what happened next."

"I don't. Tell me where I might find them?"

"Halfway up the Hill."

"Truly?" Marion raised his gaze to trace the territory of
the Hill's slope. They must have survived the disgrace
better than he thought if they were that distance above the
Below. "Do you think they'd be there now?" he asked.

"I daresay they never leave," the man muttered, smacking his lips together in thought.

"What?"

"Surely you know the story—everyone knows what happened next."

"I'm not exactly everyone . . . Tell it true."

"Shortly after the eldest was taken away for witchery—it
was a day of celebration there, if memory serves—not unlike the recent problem at the Astraea estate . . ."

"Fine, yes—a day of celebration. Go on."

"Actually—is that today's paper?"

"Yesterday's."

"Here, then." He grabbed a newspaper resting by his hip
and waved it in Marion's direction. "Page three. The writer
tells it far better than an old man might."

"Thank you," Marion muttered as he grabbed the newspaper and turned to head back up the Hill, his eyes dis-
tracted between trying to scan the printed text and find the
place his family now called their own.

He paused on the roadside not far from a stand of houses that all nearly leaned one upon the other but still managed somehow to have individual yards at their bases. Ahead the trees and buildings gave way for a clearing enclosed by a twisting metal gate. On its other side more houses sprouted up, straighter in stature, though no taller than their companions slightly down the Hill.

He froze when he saw it—the headline naming his household—and the article beginning with the name of his family's most faithful servant and the woman who kissed his scrapes and sang him songs. The woman who fed him biscuits and sneaked him sweetmeats. His nanny, Chloe.

> Chloe Erendell has been convicted by Council Court for the ruthless murders of the Kruse family five years ago and is scheduled to hang until dead Wednesday hence.

He had barely gotten to a spot to sit down when his knees gave in under the weight of reality. *Murdered?* His eyes squeezed shut and he was reduced to nothing but a rocking lump of humanity at the roadside as he struggled to make sense of news he should have known years earlier. Forcing his eyes open, he plunged one finger into the pages and shoved them flat on the ground to better read them through his blurring vision. At the roadside on his hands and knees he was suddenly as broken as a cruel child's toy.

Spots of moisture appeared on the pages below him and he snorted and sucked air so harshly through his nose it rattled with snot. He raked his sleeve across his eyes, equally as angry as he was confused. Why now?

He hadn't cried in years. He had trained himself out of

it, regardless of what method the Maker had tried. Coaxing with the cat? Nothing. The brand? Not a noise did Marion utter. He had curled it all inside, stomped down the pain and the cruelty and packed it around his heart cold as the ice that crawled free from his fingertips.

He jerked back, shoving his hands into his pockets and looking at the ground near where his left hand had rested— and the way the grass began to discolor and wilt. He needed to get up. To move away from the evidence.

He stood shakily, clutching the paper before him to obscure his face. He took a step and then another until he found himself standing across the road from the twisting iron gate—

—and the tombstones dotting its plot, halfway up the Hill. His shoulders slumped and his face fell again. The man hadn't lied. This would be where they were now and they certainly never left . . . He glanced up and down the road and strode across it, pushing the gate aside to step within.

It was oddly quiet there in the negligible shade of the few remaining trees that stood as silent witness to the dead. He wandered the rows of graves, knees weak, not quite sure what to expect and certainly unsure where to find them. They were in a small section slightly down the Hill and tucked away near an old pine. Needles covered their grave beds like a coppery quilt and sap had dried in glistening beads and long slow tears on his mother's headstone.

He dropped again, realizing.

There would be no more sitting at her feet and reading boisterous stories. There would be no more moments spent telling tales at bedtime or learning the good and proper way to sip tea before a lady. There would no longer be any niceties in his life. Or in theirs. They had all been stolen away

when he had been discovered. His mother and father's
graves flanked that of his little brother and he silently read
the inscription on each and found them to be good and accurate if not too simple. How could you boil down any one
life to only a few words carved into stone? There was so
much more to a life . . .

He puffed out a sigh and adjusted his position so that he
sat between his mother's headstone and his brother's. He
tucked his legs up under him and he opened the newspaper
gingerly, returning to the tearstained story. Slowly, and in
little more than a pitched whisper out of reverence for the
place, he read aloud.

On the second of July, five years past, servants discovered the

He swallowed hard and continued.

bloated bodies of Francis Kruse and his wife, Sarah,
and remaining son, Harold. It was quickly ascer-
tained by the investigating force that poison had
been used, leaves purported to be mint being poi-
sonous instead. By the time watchmen arrived on
the scene most of the servants had disappeared, including the aforementioned "Chloe," recently having
accepted the name Erendell, which hampered the
ongoing investigation. Chloe Erendell was discovered trying to sneak into the Astraea household recently, the evening Jordan of House Astraea was
taken in for witchery, her parents also found guilty
of Harboring. Discovered, Chloe Erendell was brought
before Council Court and, although pleading inno-

cent, was found guilty on all charges in a remarkably fast and efficient trial headed up by Lord Vanmoer. As a result of her guilt, the servant is sentenced to be hanged by the neck until dead Wednesday hence.

Marion set the paper on his lap and swallowed hard, his throat tight and scratchy around the lump lodged in it. Poison leaves? It made no sense.

Certainly Chloe had reason to be angry with Marion's father—he had used the girl ill when she probably knew no better and then lopped off her ear in a fit of his infamous rage. But Chloe loved his family—Marion knew that as much as he knew rain only fell up if you forced it to. There was something wrong about all this. His stomach pitched under his ribs and he ignored the most obvious wrongs marked by gravestones. He could do nothing for his family.

But Chloe. If he might yet help her . . . He stood, bracing himself between the two tombstones. He looked at the place his hand rested on his brother's headstone and, yanking himself up straight, realized that he knew about the leaves. He had watched his little brother gather something that day and tear it into tiny, unrecognizable bits to make the batter better.

It was not Chloe's fault. He was a witness to her innocence! He vaulted forward, dashing down the aisle of graves and out the gate. He rushed up the road, fighting gravity's downward pull with every long and rhythmic stretch of his legs.

He crested the Hill, huffing and puffing, determination pushing him onward past the burn in his side and the burn in his lungs and pressing him toward destiny.

Chapter Fifteen

~~~~~

Ill news travels fast.
—ERASMUS

The Road from Philadelphia

Rowen and Jonathan set out early the next morning, heading still farther from the negligible town. Frederick had agreed with them—"Perhaps more time and distance and then, if young Lady Astraea is truly found innocent of all witchery and allowed to come home . . ." He had paused, the worry clear in his eyes. "Then might you return as the prodigal son and reclaim the lifestyle you came from. But until then," he said sadly, "it is best to avoid most everyone. People talk. And if a reward is offered . . ."

So they turned their backs and their horses' buttocks to Philadelphia and continued on until they came to a tavern. Jonathan dismounted and tied Silver up while Rowen stared down at him in disbelief.

"Follow me," Jonathan requested.

Rowen nodded, joining him. "Why not? As they said at Jordan's party, I am no great leader of men."

Jonathan shrugged. "You led me on this particular adventure."

"Somehow that makes me feel no better."

Just inside the tavern's door, Rowen froze, his eyes darting from side to side. He'd hoped such a brief stop so early in their race from the city meant they'd outrun any unwanted attentions, but that was before he noticed two posters hanging on the wall. The one to his left announced a manhunt for the murderer Rowen Albertus Burchette, while the one to his right included an artist's illustrated rendering of a short-nosed, broad-foreheaded, thick-necked version of him from shoulders up and in stark black ink.

He was not sure which to be more offended by, the one revealing his middle name to the world or the one that claimed a "faithful reproduction of a murderer's image."

He motioned to Jonathan with his chin. The same chin now covered in an unappealing scruff. If he'd had access to a proper razor and strap he'd do the thing himself, bringing his face back to a proper cleanliness instead of allowing his sideburns to crawl toward his chin.

Jonathan frowned, running his hand across his own stubble, pulling thumb and forefinger together at the end of his jaw in a thoughtful gesture before striding forward to the bar.

Rowen blinked. Then, throwing his shoulders back, he followed, standing at Jonathan's side.

"A bit of your house ale for my friend and me," Jonathan requested of the flat-faced man behind the bar. He pulled out a coin and tapped its edge on the wood.

The man swept the coin into his meaty palm and filled two tankards, setting them down with a clank before the two younger men.

Jonathan took a long sip of his ale. "Any news of import?"

Rowen nearly spit his ale out when the bartender hooked a thumb in the direction of the posters.

"Riders came through here this morning, putting those up and asking questions. Two fellows, one of decent breeding, are on the run. Seems the ugly one"—he pointed to the image of Rowen—"shot a man of higher rank." The bartender leaned across the bar, saying, "Probably told he was ugly as the south end of a north-facing mule." He nodded, lips pursed in a smug smile.

Jonathan laughed. "He is one ugly bastard."

Rowen's face colored at the comment.

The bartender pulled away, laughing, and said, "And in my opinion a man should never be shot for speaking the truth."

"True, true," Jonathan agreed.

They drank the rest of their ales in silence, Rowen pouting and Jonathan occasionally chuckling to himself.

"What precisely was your intention—going in there and asking for news once you'd seen we are *it*?" Rowen hissed as they left. "We *are* the news, Jonathan!"

Jonathan snorted. "No. No we are not. Some other poor bastards are—and one of them is quite the ugly brute." He reached up and tweaked the tip of Rowen's nose. "Be thankful you're a handsome beast, you ladykiller, you. No one would dare imagine you and that man on the flyer are one and the same."

With a laugh, he mounted his horse, nodded to Rowen, and nudged Silver into a trot.

Even though her Making Tank placed her higher up in the tower with a small barred window overlooking the wall and the water of the lake beyond, none of it interested her today.

"What does it look like?" The voice beyond the wall, introduced as Caleb, asked.

Jordan jerked upright from where she slouched, dozing in the scant and slanting sunlight. Caleb's voice echoed in her ears. "What does *what* look like?"

"The outside—the sun, the sky, the valley . . . any bit of it."

"Do you not see it when you are taken for Making?"

He laughed, the sound sharp and cutting. "No. The Maker knows how I miss it—the outside, so he keeps it from me. I have not seen the sky in . . ." There was a long pause as Caleb thought. "Nineteen months, three weeks, and . . . two days."

"So long . . ."

"I refuse to be numbered among his success stories," he hissed. "I will not let him break me."

"You are not a Witch either?" Jordan asked, turning around and scooting as close to the hole in the wall as she could get.

Laughter roiled up again, but this time it was heartfelt. "If I have my way, the Maker will never know what I truly am. I will always control who truly knows the truth of me."

Jordan nodded and rolled up to a standing position, crossing the small space between wall and window in only a few short strides. With a new appreciation for the world outside her window, she described the scene with all the vividness and detail she could muster.

———

The Maker summoned Jordan to the laboratory early that day. The Wardens growled and shoved her inside, closing the door behind her. She pitched forward, catching herself inches from falling against a table's edge. Straightening, she brushed her hands down the front of her dress to neaten it. It was more out of habit now, she realized, than need. Her dress was irrepressibly filthy and the last things to right the damage were her own grubby fingers. She looked at her fingernails and the dirt always edging beneath them. She hooked a nail beneath another and did her best to clean away the offensive grime, but shortly gave up. Some battles were no longer worth fighting. Besides, when they realized she was innocent surely they'd give her a proper bath and a new dress to return home in.

If they realized she was innocent. Her fingers flew to the pin still nestled in the deep folds of fabric at her elbow and she traced the edges of its shape with one hesitant fingertip. The metal was cool to the touch and smooth as silk.

Rowen's heart.

Her own heart beat a little faster at the thought.

Or maybe it was the strangeness of her surroundings.

It seemed odd that the Wardens would leave her here, in the Maker's main laboratory, unattended. In the dark.

Waiting for the man who would only bring her more pain.

She stood perfectly still, her eyes roving the poorly lit space, her finger and thumb stroking the heart pinned to her sleeve.

Alone in the chamber, her eyes widened at the noise of something tapping softly near the room's dim corner, like fingers on glass. She eased her way toward the noise, her eyes wide and round to better pull in the little bit of light that showed from the resting stormlights. The room's walls were lined with long wooden countertops covered in jars, fat or fluted glass tubes, sturdy-looking beakers, and oddly shaped bottles and boxes. Some were stoppered with cork, others with rubber or metal, and disturbingly few bore labels she understood.

In a small cask a thick fluid moved, bubbles rising so frequently they sizzled through the murky liquid. She paused there a moment, watching the viscous liquid until a bubble reached its top, pierced the skin, and snapped open, belching out a smell that reminded Jordan of the docks in summer. Wrinkling her nose against the briny scent, she moved on. Her fingers skimmed the counter's edges, her chains rustling between her wrists, a reminder of her imprisonment even while she explored the dim space independently.

She paused before a ghostly shape nested deep in a dusty cubbyhole and squinted, forcing her eyes to adjust and define the curve of the bulbous thing so white it nearly glowed from the cabinet's recess. She gasped, recognizing it. Two black eye sockets peered blindly back at her, the skull leering out at her—its smile broad and amiable. Cheerful in a frighteningly alien way.

Her fingers tightened on the counter's edge.

She had only seen a drawing of a skull in a book sitting open in one of the more questionable stores in the Below, and only once. Still . . . this was smaller than she expected. Her own head was a bit bigger, of that she was quite sure. She rolled her lower lip between her teeth and eased back and away.

The cask's bubbling intensified and Jordan raised an eyebrow, her gaze drifting back toward it. On the counter a bottle shivered and another trembled, walking forward on its round glass edge. Jordan backed up farther. All the jars and bottles with liquid in them—all the containers that had contents able to slosh—sloshed and quivered and danced below the little grinning skull—a child's skull, Jordan realized—like anxious living things.

Like anxious living things with a secret to tell.

She reached out, wrapped a shaking hand around the skull, and, cradling it in hand, pulled it out of the dark pit it had been condemned to.

The bottles and flasks all stopped their chattering at once. The silence that descended was somehow more disturbing than the clattering noise of a moment before.

There was no sound in the chamber now except for Jordan's breathing and the strange and ceaseless tapping that sounded from the chamber's still unexplored corner.

She held the skull so its eye sockets were level with her own wide eyes and she peered into them, wondering what color the eyes had once been. Had they been ringed with thick lashes—was this a boy or a girl who'd lost his or her head? Slowly she turned the skull, pausing again. Jordan drew down a deep breath.

There was magick here—magick that was dark and dirty and disappointing. And had absolutely nothing to do with her.

The goose bumps on her arms raising the fine hairs there seemed to insist this magick wanted to have more than a little to do with her—regardless of her own wishes.

She tried to force her hands to stop their trembling but that only intensified the rattling that shook her straight to her bones. With all the care she could muster, she set the skull back in its cubby and stepped away once more.

Dread uncurled in her stomach, but Jordan headed toward the noise, her feet pulling her body, unbidden, forward. The child's skull was behind her, and the blackness nestling around it felt just as heavy as the darkness cloaking the corner before her.

Light slipped like quicksilver across the domed surface of a large bell jar. The tapping sound grew louder, more frantic, and she saw a flicker of movement behind the glass's surface. She drew nearer and the sound intensified, the tapping becoming a soft drumbeat as a dozen pairs of wings—of all shapes and patterns, colors and sizes—beat against the glass in protest of being confined.

Butterflies flew in a controlled panic, wings stroking the glass.

Jordan's hand flew to the pendant at her neck.

Light blared in the chamber and she stumbled back.

"They're beautiful, aren't they?" The Maker's voice scraped down her spine and Jordan swung around to face him, her chain swinging between her wrists.

She was as free as the butterflies in the bell jar. She could move, but not far enough to mean anything.

The Maker strolled across the floor and flicked a finger against the jar, sending the butterflies into a full-blown panic, their wings clattering en masse against the opposite wall. "Did you know their wings seem to have similarities to the stormcells?"

Jordan shook her head, mute in his presence.

"They build and hold power in their wings thanks to sunlight the way Witches pull storms into themselves. Some believe they bring sunlight—that's why they've been nicknamed sunseekers—that they have a symbiotic relationship with the sun itself, calling to it the way your kind calls to darkness and storms." He looked her up and down. "Nothing to say?" He frowned. "That is so very frustrating—talking at someone instead of *to* someone. You should speak freely, Jordan."

She looked down, focusing on the spot she knew her feet were hiding beneath the hem of her dress. "*My* kind calls to nothing. *My* kind is Grounded."

"You're just like the rest of them," he said, disappointment clear in his softening tone. "You resent me. You resent this gift I am giving you—this freedom from being Grounded. Do you know what I would give to no longer be Grounded?" His hand dropped forward and he snagged her chain, yanking her forward.

"Let us begin then," he said, placing her in the chair and pulling the buckles tight across her wrists. "I do not hold your words against you, Jordan. You should speak freely," he insisted, his mouth so close to her ear as he cinched the final strap that all she heard was the rasp of his words. "Yes, Jordan, if thoughts or words well up in you, you should always speak freely. Or, better yet—*scream*."

On the Road from Philadelphia

It was Rowen who suggested he stand guard at the river's edge, letting the horses drink from the shallowest part of the water. "Perhaps we should head directly to Holgate. When Jordan is cleared of these charges, she will need someone to bring her home."

Jonathan kept his head down, settling Silver's mane with the brush he'd wisely packed into the saddlebags. "That is a good point, young sir. And as good a direction to head as any." He tugged at Silver's ear and the horse flicked it and whinnied good-naturedly. "You could be Miss Jordan's escort—if not her hero," Jonathan teased.

"I'm only hero material if your cousin Frederick includes me in his fiction," Rowen mused darkly.

"There is more hero to you than I think you've ever imagined," Jonathan said, pausing in Silver's grooming to look across the horse's back to Rowen. "I tend to believe, if you will indulge me a moment, that a man can never be disproven of heroism unless he fails when pushed to perform. Untested, who knows? You, *friend*"—the word choice was not lost on Rowen—"have only now begun to be pushed. To be tested. Your potential is yet unglimpsed. There is the stuff of legends within you. Of that I am sure."

Rowen looked away. "So we head to Holgate."

"Yes. And you consider that you might yet be Miss Jordan's hero. She is a damsel in distress. What is more worthy a hero's task than to be a knight in shining armor for a damsel?"

Rowen laughed. Rudely.

Jonathan was not amused. "Consider that you might be the happily ever after to her currently tragic tale."

Rowen mumbled something devoid of commitment and said, "You read too much fiction." He cleared his throat. "Perhaps. If I am to be her hero—the happily ever after to her currently tragic tale—then I must say you are a good part of that story. This madness is all made more bearable by the assistance of a fine friend such as yourself. A fine friend is just as important as a fine woman in having a true happily ever after."

Jonathan snorted. "You might disagree with your current sentiment if you spend more time with Miss Jordan. Unchaperoned."

Rowen blinked and then burst out laughing. "Perhaps!"

They didn't hear, see, or smell it until it was on top of Jonathan, its broad flipper hands catching his head and twisting his neck with a crunch so loud Silver bolted as Jonathan crumpled to the ground, the Merrow sinking down with him.

Rowen shouted and fired a shot, but the Merrow sprang away, using its slick tail as a coil and propelling itself after Silver as he streaked into the woods.

Ransom's nostrils flared, ears flattening against his skull as his lips pulled back from his bright white teeth. Rowen reloaded and watched the tree line as he stumbled over bits of river debris on his way to Jonathan. He didn't dare go to his knees, didn't dare turn his back to either the woods or the water as he crouched to check his friend for signs of life.

It took but a moment.

"Damn it!" Rowen shouted, rising. "Damn it all to Hell—it's not supposed to happen this way!" He headed into the woods, hunting for the Merrow that couldn't be too far ahead. He stopped, hearing noise behind him.

Ransom blew a burst of hot air out his nose, nearly baking Rowen's face.

"Didn't want to be left behind, did you?" Rowen asked, sparing a quick touch for the horse. "Me neither." He stepped to his steed's side and climbed into the saddle, mindful of the loaded pistol. "Let's us go and see just where our slimy little friend got to, shall we? I have a bullet with his name on it." He nudged Ransom forward with his heels, watching for any signs of either horse or the Merrow's passage. Plants bent a different way than the rest or stems or branches broken—all were telltale signs of movement. As was the sudden noise of a terrified horse's scream.

Rowen kicked Ransom forward and the horse barely

even flicked an ear at being commanded into danger instead of being directed away from it. They plunged through the brush and thin briars lining the already torn pathway, bolting toward the source of the sound.

Ahead of them Silver stood and stamped, his eyes rolling and head lowered, focusing on something low to the ground and obscured by the bushes before them. They crashed through the last bit of brush and came to a sliding stop beside the horse, their haunches touching.

Silver broke free of his staring contest with the Merrow for a moment and Rowen lowered his pistol and took a shot.

The Merrow squealed and flew backward through the brambles as fast as if the bullet carried it. This time they tracked it the whole way from the noise alone and Rowen struggled to reload his gun as Ransom carried him after the beast to finish it off, leaving Silver back in the thicket. He would avenge his best friend, escort the damsel, and put things to rights in Philadelphia.

Blackpowder spilled from Rowen's powder flask and his wadding was a sloppy job at best. But he dropped in the lead and rammed it home and was ready when they burst back to the river's edge.

At least he had thought himself ready.

At the water's edge three more Merrow crouched, petting and cooing to soothe their wounded comrade as they stuffed his wound with the gooey growth that always tangled Rowen's line when he dared to go down to the Below's dockside and fish.

They looked up at him, sitting there on top of his beautiful horse, and they gnashed their impossibly large teeth, drooling.

"Damn it," Rowen repeated, letting Ransom dance

backward beneath him. "I am fairly certain *this* is also not supposed to happen . . . I want my damned happily ever after!" He reached down and loosened the sword at his side and then, refocusing on his gun, took aim and fired.

The blow knocked a Merrow back into the water in a splash of blood. Something moved just below the surface, causing ripples and then another ripple, and another, as spines circled the rising blood in the river and then, in a furious fit of splashing water and high-pitched wailing the waters frothed with foam and blood as the Merrow tore each other apart.

Ransom carried Rowen another long slow step backward as Rowen reloaded and fired.

The Merrow shifted, anticipating his shot, but the ramrod sliced through one of them, launched from the pistol's barrel in Rowen's haste, and flew like a spear into the water beyond as the bullet went wide and grazed the other.

The remaining Merrow snapped their jaws together, teeth clicking wetly as saliva dripped and they scurried forward, propelled by their coiling and then stretching tails. They leaped at Ransom and Rowen swung his pistol like a club, connecting with a sickening sound with the skull of one of the Merrow and knocking it to the ground, unconscious and bleeding.

Distantly Rowen wondered if they'd drag that one down into the swirling waters for a fleshy feast, too, and he cursed and freed his sword, slashing wildly as the Merrow dug claws into Ransom's flank and he squealed like a hog at slaughter.

He bucked and Rowen flew from the saddle, landing hard. Catching his breath and climbing to his feet, Rowen watched the prize stallion whip his spine so loosely that it seemed he had no bones in his back at all. His adversaries flew free of him, unable to maintain a grip with tail, tooth, or claw and Ransom spun on his hooves and, with one quick look at Rowen, bolted back into the dry cover of the woods they'd just come from.

Rowen stood his ground, slashing out with his blade and retreating into the woods the way Ransom had gone, his eyes on the snarling and still advancing Merrow, his last glimpse of the best friend he'd ever had the lifeless body at the river's edge, the waters lapping at his side.

Far past the fringe of the forest, nearer to its light-dappled heart, the Merrow gave up the chase and slunk back to the relative safety of the river. They'd slip downstream soon, seeking saltier water.

When he was certain they intended no ambush, Rowen bent over to catch his breath, his sword quivering in his grip. He willed himself to release the weapon and watched it fall to the ground with detached interest. He set down his pistol and began to rub feeling back into his right hand. He crouched by his weapons, stretching and flexing and checking himself for wounds. His beautiful pants were ruined now, covered in dirt, Merrow slime, and blood. He tugged a small briar branch out of one leg and winced as the thorns pulled out.

But beyond all the small indignities of battle—the dirt, the grime, and the blood—was the loss.

He turned back toward the distant river and the place where Jonathan had gone down.

If he'd had any doubt before about going swiftly to Holgate to find Jordan, it was as gone as Jonathan's life. Jordan was his last remaining close friend. Jonathan had not abandoned Rowen in the time of his greatest need, so neither would he abandon her in hers.

"Damn it," he repeated for good measure. He stood, shook out each of his limbs, and rolled his head to stretch out the pinch of tension in his neck. He rubbed his face, surprised when his fingers came away damp. "Damn it," he said again, this time the words but a whisper. He picked up his sword once more, slipped the empty pistol into his belt, and peered up through the overlapping canopy of thick leaves to try and find the sun. He decided he would again match his path to its own once he recovered the horses.

Holgate

Caleb's voice surprised Jordan. "You do not feel her there? With you?"

Jordan shook her head, confused. "I truly do not know what you mean . . . There is no one here with me."

"Sybil is," Caleb insisted. "You may not see her, but she remains. In the walls and in the water. She is a part of this place. She is rooted here."

Jordan shivered. "A ghost?"

"The spirit of a little girl," he corrected. "I might become a ghost someday, but she? She is Rusalka."

Jordan tested the word on her tongue, rolling its foreign sound in her mouth. "Rusalka? What is that?"

"It is the spirit of a murdered girl bound forever to water."

"How could that be?" Jordan's finger traced the chink of mortar running between the weeping stones. "If she was a murdered Witch . . . would she not be tied to a soul stone? Not water?"

Caleb grew quiet a moment. "Why not both? I still feel

her. Part of her remains there. I am certain. She was sweet.
Just a scrap of humanity. Taken too soon from this world.
Not I. For me the end comes not soon enough."

The Warden slammed Jordan's door open and grabbed
the chain hanging between her leather shackles. At the top
of the Eastern Tower, Jordan next saw the child who had
called her an abomination as the Maker prepared to do the
less than gentle parts of his job. The child carried a floppy-
eared toy that seemed somehow less substantial than previous. The little girl looked at her with wide eyes and handed
the Maker a bowl of some food and piece of bread so fresh
and warm Jordan could smell it from where she stood with
the Warden, eyeing the boards, the straps running across
them, and the table that held a roll of dark-colored cloth.

Her mouth watered the tiniest bit but her stomach grumbled so loudly in response to the scent and sight of freshly
baked bread that the Maker even turned to look at her.

"The pretty lady is hungry," Meg said, tugging gently at
her father's shirt. "Do you have any to spare her?"

He looked at her as if it was the oddest thing anyone had
ever suggested to him. "What a very sweet girl you are, Meggie. But you must remember what she is. Yes, she looks like
a pretty lady, but . . . she is a powerful monster under that
smooth skin of hers. An *abomination*," he reminded. "Now
run along."

"Yes, Papá," she agreed. "I think I will visit Maude first
for a drink. I am parched."

"Go then, little dove," Bran said. "Have a care on the
stairs—I will meet you in the library in less than an hour."

She nodded and he helped her through the door and
watched as she started her descent before he closed the door
once more.

"She is an interesting child, do you not agree?" he asked Jordan as he approached her with the bread and bowl. "If I follow her suggestion, give you this piece of bread, could we dispense with the unpleasantness and shoot straight to you calling up a storm?" He picked up the bread and held it before her face. "It is fresh. And warm . . ."

"I cannot. I am no Witch," Jordan protested. Her wounded finger flinched, curling toward her palm in response to his nearness.

"Not even for a nice piece of bread? Can you smell it over the stink of the Tanks and your magick?"

Her nostrils flared involuntarily. "Yes, I smell it," she whispered, her eyes reflecting back the frantic hunger that threatened to crawl up from her stomach and out of her throat. "But I cannot call a storm. I have no magick."

The Warden strapped her to the boards.

Bran shook his head. "I wish you would stop repeating such nonsense." He set the bowl down on his table and unrolled the cloth that held all the instruments of his particular trade. He picked up a scalpel and bit into the bread. "Oh. It is delicious," he said around a bite of the stuff. "And so, so very soft . . ." He crossed to her side and looked her straight in the eyes as he said, "Just like a lady's flesh."

And then he made her scream.

Philadelphia

All the way up the Hill Marion left signs of his passing. Small patches of wilting grass marked his every footstep and the air became unseasonably cool wherever he passed.

His breath came out in frosty puffs as he pushed on to the Council's chambers and then, standing before the doors, he hesitated.

Yes, he could clear Chloe's name. Yes, he could prove her innocence, make an ass of the Council Court and . . . and name himself as witness. Put himself at the scene of the supposed crime, thereby admitting his true identity.

Showing that he was the son that was taken for witchery, the one Witch that had escaped Holgate.

If they tortured Witches to *Make* them, what might they do to a Witch who had escaped and wreaked wintry havoc? His fingers flexed at his sides. They had stolen him from the family their laws had ruined. He should have died that night beside his parents and his little brother but instead the Council and their Weather Workers had taken and tortured him. Made a monster of him. What more could they do to him that they hadn't done already?

What could they still do to hurt him? What was left for them to take that they hadn't already ruined? He should have died that night five years ago. Why had destiny spared him then? If the Council discovered him now, killed him now, at least he'd die knowing he saved one person who was important to him. And, if God was just (if there was a God), perhaps he'd be reunited in Heaven with his family. He decided he had nothing left to lose and the rescue of Chloe—even if it meant a much sooner heavenly reunion with his parents and little brother—was quite the gain.

He squared his shoulders, set his jaw, and climbed the last set of stairs into the Council's main hall. Automatons shifted along the walls, watching him as he moved toward a central desk and a reassuringly human watchman. "I am here to speak to the Council Court and present them with new evidence."

The watchman looked up at him. "The Council is adjourned for the day to oversee the administration of justice."

Marion's brow creased. "But I have new evidence that can clear the accused named in the case of Chloe Erendell."

"Oh." The watchman's mouth dropped open and he looked over his shoulder to the broad expanse of doors and large windows overseeing the Council's broad courtyard.

And that was when Marion saw them—a crush of bodies all turned to watch something ahead of them. "No," he whispered, realizing. "No. The paper says Wednesday *hence* . . ."

"Yes," the watchman yelled at his back as he sprinted across the room's length, "they confused the dates—the paper was very apologetic—we usually have more spectators for a noon hanging—quite the event . . ."

Marion was at the doors and shoving through them, pushing past people when he could not slide between them and shouting—always shouting, "Stop! Stop!"

But the crowd was cheering and laughing and there was no more place for him to run and so he made his way to the one tree in the courtyard and shimmied up its trunk just high enough to see the gallows and the hooded figure in a simple shift who stood there, noose about her neck, dark hands and feet bare, her head bowed as she gave her final confession. There stood his nanny, his last connection to a more innocent time, and he knew then just what he still had to lose.

He screamed her name, cried out her innocence again and again, and snow billowed out from his mouth but was whisked away with his words by the breeze and evaporated in the day's heat and the crowd's fierce haze of human musk.

The floor beneath Chloe's feet dropped away and she fell

toward the ground—only stopped by the sudden tightening of the rope round her neck. Her feet kicked out a moment and Marion gasped, ramming his knuckles into his mouth to keep from crying out to her—or anyone again.

Then she was still.

And he was all alone in the world.

This time for certain and for good.

The cold seeped out of him, cruel and deadly, burrowing into the tree that held him in the same insidious way the cold clutched his heart, so that, after the crowd drifted apart and Marion finally climbed down from its branches, only then did the tree's leaves begin to curl and blacken along the edges. Only then did the cold begin to kill it from the inside out—the same way the cold was killing its young master.

Chapter Sixteen

~~~

Everybody talks about the weather,
but nobody does anything about it.
—MARK TWAIN

Holgate

That night Meggie again awoke to soaked sheets, a wet gown, and a perplexed Maude. Maude had decided to sleep on the floor at her side, as cramped and uncomfortable as it was, although Meggie had innocently suggested Maude share her papá's bed as it was so big and he was quite alone in it every night. "And a spot of warmth and kindness never hurt a soul, my mother used to say," Meggie said loudly enough that Bran couldn't help but hear it.

"A spot of kindness, yes?" Maude said with a smile. "Such things do quite frequently help situations one might think beyond help . . ." She sighed. "Quite alone in it every night, is he?" Maude had asked.

"Most certainly so," Meggie quipped. "And I think I know why," she said with a solemn nod.

"Oh you do, do you?" Maude asked, tucking her in after

one last story. It was harder than ever to get her to go to sleep now that every night she had a friend staying over.

"Yes. It is the snoring," Meggie said sagely. "It is a dreadful racket," she disdained. "It sounds like an elephant trying to blow its nose!"

"I heard that," Bran called from the other room, sending both the girls into a wild fit of giggles.

"A rabid elephant blowing his nose," Meggie squeaked defiantly.

"Oh, is that so?" he bellowed, racing toward them, a grin on his face. He jumped onto the bed and bounced Meggie so hard she was lifted into the air and gave a little scream. But she dissolved into laughter again when she landed and snuggled back down into her pillow, dragging the covers up around her ears to better ignore her father's silliness.

A tickle battle then erupted between the two and Bran attacked, shouting, "Come here, you! You're a soft little thing, aren't you?"

Meggie squealed between giggles, "A lady should be *soft*!"

Bran froze on the bed, arms outstretched, body stiff but rocking to the swaying of the mattress beneath his feet. The smile fell from his lips and shadows hardened his expression. He swallowed hard. Something in his chest tightened and he turned to look past the girls. To the door.

But Meggie pounced on him, knocking him onto her bed and knocking whatever dark thought had been in his head right out with her relentless joy. Maude just sat on the floor beside the bed, watching and marveling at how free Bran was now with the child—how very different—how young he seemed when it was just the three of them together.

He was a man unburdened—because of what they were all certain would be a burden.

"What?" he asked, stepping off the bed and hopping over Maude on his way back to his room and his too large for one man bed. "Why are you looking at me that way?"

"Because I see them again," Maude whispered, her cheeks heating with a sudden and surprising blush.

"What? What do you see again?"

"Your dimples," she said. "Only when you smile that much do they appear. But there they are." And with a sleepy smile she leaned back onto her makeshift bed and curled onto her side, tugging her own blanket up, a smile on her lips.

He stood there in the doorway between the two rooms like a man caught between two worlds, and he reached up to touch his own smiling face, amazed that she had found something in him he had never even noticed about himself. He uncrossed his arms and watched them for a moment before leaving for his own bed—watched the two most beautiful, gentle, and amazing girls in the world.

And they were both, in at least some small way, his. And he was ready to try and offer a spot of kindness himself.

Philadelphia

Marion tried to sleep that night in the park but his dreams were as dark as the farthest corner of the sky. When dawn finally came he rose from where he'd hidden by the public hedge-maze and staggered onto the main thoroughfare. He touched things at random as he stumbled back down the Hill to the Below. No longer did he worry who saw or who screamed. No longer did he bother with anonymity or soft action. These were the people who destroyed all he ever loved. These were the people who built on the backs of his kind and ruined anyone who loved the Witches. The Witches who provided stability for their country—their government's country.

"An election year," the boy had said.

Marion grinned and reached out for a window box hanging in front of a cheese shop's painted window. He trailed his fingers along a single fringed dianthus petal and watched the frost spread out like tiny snowflakes flattened flush to the flower. Wrapping round its stem, cold consumed its leaves. The frost scrambled the short distance to the next plant in the box, leaving a glittering path of destruction that wiped the entire window box of life in under a minute—all while Marion stood silent and watched his talent seek and destroy.

He would bring them all down, he promised himself, make them all suffer the unseasonable cold that was ever in his heart. He began his journey down to the Below once more, his eyes on a certain bridge and the warm glow of firelight peeking out from beneath it already. The sun was still low in the sky when he began to formulate his plan. Destiny had saved him five years ago and Made him who he was for this purpose. And if he was to get his revenge in a proper way, he had best research and prepare.

Bringing down the Maker would require planning and transportation.

But if revenge was a dish best eaten cold he was surely the best man to enjoy both its taste and temperature.

"Today we will try something new," the Maker told Jordan.

Her stomach flopped like a fish caught in the net of her gut. Silently she assumed her spot by the board, offering her manacled wrists to be bound for the day's new torture.

"No, no," he corrected. "Today we will have a spot of kindness. And a spot of tea." He smiled and opened the door to the laboratory. In walked Meggie, carrying a tray with a teapot and cups and saucers balanced on its surface.

"Sit, please," Bran requested, motioning for Jordan to perch on a chair.

It was then, as she sipped tea with her torturer, that Jordan realized he was quite insane. It was also then that she wondered if perhaps she would not soon follow in the same manner.

Following the new treatment he asked her if there was anything he might do to make her feel more comfortable. He made it clear he would not remove her from the Tanks, but was there anything else she might appreciate? Her eyes fell on the tea set and narrowed. "A daily cup of tea in my Tank."

His eyes crinkled at their edges and he nodded. "That I can most certainly provide."

And for the next several days, he was good to his word, hoping that kindness might make magick blossom when nothing else would. For those days tea became the shared ritual of Jordan and her cell mates—a spot of sanity amid the pain and darkness. And on those days, unbeknownst to Jordan, the Maker was a kind, gentle, and happy man.

One day Jordan would take a sip and pass the cup and saucer through the hole between her cell and Caleb's, the next she took a sip and passed it the other direction to Kate.

But the happiness was short-lived. Jordan still summoned no storms and, having proof that she could, the
Maker had to presume she was refusing or required a different method to trigger her skills. So the torture resumed, but
the tea kept coming.

It was on one such a day after Jordan had returned from
her time on the Eastern Tower's top, her hand aching all
over again from the Maker's attentions, that the trio first
argued over who received the precious liquid.

Jordan passed the cup through the hole in the wall,
her shaking hand making the cup clatter against the saucer. "Apologies," she whispered, tea spilling onto her fingers.

"Stop," Caleb insisted. "You need it more than I . . ."

"No," Jordan said.

But the cup and saucer paused and Caleb scooted it back
so it rested just in the shared shadow of the wall.

"I will leave it there," Jordan challenged. "You should
drink it—enjoy it so it does not go to waste."

There was a groan from the wall's other side. "It is on
your side of the wall."

"It is not," Jordan protested.

"Indeed it is."

"Not."

"You are the most difficult neighbor I have yet had," Caleb muttered. With a grinding and chattering noise the cup
and accompanying saucer walked closer to her in the grip of
her mysterious neighbor's hand.

It was the most Jordan had ever glimpsed of Caleb and
just one look made her stomach do flips. The hand was as
dirty as hers—that was far from surprising, but the marks
that crisscrossed the back of Caleb's hand were a system of

cross-hatched scars, white and rising from the skin's already pale surface and a testament to Caleb's continued courage.

He said he wouldn't give in to the Maker and he hadn't, though it had cost him.

Before Caleb could withdraw his hand, Jordan knocked the cup awkwardly aside to grasp his fingers.

For a moment they were still and silent that way, tea leaking from the overturned cup, Jordan's hand clenching the fingers of the boy next door.

"Please don't," he whispered, his voice rasping to finally break the shared silence. "You're wasting good tea."

But she wrapped her fingers more tightly around his. "How did you come to be here?"

"Although I do not mind your questions normally . . ." He shifted in the straw on the hole's other side. "You must not ask me that."

His fingers twitched against her palm.

"You must let me go," he said.

"Not yet." She twisted closer, trying to get her face close enough that she could see his face.

But the darkness between them was too deep.

"I don't wish to let go just yet."

"We never do." He groaned. "Who are you really holding on to, Jordan? It can't be me . . . You barely know me . . ."

She sighed.

"Who was he?"

She released him then, pulling away to tuck her knees up and wrap her arms around them. "I don't know what you mean."

"Liar. You're holding on to someone. In your heart. I know it."

"How would you know?"

"Because we do that—hold on. It's what keeps us going. It's all that keeps us going."

She heard him move in the straw again and she imagined him mirroring her position just a wall away. "*Is* that what keeps us going?"

"Well, it certainly isn't the love of one's family . . . not for me." Silence soaked up the moments like a sponge falling into water for the first time. He reached through the gap in the wall again, this time even farther into the grim space of her cell. His fingers fidgeted, wanting hers, and she could not help but take them again.

"Who keeps *you* going?" she asked into the dark.

"Thomas."

She nearly pulled back in surprise at him naming another man. But his delivery of the name, so soft and sweet and . . . *loving,* made her brow furrow, and not thinking of her own imperfections or the wrinkles she'd surely earn, she squeezed his fingers tight, whispering, "Tell me all about him."

And they rested that way in the dirt and the straw, neither of them worrying over filth or social convention, holding hands and remembering a brighter, better time when love was fresh and new and within reach. It was remembering those things that next spurred Jordan to action. Caleb was right, she was holding on to someone and realized then in her Tank how lost she felt without him.

En Route to Holgate

Rowen was lost and he'd been lost for days. How was it that a man of his education and breeding could be so utterly turned around in a forest? He sat with a huff at the base of a tree and ran his hands across his face, scratching at the stubble growing there. He growled out his despair. He no longer had clean clothing, a ramrod for his pistol, or his horse, and, to make things worse, he was growing whiskers to rival his grandfather's. Soon he'd have a full beard and mustache and children would flock to him and call him Father Christmas . . .

How did people stay reasonably clean shaven before barbers and razors and straps? Did they use other knives? He looked at his sword. He'd cut his head clean off if he tried to shave with it. The natives. What did they use? Flint? He glared at his pistol and its firing mechanism. No flint to be had as they'd made the fashionable switch to percussion caps not long ago. They fired better most times, but one could hardly get a good shave from a percussion cap.

Flint was merely a piece of rock that could be sharpened. Surely he could find that. Even if he couldn't find the horses. Or Holgate. Or Jordan.

His stomach rumbled. Well, no one would mistake him for Father Christmas, as lean as he was becoming. He threw a rock he'd managed to sit on and cursed at the thought it might have been flint. And no one would ever mistake him for being jolly.

Damn it all! His best friend was dead, his steed was missing along with most of his remaining possessions, he hadn't had a meal of substance since Frederick's house, and he was absolutely certain he had sat beneath this same exact tree raging about his failures before!

By the time he reached Holgate Jordan would already be gone. If he ever reached Holgate. His chance at a happily ever after was slim at best and his chance of being a hero? Worse.

He dragged himself back up to his feet and held onto the tree. He had to take desperate measures. He had to find Ransom. Or Silver. Or both.

And he might just have to do the thing he'd never dreamed of doing—ask for directions.

Damn it all!

Holgate

There was something about a child and spreading kindness that did not sit well with Bran and his title of Maker, so he summoned Councilman Stevenson to his laboratory to conclude business. "I have not the stomach for this job anymore," Bran admitted, his gaze traveling over the Councilman's head to rest on the sightless skull in its makeshift place of honor—the skull belonging to the child who reminded him so much of the little girl who now frequently shadowed his steps. The same little girl that looked up at him with worshipful eyes and suggested he try patience above pain.

"And precisely what do you mean by that?"

"I mean . . ." Bran looked down, his brow pinching together over the narrow bridge of his nose. "I cannot be your Maker any longer."

The Councilman hopped back, shaking his head in surprise. "You cannot . . . ?" Again he shook his head. "I fail to see how you have come to believe that you have a choice in such matters."

"Of course I have a choice. I have a family now. I must make this choice for their good as much as my own. Perhaps more for theirs than mine."

"A family?" the Councilman chortled, holding his stomach with one hand. "You have a bastard daughter by a whore and a maid warming your bed until you tighten your purse strings or she finds someone more interesting." He shook his head, still laughing. "A *family*?"

Bran crossed his arms over his chest and spread his feet in a broader stance. "I will Make no more Conductors."

"Then who do you think will? Who will provide our most valuable energy resource except you? Who will power our lights and our carriages and our airships?"

"There is talk of a better power source: steam," Bran suggested.

The Councilman's head snaked forward. *"Steam?"*

"Yes. Steam."

Lord Stevenson raked a hand through his thinning hair. "Do you have any idea of how a change to steam—only a possibility of power, truly—would change our entire society? Can you fathom what such a thing might mean?"

"It might mean that Councilman Braga was right. It might mean revolution," Bran said matter-of-factly.

Stevenson snorted. "My *God*." He turned his back to Bran, smacked his palms onto the countertop, and lowered his head, rolling it back and forth on his thin neck. "And you would do this because you no longer have the stomach for your family's line of work?"

"And because of my *family*," Bran said, grating the word out from between his teeth.

Stevenson raised his head and a chill raced over Bran's arms when he realized what the Councilman's gaze had come to rest on.

Sybil's fragile skull.

Stevenson's tone of voice changed, frustration falling

away and, although Bran could not see his expression, he was certain he now spoke through a smile. "For the sake of your family," Stevenson said, "I would continue being the Maker, if I were you. Such a dramatic upheaval as you suggest can be especially hard . . . on a child."

"Are you threatening me?" Bran asked, his voice thin, eyes dangerous.

Stevenson turned to face him. "Threatening? Why, no. I am merely suggesting—strongly—as I did to Councilman Braga before his untimely disappearance that you reconsider what might happen if things around here changed too much. Perhaps with a good night's sleep and a bottle of bitters you might find you still have the stomach for this work after all."

Jordan folded the paper star and tucked it back up her sleeve not far from where Rowen's heart was pinned, and, standing, waited by her Tank's door. The watchman shuffled by on his rounds, pausing at her door. There was a clatter as he adjusted the things on the tray. "I have no care to know what it is you do to have curried the Maker's favor enough to give you a proper tea, but I sure as Hell wish you'd give it a rest." He fumbled with the keys and she envisioned him balancing the tray, teapot, and teacup between his hip and the door like any good servant would when struggling so.

With a grunt he opened the door and Jordan took the tray from him with one hand and a gracious nod while slipping the folded star into the void the door's handle needed to connect with in order to give a proper lock.

"Oh!" she exclaimed, jostling the tray so that tea spilled and soaked the watchman as he struggled to catch pot, cup, and saucer all at once. "How horribly clumsy of me . . . so very sorry . . ."

He righted the tray and its contents and scrambled back from the door cursing. The door slammed shut and Jordan heard him storm away.

"Take your chance now," Caleb urged. "While he's gone. Take your chance!"

"I'll bring you with me," she said, slipping out her door to stand outside his.

"No. There's no time for such foolishness. Grab his cloak and throw it over your chain to make it look like you're carrying something. But go," he urged. "This is your chance. Run with it!"

Exasperated, she did as he ordered, promising, "I'll come back for you!"

The door at the end of the hall closed behind her and she never heard him say, "No, you won't."

She pounded her way down the stairs and burst out the bottom door and onto the main square of Holgate before the watchmen spotted her and neatly brought her down.

"I promised I would come back for you," she announced to Caleb, moping as the watchman threw her back into her Tank and slammed the door, this time making sure the lock held.

"Although I find your willingness to keep your word awe-inspiring, I did not quite imagine it happening like this," Caleb admitted.

They said nothing else to each other then because after such a defeat there was truly nothing to say.

It was not long before the Maker summoned her.

"You realize what this means?" Bran asked.

Jordan looked away, unwilling to answer.

"I cannot trust you. Now I must chain you to your Tank's floor. I wanted so badly to avoid this," he said, spitting the words out. "I wanted so badly to avoid *all* of this," he said, the words somehow about far more than chaining Jordan and distrusting her.

"How do I explain to Meggie what I must now do to you?"

"Meggie?" It was the first time he'd dropped his guard enough to name his daughter. "Tell her the truth," she suggested, raising her chin as he strapped her to the boards. "Tell her that you are a cruel man who has nothing but dark designs." She screwed her face up, eyes squeezed tight, and braced herself for his inevitable retaliation.

Finally she opened her eyes and relaxed her jaw.

He stood a few feet away. Silent. His eyes seemed fixed on the floor as if he'd suddenly discovered some great secret about its construction. No hand was raised against her, no tool was poised to bite into her flesh. "I wish things were different," he muttered.

"You are certainly not alone in that wish," she scoffed.

He puffed out a deep breath and stepped forward to check that she was cinched tight. "But we are both the products of our environment and our parentage—whatever yours might be," he added. "And so we must do some unpleasant things from time to time to get by. Sometimes we have no choice."

Then he did a new variation of her treatment. Still she remained Grounded and unMade. When the Wardens finally came to take her away, she was crying.

Bran stumbled to a bucket in the laboratory's corner and, crouching before it, watched everything he'd eaten earlier in the day rush back out the same way it had been put in.

Jordan was an aching lump in her Tank. Today the sunlight was not enough to lighten her mood and being surrounded by the same grim walls was far from inspirational. Her right hand flopped out, limp, on her lap, wrapped in a hasty bandage that had soaked through with a stinking salve. "To heal the burn," the Maker had promised.

The burn he had given her with the brand.

Even blind with pain she hadn't produced a mist or a drizzle.

The Maker had said she must have a tremendous will to continue to hold out so fiercely.

Pain was her constant companion now. Long gone was her naïve belief that Weather Witches were just a segment of society that worked hard for their living, a segment of society that had some small control over their destinies. Maybe no one had choices.

Further gone was her halfhearted hope Weather Witches held some modicum of respect from society.

Hope was no longer a word she recognized.

There was a flutter of sound at her windowsill and a shadow fell across Jordan, marring the crisply split beams of light that divided her curled form in slices cut by the bars that kept her from the outside. She stirred, raising her head off her knees. Something had changed. She looked toward the morning's light and the thing that now blocked part of it.

A hawk paced the stone sill, its tail feathers and wing tips brushing the bars in a soft and rhythmic way that reminded Jordan of the lightest touch of Rowen's fingers across the strings of the guitar he'd shown her once. It was beautiful, this hawk—large and covered with feathers full of various shades of brown, cream, and red. It turned and cocked its head, looking at her. A beak the color of old butter and tipped with ebony hooked cruelly between two golden eyes that glinted as brightly as her mother's favorite earrings right after a good polishing. Its pupils were broad and dark, black pits marring its shining eyes, and Jordan shivered but unwrapped her arms from around her legs and slowly pulled her feet beneath her so that she could crouch there.

Hearing something, the hawk hopped, turning its back to her.

What was it like, Jordan wondered, to have such freedom and power you could soar through the sky, wind ruffling your feathers? Did it tickle your skin—the pull of air on your feathers? Did it make your eyes tear as the wind whipped past? What did eyes like that see from high in the heavens?

Carefully she stood.

The bird cocked its head.

Something interesting in the courtyard so many stories below or had it spotted something in one of the trees lining the lake that fascinated it?

She took a step forward.

And another step forward, quietly closing the distance between the bird and herself.

It gave another little hop, excited by whatever it had spied. Then it froze and only the faint breeze that always twisted around the tower and through her Tank gave it the appearance of life, teasing the edges of its feathers.

What were those feathers like when stroked against the skin—could you feel freedom in their touch? Did they carry the sensation of rising winds as easily as the winds carried their owner? Her hand stretched out, fingers open and trembling at the question and the desire that now tingled at their tips.

Straw crackled beneath her foot and the hawk's head spun, its eyes widening and glinting, seeing her so close. With a shriek it leaped off the sill, plummeting. Jordan's heart dropped into her stomach and she lurched forward the last few feet, hands wrapping around the bars as she pressed her face between them and watched the bird throw its wings open—the movement audible—and slowly, lazily loop over the crowd below before beating its wings and climbing, rising above the shop rooftops and up above the wall that hemmed in Holgate and kept it from the bridge, the lake, and the outside world.

From freedom.

The hawk soared over the wall and shrieked again as it headed out over the water and teased the treetops with its wing tips.

She sighed.

To have that freedom . . . She'd never had that. Society did not allow for a young lady to just . . . go anywhere or do anything on her own. Even her time with Rowen had been chaperoned.

Mostly.

She smiled and remembered.

Rowen had stolen her away one morning. It all seemed so innocent.

One moment they were seated in the parlor sipping tea and munching on delicately crafted watercress sandwiches and then Rowen (who delighted in balancing his cup and saucer on his knee) had broken them both, sending their chaperone scurrying for a mop. He stood then, grinned in that devilish way that was only Rowen's, set her cup and saucer aside, and, grabbing her by the wrist, tugged her out the back door and into the glassed-in rooms where the thick-scented exotic plants thrived.

"Quickly now," he urged, his smile so deep it dimpled. He took the lead, his hand slipping down her wrist to grasp her hand. "And quietly," he added, giving her fingers a gentle squeeze.

What could she do but follow, her heart racing and the most insane smile stretching her lips?

Out the back of the glass and steel building they'd gone, Rowen tugging her along and only glancing back twice to make sure he wasn't going too fast for a companion in heels and a tightly cinched corset.

But each time he looked back he'd snared her with those changeable eyes of his and she'd quickened her pace. Because wherever he was leading she wanted to go. In Jordan's book, Rowen was synonymous with adventure.

They'd raced through the gardens dotting the Astraea estate's back lawn and into the hedge-maze, Rowen guiding her through with such accuracy it seemed he'd often made the trip blindfolded. Or in the dead of night, like Jordan had several times when she had needed to clear her head.

Out the back of the hedge-maze they went, only pausing at the very edge of her family's property—the edge with the walled lip that overlooked the Below so dramatically it made her clutch his arm and close her eyes a moment to quell her sense of vertigo.

The Astraea holdings had been built as high into the granite face of the Hill as anyone could get and was nick-named "the Aerie" for more than one reason.

Rowen had grinned down at her, his eyes lingering on the way she held his arm so tightly before he slid his fingers under hers, pried them free, and wrapped them into his hand. He gave her hand a little squeeze and said something.

At the time she hadn't heard what he said and for weeks after, when she remembered that moment, she tried to convince herself that the loss of his words meant nothing since she could read so much in his face. But now, her hand aching and her head pounding, she wanted nothing more than to know what words his lips had formed at that instance a heartbeat before he led her through a narrow break in the hedges at the wall's edge and onto a set of stone steps she had never even known existed.

They stood on a winding slate stairway, above what suddenly seemed to be the rest of the world as all of the Below spread out in a rambling and colorful variety of houses and shops of different shapes and sizes. They were so far up it seemed the Below was nothing but a set of odd miniatures designed for a wealthy child's dollhouse.

There was no banister to hold, no place to stop and rest during the long descent, and she hesitated there, looking back over her shoulder toward the safety and manicured simplicity of life on her family's estate.

But his hand touched her face, turning her back to look at him. "Don't look back," he whispered. "Forward. Onward." He seemed such the bold adventurer then, standing like a mountain king with the backdrop of an entire wild kingdom behind him.

She could do nothing but follow.

Down the stairs they went, her knees wobbling by the time they reached the bottom.

"Next time you must give me fair warning," she had scolded, "so that I might wear more sensible shoes."

"Next time?" he asked, one eyebrow arching rakishly. "You are already imagining a next time?"

She blushed so hard her face stung with heat. "I do own sensible shoes," she said in answer.

"I'm sure you do," he replied. "Here." He tugged on her hand and drew her into the back of an alley.

She tripped after him and fell against him, her hands grabbing at him so that she kept her balance.

His arm wrapped around her instinctually, holding her close until she regained her balance.

But she never truly had regained it after being held so tightly against him.

There in the shade of the buildings stacked around them as awkwardly as toy blocks, Jordan first heard Rowen's heart beat and felt the strength of him just beneath the comfort of his slightly soft frame. He became synonymous with adventure and safety all at once.

"My head is spinning," she had whispered.

"We took the stairs too fast," he apologized. "I did not want us to be spotted before you'd had a bit of an adventure . . ."

She drew back from him then and maintained a more respectable distance between them.

He smiled and said, "Come now. There are a few spots I would take you before we must make our ascent."

"You have done this before?" It was a stupid question. Of course he had, how else would he know about the slate stairs?

But instead of saying anything sharp or hurtful, Rowen winked at her. "Here." He grabbed her hand and wrapped it around his arm. "It will be safer if they believe we are officially together. There will be fewer questions asked. The Below is not the finest place for a woman unescorted."

"Oh. Of course," she agreed. She rested her other hand on the top of his forearm as she had seen her mother do with her father.

"Try to keep your eyes in your head," he suggested. "Best to appear we are well versed in the neighborhood although we obviously do not belong to it."

She nodded and made a conscious effort.

It was tremendously difficult not to gawk, though, especially when they stepped out of the alley and onto the main street. It was crowded with colorful shops, and windows were stuffed with displays of wares from different lands and painted with gilt and silver paint using words like *New, Improved, Startling, From the Orient, Unique!*

Tiny automatons puttered in circles in one shop window and wriggling puppies filled another. Hanging in the next were a variety of meats—smoked hams squeezed tight in netting, sausages in long skins, whole roasted ducks, chickens, and rabbits, dark, gutted, and strung up for display with a shelf of cheeses below them, waxed or wrapped in paper, with flesh white as the moon, yellow as the sun, and dark as tanned leather.

They paused at a flower shop, a young girl with a basket full of wildflowers standing before it to shout to passersby. Rowen pulled out a coin and gave it to the child, who did a dainty curtsy and passed a bundle of flowers to Jordan with a grin that surprised Jordan with the child's lack of front teeth. The child giggled and began to bellow about her wares again.

Jordan sniffed at her gift and gave Rowen a smile before returning her hand to its place on his arm, now with the bouquet pressed and perfuming the air between them.

They wandered down the main street, pausing before

windows and tables stacked with assorted wares, commenting quietly about the large carved wooden signs that stuck out from second stories on heavy metal supports and wasted no time on words but spoke to a less literate crowd. The cobbler's shop was represented by a sign in the shape of a shoe, the baker's sign was in the shape of a steaming loaf of bread, and the tavern on the corner had a spotted dog with an assortment of empty pewter mugs chained upside down beneath it so they clanged together and drew attention in any breeze.

But the doorway Rowen dragged her through had no sign that she could see and it took a moment for Jordan's eyes to adjust to the dim lighting inside.

Behind a workbench an older man was bent over something small that shimmered and threw back the light he had tilted to focus on it. He wore a strange assortment of glass lenses over his eyes and reached up to tug one aside and then cranked an adjustment on the contraption's other side, making one of his eyes appear amazingly large in comparison to his other.

A chime sounded behind them and the man looked up, blinked, and then readjusted the lenses, sliding most of them up and to the side so that it seemed he had as many eyes as an insect. "Well hello, milady," he said, rising to his feet only to bow. Then he noticed Rowen and laughed, dodging around his workbench to shake his hand. "How long has it been?" he asked, looking Rowen up and down.

"Almost since you broke with the family."

The man rolled his eyes. "You have an awkward way of expressing yourself for a nephew of mine," he muttered.

Jordan blinked. "Nephew?"

The man looked at her, his eyes crinkling when he smiled. "Our dear Rowen is a bit of a man of mystery, is he?"

Rowen simply smiled and puffed out his chest. "Jordan, this is my uncle, Nicholas Burchette. He and Father had a bit of a falling out some years ago over the family holdings and rather than battle it out in Council Court as most of our rank do, he decided to cut all ties with the family and move to the Below to set himself up as a craftsman."

"To be fair, it was not your father who instigated the issues, it was your mother."

"It always is," Rowen agreed darkly.

"And I already had the skills of a craftsman and had already served my required military time, so rather than lodge a proper complaint and drag my own family before Council, I did the truly noble thing and removed myself from nobility." He shrugged. "I have never looked back."

Rowen looked at Jordan and nodded. "As it should be."

"And now you—" Jordan took in the shop's interior for the first time. The place was lined with tiny shelves and hundreds of clocks and timepieces chattered and ticked along, some in eggs decorated with cut and colored glass, some giving life to pocketwatches that were chained to their shelves, and some mechanisms in wooden boxes that looked like miniature cottages. And some . . . She stepped forward to investigate the thing under the workbench's bright light. "Is that a ring?"

"Yes. My newest project." He slipped between the counters and her, excusing himself, and lifted the thing up, holding it between his index finger and thumb, so it was more readily viewed. Rowen stepped forward and all three of them pressed their faces close to the thing that was only the size of the stone in Lady Vanmoer's anniversary ring. It was a metal ball perched on a narrow band with a tiny bump on its top.

Jordan squinted at it. "Would it not be heavy on one's hand?"

Nicholas smiled at her and pressed the tiny bump on its top. There was a click and the ball split into three equal petals, opening to reveal a tiny timepiece no larger than a pearl.

Jordan's head snapped up and she looked at Nicholas. "That is truly remarkable. However did you . . . ?"

He smiled and shook the ring once, and the petals closed. "I use very small tools and remarkable magnification." He set the ring down on a tiny pillow and stepped back. "Many years ago I had the great fortune of meeting a man (much my senior) who worked on a device much relied upon in your own household. A Russian."

Jordan tilted her head, considering. "The elevator?"

"The same," Nicholas responded. "Ivan Kulabin. He had a gift for mechanics and showed me a few things. And shared some amazing things far more tangible than his knowledge."

She took a moment to admire the tiny tools spread casually around his workbench's surface. They sparkled, gleaming there, tips and edges like tiny fingers or blades—

The pleasant memory was ripped away and Jordan whimpered at the thought of the glimmering tools. They could make so much beauty and wonder or wreak such cruel havoc . . .

Where was Rowen? Her good hand reached into her sleeve and she was briefly reassured by Rowen's heart hidden there. She lowered her head and bit her lower lip. How much longer until the Maker gave up and realized she was no Witch? How long could she continue without breaking?

It was more than the torture, she realized, touching the fresh wound tenderly. It was the exhaustion that wore at her the most. The worry and fear. The Maker seemed never to follow a schedule. There was truly no time one might feel safe—no time she might simply let down her guard.

She glanced toward the door and the small window in it, assuring herself that no one was watching before she tugged on the heart-shaped pin, pulling it free.

The pin's back sported a blade akin in shape to a long slender nail.

She slid its tip beneath her manacle and turned it experimentally to see if its point might cut the leather. She winced realizing it would, but not before it cut her, too. She dragged it back out from between her wrist and the restraining cuff and set it on her lap. Then she looked at the lock on her cuff and grabbed the pin again, prodding its tip into the locking mechanism and wiggling it. But, long as it seemed, it still was too short for the lock.

Her head snapped up and she looked at the lock on her Tank's door. The keyhole was much different than that of her cuff's. Quietly she slid over to the door, and on her knees in her ruined party dress she carefully slid the pin's tip into the lock's hole. She heard it make contact with something inside and her breath caught. She fell onto her rump in surprise. It might be possible.

If she could somehow slip off the cuff . . .

. . . then out the door and to the gate . . .

And what then, she wondered, standing to go to her window. She wouldn't get far dressed as she was and on foot. She knew that much now. She would need transportation to take her away from Holgate. A horse, a carriage, hidden in a wagon or . . . Her eyes lifted to the other broad tower marking the horizon of Holgate and making it a truly unique silhouette standing stark against the horizon.

The Western Tower was tall but squat in comparison to the tower holding the Tanks and the Maker's rooftop laboratory.

And projecting out of the uppermost story of the Western Tower was a heavily reinforced balcony upon which cabled tethers extended to waiting airships. Everyone had heard tales of scoundrels stealing away on an airship or a Cutter— stowaways.

Granted, most of the stories ended badly, but she was not facing a happily ever after if she remained here either, she knew. Out of the frying pan and into the fire, perhaps? She shrugged and considered. Perhaps it could work. Trying it— trying *something*—was at least far better than waiting around for her destiny to be assigned to her. In this she had a choice.

She pressed her face to the bars, watched the goings-on of the Grounded with more fascination than she'd ever spared anything but her clothing and her hair, and set her mind to plot out an escape plan. As soon as she could find a way to escape from her cuffs.

She could do this, she thought. She could rescue herself or die trying. And if she succeeded perhaps she could return to rescue the others. She swallowed hard and forced down the fact she really would prefer someone else doing the rescuing.

She was, after all, a lady held prisoner in a tower . . .

Was such a rescue not exactly the sort of mission heroes aspired to succeed at? Where then was her hero? Where was Rowen? Did he simply no longer care a whit about her?

Her good hand wrapped around the bars and she steeled

herself against the idea that the one young man she had taken a vague fancy to no longer desired her company.

And that she would need to become her own hero and never again wait on rescue.

Chapter Seventeen

❧

A horse, a horse! My kingdom for a horse!
—WILLIAM SHAKESPEARE

En Route to Holgate

Rowen was still having little luck with the horses. He had seen them both a distance away as they grazed together, but they wanted no part of him—especially Silver with his battered and still bloody sides. Ransom seemed less concerned with Rowen's occasional attempts at approaching them, but given the choice of indulging in lush summer grass or being ridden into danger?

For a hungry horse there was no choice to be made.

A bird alighted on a tree branch nearby and, appraising Rowen with a cock of its head and a quick glance from its beady black eyes, determined he was no threat and so puffed out its fluffy breast and began to warble a tune.

Rowen sighed and sank down against the tree trunk.

When he'd been a child he'd heard stories—nursery tales and lullabies of places the birds sang nothing except a single

note. Of a place where there was no song in the world except a single prophecy of such dark sacrifice it leeched all
the music from people's souls. Of a time all dreams and
nightmares came from a mystical dreamland tree that became poisoned and started to tear apart the world with a
dark magick that brought nightmares to life. But the magick
was defeated by a young man—Marnum—a hero who found
that music was the earliest magick and reintroduced it to
their world. A hero.

It was always some damned hero.

Some golden-haired godlike young man with all the tools
he needed and all the right answers at all the right times. A
hero who instinctively knew how to conquer evil and face
down temptation.

Hell, Marnum would probably have kept from ruining
his clothing as he adventured.

Rowen looked with disdain at his boots (covered in mud
and an oozing green slime that reminded him distinctly
of . . . something distinctly unpleasant) and his pants—he'd
torn even his buckskin breeches.

He was no hero. He was a filthy, fumbling vagrant.

A man like Marnum—a real hero (even if he was just a
legend)—always got the girl.

A man like Rowen . . . All he'd probably get was the
plague.

He sniffled and rubbed at his nose. Yes. *There*. Right on
time (since nothing else ever seemed to be). The potential
beginnings of the plague. He tested out a cough, listening
intently to the end of it. No wheezing.

Yet.

Well. As it was only a matter of time before he died, he
might as well make the most of his death by dying in the

cause of rescuing Jordan. He had no other place to return to, no one else who might wish to see him now.

He was a most unwanted wanted man.

He looked at the bird, still merrily trilling away with no concern about his proximity. And the damned thing was right. He was no threat. Except to himself.

The bird let out a shriek and dove for the bushes as something larger rocketed through an opening in the canopy and landed right on the branch the little one had been seated on. The branch wobbled beneath its weight and Rowen looked up to see a hawk scanning the area around him.

He dragged out his sword and sketched in the dirt around him a moment before he thought better of it. He already needed a good whetstone to sharpen his blade; he'd best not dull it further.

He set down the sword and tugged off one of his boots, turning it upside down to empty it. A pebble bounced out of it. And a small stick. He needed his spatterdash gaiters to better protect his feet. He slipped his boot back on.

He needed his saddlebags. He needed his horse. He needed to be ready to get Jordan when they released her. He dragged himself back to his feet and the hawk took off.

He set out to find the horses and this time succeed with getting them back and on the way to Holgate.

Holgate

It was true that Jordan Astraea seemed to be an anomaly in the world of Weather Witches. No other Witch had held out as long as she had—no other Witch had continually insisted so vehemently that she was not what Bran knew her to be.

Perhaps he was losing his touch. Perhaps the appearance of his doe-eyed daughter had caused him to go soft. He shook his head and looked at the child once again seated not far from his feet. Yes, he was gentle around her, but was he too gentle at his job? Surely not.

So Bran found himself doing something he seldom did: he dusted off the dustiest of his books and began to do some more thorough research.

He traced all sides of her family tree, pored over each family members' physical and mental descriptions. She was, as completely and truly as any child might be, the very definition of what should happen given the union of an Astraea and a Wallsingham. And if she was exactly as she should be . . . she should not be a Weather Witch. There were none in either of her family lines.

Witchery could be traced as clearly as the results of Darwin's work aboard the *HMS Beagle.* It was very much like the split in the evolution of a species. There were clear connections. Lines connecting Witches like a spider's web. Except in the case of Jordan Astraea. So much of her was directly from her father, from certain physical features to attitudes. Too much of her was him for Bran to dismiss her claims of innocence. And if she was his offspring, then there seemed no way she could be a Witch.

He sat back in his chair and scrubbed a hand across his face. No Weather Witches or magicking of any discernible type anywhere in her background and all signs pointing to her background being what she claimed.

He groaned and Meggie hopped up, asking, "Are you well, Papá?"

He smiled, assuring her that most indeed he was, though the truth of the matter was that the thought of doing what he did to Make Weather Witches—doing *that* to an innocent who was truly Grounded—his stomach clenched. The idea made him ill.

A siren sounded, blaring from the corners of the compound's walls and making Meggie jump into his lap. "There, there, little princess," he said, pressing his hands over her own smaller hands. "It simply means we have airships inbound."

The noise stopped and Meggie twisted round in his lap to look him square in the face. "Can we see the airships, Pápa?"

He nodded. "Yes, yes, I think that's a most excellent idea. We can watch them dock tomorrow before lunch, I expect."

She clapped her little hands together and slipped off his lap. "That sounds wonderful!"

"Good. But now, let's straighten things up and prepare for bed."

Meggie returned the books to any shelves she could reach and patiently held out the ones she couldn't reach for Bran to return himself. She straightened the papers on his desk and put things in their proper drawers and then waited for her father to say it was a job well done. Which he always did, even if he still fixed a few small things himself afterward. The library's door closed behind them and they returned to their private chambers to find Maude already preparing for bed.

"You two are late," Maude scolded, but it was a soft and joking tone she used. She grabbed Meggie and quickly helped her change, running the brush through her hair a dozen or more times so that her hair had a gloss that made it look remarkably like moonlight. Maude cleared her throat. "It is time for a bedtime tale," she began.

"And this time, I shall be the tale-teller," Bran said, stepping in.

Maude smiled and sat on the edge of the bed with Meggie, delighting in the story Bran told, which included a pantomime of dancing bears and assorted animal noises. At the story's conclusion, both Maude and Meggie were laughing and clapping.

Bran took a bow.

Together the two adults tucked Meggie in and kissed her cheek and forehead.

It was then that Bran realized something was missing. "Where is your bed?" he asked Maude.

She wove her fingers together before her and looked out from beneath her eyelashes at him. "I did consider what Meggie had suggested regarding your far-too-large-for-one bed. And considering that I hear the snoring nightly all the way in here, I think I might somehow adjust to the noise being—a bit closer?"

Bran blinked at her. "Oh. Why, yes, of course." He motioned to the bed and followed her, curious.

She closed the door between Meg's room and Bran's and turned off the remaining stormlight.

Bran stood there beside the bed and in the dark, both literally and figuratively. He heard the rustle of fabric and the sound of cloth hitting the floor. "If I asked you to leave here with me and Meggie, would you?"

The noise at his bedside ceased a moment. "What? Fly away with you on some airship on a grand adventure?" Her tone was hard to read and he wondered if she was mocking him.

But hearing another piece of clothing hit the floor he re-

alized he didn't care at the moment. She'd know he was serious soon enough. "Yes."

"Then yes," she replied. "I will go away with you, Bran
Marshall. I will let you fly me straight to the heavens, if you
like."

She slipped beneath the covers.

As did he.

Maude rolled onto her side to face his side of the bed.

As he rolled onto his side to face hers.

They lay in the darkness together but apart until she
stretched an arm out and rested her hand on his side. He
snorted at the touch of her and she said, "Hush now. You stay
on your side and I shall stay on mine."

But neither of them obeyed the mandate and neither of
them found reason to complain afterward, either.

En Route to Holgate

Rowen was so close to the horses he could hear the swish
and slap of their tails on their hides as they defended themselves against the last flies of the season.

Ransom's saddle had begun to slip to the side and Silver's
was obviously annoying him as he tried to rub it off against
the nearest tree. Not wanting to startle them, Rowen began to
sing a song, softly at first, but then he picked up volume until
both of their ears pricked in his direction and then he stepped
out and stretched his hand out before him as if he held a
sweet. He had seen his father use a similar trick once before
and remembered his words of advice: "Act as if you have
something they want and they will be yours for the taking."

So with every move, he made his body tell a story of having something that surely a horse would want.

Ransom looked up, still working grass around the bit of his bridle to chew it. He tilted his head and ambled over to investigate and as his velvet-soft nose brushed Rowen's empty palm, Rowen slid his other hand along the stallion's cheek and wrapped his fingers around the bridle's leather straps.

Ransom blew out a hot puff of air and shook his head to rattle his dragging reins but conceded to his capture. Rowen worked his way around his steed then, never fully releasing him and carefully tightening everything from small buckle to girth strap. "I promise a proper stall tonight," he said, "but now we have a mission to complete and a lady to rescue. Surely you can broach no argument in that regard." He climbed into the saddle and encouraged Ransom into an easy walk, glancing over his shoulder from time to time at Silver.

Silver stayed with them, only a few lengths behind and tearing at grass as he went.

In the saddle Rowen nodded in time to Ransom's pace and eyed the position of the sun. He nudged Ransom and they moved into a trot, Silver still keeping pace.

Also En Route to Holgate

Marion's travel, hidden in an oversized carriage, even hidden among the baggage, was far faster and on a far straighter route of main roads than the winding path to Holgate that Rowen's solitary journey had required of him. Marion tried to get comfortable, pinned as he was between two trunks and a fabric bag that smelled of cat urine. It was no easy task and finally he gave up on that least important bit of his mission, abandoning comfort for the assurance of not being discovered.

So he bounced along, cramped but invigorated by the fact that he was moving ever faster toward completing the cycle of his destiny. That if he did this one thing, if he ended things where they had truly begun, perhaps he—and others like him—might then be free of the tyranny of their enslavement as Weather Witches. And perhaps no more children would be snatched from their parents and no more lives would be ruined for the sake of the minority's luxury and their fear.

Holgate

Shortly after breakfast Bran and Meggie met Maude outside the kitchens. She was tidying her hair as best she could and taking off the broad apron that protected most of her outfit from the normal hazards of cooking large quantities of food in a space shared with a dozen other people. She folded the apron and set it on a stack with others to be laundered. "You should not be down here," she said to Bran. "It is not a proper place for a Maker or a wee lady—now that she has better."

"You stay on your side and I stay on mine?" Bran asked.

His dimples were obvious and Maude grinned a response.

"Let us go out into the town," Maude suggested. "The weather—"

"Will be perfection for viewing an airship docking," Bran assured. "I have seen to it."

They left the interior of Holgate's mightiest structure and blinked against the brightness of the sun.

"Gorgeous," Maude said.

High above them and to their west an airship was in view, its back a long egg-shaped balloon with long frame and fabric wings on either side and a rudder like a fish's tail. Its belly was a large enclosed basket woven out of glass and metal.

"There," Bran said, leaning over to be closer to Meg's perspective. "The basket holds all the cargo and most of the people," he explained. "The big balloon above it helps to keep it floating in the sky when the Conductor can no longer do it."

"Why would a Conductor not . . ."

Bran's expression darkened. "Sometimes they simply cannot. Or, rarely, they will not. But that almost never happens."

Meg nodded, watching the lumbering beast of a balloon slowly drift toward the tower.

People stood silhouetted at the balcony's edge, cables tied about their bodies and linked to the side of the building. In their hands they held cables of another sort, just as heavy-looking and also linked to the tower's fat wall, but at multiple spots. Those on the balcony leaned forward as others leaned out of the balloon's basket and tossed tethers toward the balcony. They were caught and looped around yet another tether point and the airship slowly turned so that its snout faced them and it sidled up to the balcony.

The waiting people holding the cables launched themselves at the massive ship, reaching up and out to grab the rope net holding the balloon and basket more fully together. They climbed as quick as monkeys, hauling themselves ever higher on the ship until they clamped their cables to the netting's top and leaped the impossible distance back down onto the balcony.

Meg clapped her hands together and did a little dance. "Oh, Papá, that was amazing."

He grabbed one of her hands and, swinging her arm with his, started them walking down the row of shops.

Maude looked at him suspiciously. "Don't you have work to do on the tower top?"

"I changed my schedule. That can all wait."

She rounded on him. "I do not recall you ever deviating from your schedule before."

His eyes rolled heavenward as he thought about it. "That would be because I never have. But it is a beautiful day."

"And?"

"And I would like to at least spend the morning with two of the loveliest women in Holgate."

"And?"

"And," he said, and sighed, shaking his head at her, "I need a little time away to think upon a particular situation. An issue that may actually be an anomaly of sorts."

Meggie peered up at him and tested out the word herself, "A-mom-molly?"

He tapped her nose. "Anomaly. It means something very much out of the ordinary."

Maude nodded. "And this anomaly may be a very bad thing?"

"Bad enough. But let's not dwell on that now," he said. "Let us search out some fun—perhaps purchase a fresh croissant, some tea, and jam and sit at the café . . ."

Maude smiled, and as she grabbed Meggie's other hand they started down the cobblestone roadway, swinging her between them so she squealed as her feet left the ground.

The hawk was back and Jordan watched as it crept across the broad sill of her barred window, its tail scraping the stone and then thudding softly against each bar as it walked the length of the ledge. Jordan pulled herself to her feet and quietly stalked the distance to the window. She had never wanted to touch a hawk so badly. Her father had a few hunting hawks at the estate (another reason it bore the nickname "the Aerie"), but she had never bothered with them. They ate dead chicks and brought down bunnies and smaller birds with cold eyes, sharp beaks, and cruel talons. They were predators and Jordan more frequently identified with prey.

But this one was quiet and curious, fascinated by the world below Jordan's window, and likewise she was fascinated by the way it stalked from so high above. She was tantalizingly close to it when a link of her chain changed positions and clanked—and the bird shot into the air with a cry and a popping out of its wings that was so fast a feather came free and fell into Jordan's Tank, floating lazily back and forth until it settled on the straw. Reaching out to retrieve it, she saw something sparkle under the straw. She picked up the quill, tapping its end against her fingertip, before she slowly slid the straw away from the drain grate centered in a depression in her floor. Looking into its iron slits, she again caught the reflection of something inside.

She set the quill down and took off her pin again. With a grunt, she dug the pin's back all around the drain, slowly freeing the thing from the rust and grime cementing it in place. It screeched as she removed it, but the prize inside was worth the worry.

Victorious, she withdrew a tiny crystal.

It glowed blue, growing brighter when it rested in her hand. She slid it into the top of her bodice and, replacing the grill, retrieved the quill once more.

She crouched in the corner out of view of any passing watchman and inserted the quill's tip into the lock on her cuff. It certainly fit . . .

She wiggled it around and heard a click when she applied a bit of pressure to the right spot and the cuff's lock sprang open. The first cuff dropped to the Tank's floor. She started work on the second cuff's lock but the lock was not as easy to trigger and although she tried again and again, each time trying a slightly different angle and a slightly different pressure, she nearly cried when the quill made a crunching noise and split along its length.

She wanted to tell Caleb what she was working at, but the sound of his snoring kept her quiet.

She pulled the broken thing out—it was no stronger than a thick piece of straw now—and certainly no more useful. One cuff open and one hand free . . . She quietly maneuvered the loose cuff and the chain through the iron ring bolted to her cell's floor and stood up, freer in her cell than she had been for a while.

She swept the straw aside with her foot and stooped to retrieve her pin. She waited until the watchman walked by on his hourly tour of the Tanks and then she crouched before her door's lock and wiggled the pin's sharp tip into its opening.

A wiggle, a turn, a click, and the lock reacted.

For the longest moment she remained crouched there with her face by the lock, completely stunned by her success. Finally she slipped on her shoes, stood and gave the

door a little tug. It moved. The door was unlocked—open.
She was free and if she made it far enough this time, she
could return for the others. She looped the chain around her
free arm and pulled one side of her skirt up to obscure it in
the folds of the fabric and, truly opening the door now, she
slid out into the hall and bolted for the door at its far end.

En Route to Holgate

Rowen had allowed the horses one break, during which he
had finally gotten his hands on Silver. He adjusted all the
straps and buckles and rubbed the horse while reassuring it
with soft words and firm hands. Looping Silver's reins
around his saddle horn, he kicked Ransom into action, a
feeling growing in his gut that soon, very soon, he would
see Jordan.

With that thought in mind he set the horses into a gallop
and lowered his body over Ransom's back and neck, making
them as sleek a shape as possible for cutting through the air.

Holgate

She burst through the door and took the stairs at a dead run,
leaping over them two at a time. The feeling of freedom—
the exhilaration of escape—overrode every bit of discomfort
she felt and the moment she burst out the tower's lowest
door and stumbled into the bustling and shop-lined street of
Holgate's eastern side she sucked in a breath that seemed

sweeter than any she had ever taken before. It was only a short distance from the street to the Western Tower and then a climb up even more stairs than she'd come down to make it to the top . . .

Her eyes traveled the length of the tower to where an airship floated, tethered as tight as they dared, at the edge of the jutting balcony.

She steeled herself and sprinted across the street.

That was when she heard them.

"Witch on the run!" someone shouted, and an alarm bell rang.

Jordan doubled her speed but suddenly every face turned toward her was fierce and cruel—nowhere did she see a speck of compassion. Men she hadn't even noticed before reached out to grab and hold her—she shook free of them, but her skirt dropped and the chain fell loose and she was running as much as dragging—

And then she saw the Maker and his little girl. The child's mouth stood as wide open as Jordan had left her cell door standing, the child's eyes wide.

A whip lashed out, wrapping round her waist and pulling her off her feet. The men had her. The Maker was shouting and the little girl was running and she grabbed Jordan's chain, screaming, "Don't hurt her!"

And then there was a bolt of light and everyone was suddenly flat on the ground. Sparks ran across Jordan's chain and made her gown glitter with light.

Stunned, Jordan tried to stagger to her feet.

But the Maker had his gloves on and took the chain from his daughter's hands.

"Don't let them hurt her, Papá," the child pleaded. "She is so scared . . ."

He looked from the one to the other of them. "I know, Meggie," he whispered, "but she is as the Witches are—an *abomination*." And from the look on his face Jordan knew that any previous doubt he might have had was gone.

She tumbled out of the doorway and onto the tower top's stone floor. Her foot caught up in her own skirting, she landed hard on her hands, jarring every bit of her.

"I cannot believe it," the Maker exclaimed. "I do not know what to think when it comes to you, Miss Jordan Astraea." He paced by her, his shoulders slumped and his back bent, hands twisting in one another before him as he thought. "The very moment I am truly doubting that you are a Weather Witch— that you *can* be a Conductor, you Light Up faster and brighter than a Councilman at a cocktail party! I was ready to admit I was wrong . . . I was ready to give up on you, accept you as Grounded . . ." He turned and faced her and the sun framed him so harshly she had to look away. "What am I to believe now? I thought for a while that you were right—that I was wrong, that somehow—for some godforsaken reason—the Maker had managed to torture an innocent member of the Grounded. Do you know how that made me feel?"

"I hope it made you sick," she hissed.

He straightened. "It did!"

"I *am* Grounded," she said.

"The same words, but you showed a far different reality out there on the street. So do it again. Do it now. Admit what you are once and for all and let us end this farce!"

"I am Grounded," she spat out the words. "I do not know why what happened out there *did* happen out there."

"Admit what you are and we can move past the Making.

I can get you out of here tomorrow. On that airship." He pointed to the bulbous thing tethered to the Western Tower. "They need a new Conductor and can train you to the finer points of the job. Imagine. Being out of the Tanks. Being the captain of your own ship."

"A Conductor's no more the captain than a maid is the head Councilman," she snapped. Lying there on the floor, she tried to get her feet free of her skirts. The right one had no trouble and she rolled onto her back and sat up, seeing her shoe peek out from under her hem.

He nodded once. Slowly. "But still it is better than the Tanks. So admit your true nature. Tell it true."

"Tell it true? I am Grounded." But her right foot . . . She shook it, but it would not come free. She pressed with it and heard stitches snap and gave a little start, immediately stopping the action. Her lips turned down at their ends and she bit the lower one, worrying it between her teeth. She did not want to ruin what might be the last dress she was given by popping stitches in a place that would surely not allow her a needle and thread. Bending, she reached forward to flip her skirts up and see the problem, but she froze, her hands curled above the hem.

The door opened and Meg stepped out onto the tower's top.

The Maker looked at his daughter. "I do not think you will want to be here for this," he advised her. "The lady insists she is Grounded."

"Then let her go."

He blinked at her. "Oh, Meggie. You are so young and so innocent. She is not Grounded, little dove. You saw what she did on the street." He turned back to Jordan and muttered, "Even if she was Grounded, I couldn't let her go."

Jordan swallowed and tugged the fabric of her skirt back, immediately seeing the issue. Her heel was snared in a web of the same beautiful thread that ran throughout her ball gown. Light winked off the metallic thread and she curled over her leg to untangle her shoe.

Her foot freed, she hesitated, fingers tracing the intricate work she would have never appreciated had she not looked beneath her skirts.

"Papá, you are the Maker. You can do whatever you wish," Meg insisted.

"Hush, Meggie. Nothing is quite so simple as all that." He looked at the blades. "I would have to make you disappear to save my reputation," he explained slowly to Jordan. "Only it's not just my reputation I'd be saving—I have others to watch out for now, you see. I am a provider—a family man."

Meg was beside him, holding his shirtsleeve, but Jordan paid them little mind, listening halfheartedly. How such a sweet child could be the offspring of a monster like the Maker . . . But the strange threads running like a spider's web caught her attention again.

Why would anyone invest such time and attention to detail . . . Such *money* (for she knew metal spun into thread was no cheap purchase) . . . all for something no one would ever glimpse or appreciate?

The web ran everywhere her skirt did. And it was fine—nearly soft—not something like a hoop that added body and support to a dress. She popped up straight for a moment, eyes darting as her mind chased a thought as doggedly as a terrier after a rat.

"Besides, how else would you explain away all the potential anomalies then? What? You have demonstrated witchery at your birthday party—twice, at the Reckoning and just now on the streets of Holgate. That seems rather damning to me . . ."

"No," she whispered. "Think on the science of it—you are a man of science . . ." She slipped her right hand up her left sleeve, flipping the remaining ruffle as she went. Intriguing. The ruffle was simple cloth—granted, a high-class weave and thread count that created a supple fall of fabric, but . . . Her fingers reached higher.

She barely kept from giving a little shout at her discovery when her fingertips brushed the same netting lining her sleeves as lined her skirting. But why?

"We must all be men of science here in the New World," he pointed out.

"What if there was another Weather Witch present at each of those moments?" she asked. "What if I was mistaken for being something I am not?"

"Accidents happen," Meggie said with a slow and solemn nod.

"Accidents . . ." The Maker shook his head. "No. How? If there was another, we would have to find it. Gather it in and do whatever I must do to Make it. But . . ." He ran his hands through his hair and shook it out. "How? How?" he demanded, and Jordan scooted away, more frightened of him now than she had been before. "By some strange transference of power? That is the only imaginable way . . . No. Highly unlikely at best." Still he paced, his hair becoming wilder and his face more frightening with every turn he made. "There are no people around you who have been in each place. It would mean the involvement of at least one additional Witch. It would mean there is one loose in Philadelphia and one loose here."

"Yes. Perhaps," Jordan whispered, her voice soft with desperation. "Think on it. At the Reckoning the Wardens held both my body and my chain . . . Are they not Witches, twisted as they now might be?"

The Maker paused and stared at her. "Yes."

"Could they not have transferred a charge . . . if excited? What Makes a Witch?"

"Heritage and the proper trigger. Most frequently pain."

"Must pain always be physical?" Jordan whispered. "Is not emotion as powerful as physical pain? Perhaps even more powerful?"

He dropped suddenly into a crouch before her and she drew back in fear. "Yes, I guess so. But pain can be regulated. It teaches control. The metal of the chain . . ." His head tilted, his eyes searching her face for some clue. "But the party . . ."

"Was emotionally charged," Jordan said, recalling the debates, the entertainment, all of it.

Meg came forward and stood between them, her small hand on her father's shoulder.

"A Witch had been found once before in my household; could there not be another lurking? Leaving us unawares?"

He rubbed a heavy hand from his chin up his jaw and snarled his fingers into his own hair again. "The chain conducting I can fathom. But . . ." His gaze raked over her, examining her body language but finally falling frozen on her underskirt.

Jordan blushed and flipped the fabric back down.

"No," he said, grabbing the hem and throwing it back so fiercely Jordan and Meggie both gave a shout of protest. "This is the dress you wore at the party?"

"And ever since, minus my corset and stockings. And

shawl," Jordan mumbled, barely keeping herself from smacking his hand—it was unnervingly close to her thigh.

"What is this web?" he demanded, tugging at it. "It is not
even attached"—he turned it to examine the artistry of the
decorative front—"to the design. It is no clever method of
uniformly working the back of someone's embroidery hand-
iwork." He ran his hands roughly up the outside of the rest
of the skirt and the side of her bodice, saying, "It is something entirely separate, something designed to nearly encase
you in a shroud of metal . . . In a cage of conductive material. Expensive conductive material . . ." His expression
shifted from one of horror to one of wild wonder. "Someone
must hate you with a finely burning passion," he concluded,
flipping her skirts back down and staring at the wall, his
mind puzzling things together. "Someone connected to this
dress."

"It was a gift from my very best friend," she said.

His eyebrows rose simultaneously.

"My very best friend," Jordan repeated. "But it was
crafted by a strange little woman from the Below . . ."

On one of the most special days of her life as a young lady
she had worn a very special gown—so special she hadn't
even realized . . . A gift from her very best friend.

A gift designed by a most peculiar modiste with a reputation for churlishness and oddity. Jordan jumped to her feet.
It was the modiste! She had planned things out to bring her
family down by first destroying both Jordan's and her mother's reputations.

Meg clasped her hands together and her face lit as if fired
from within as she hopped from foot to foot. "See? Accidents
happen! The lady is a lady, not a Witch."

Jordan's heart soared in her chest, exhaustion turning to

elation. She was Grounded. She had been a victim of some other Weather Witch, but she was Grounded. Her mother's name might yet be restored and the Astraeas returned to their appropriate rank.

The Maker winced at the oversimplification. "So you are not an abomination . . . ?" He smirked. Standing, he rested his hands on his hips. The smile fell away from his face. "But you are a failure. And I can have none of those to my name. I have no choice."

It seemed a most frighteningly desperate apology.

"I will never say a word . . ."

"Yes. Yes you would. You are bred to a certain standard. Your type talk if only to complain and bring down those around you."

"No," she insisted. "Release me and I will find my family and move us all quietly away. We will live out our days in solitude in the countryside and I will never ask nor want for more than this—just my freedom . . ." Her heart, so briefly flying with relief, tumbled into her stomach.

"Papá, please," Meg asked, slowly realizing that not being a Witch could also be bad.

"It would be so much easier if you were a Witch . . . and there is the little matter of this morning's strange display of magicking . . ."

Jordan threw her hands into the air. "I am Grounded! There must have been another Witch there."

"He would have needed to be touching you or your dress or chain."

"He or . . ." Jordan's eyes widened and she turned slowly to the little girl still standing between them both. The little girl with big, soft eyes who wanted nothing more than for Jordan to go free and for her papá to be blameless—who wanted nothing more than for everyone to be happy. And the word tumbled out to damn and doom them all in far different ways. ". . . *she*." And then Jordan felt it—a pain so sharp it had to be heartbreak.

Meggie gasped, hands flying up to clap over her mouth, her tiny heart-shaped face stretched and stunned. Her eyes went from Jordan to her papá and then to the board with its thick restraining belts and buckles and finally her gaze fell upon the array of her papá's sharp tools that she cleaned daily—tools she never asked about, never dared to wonder aloud about what he used them for or why they always came to her sticky and covered with a red so dark it was brown . . .

He caught the child—his child—as she fell, weeping. The water nearly poured from her then, a deluge from her eyes and ten tiny rivulets running from her fingertips. Clouds moved in above her and liquid crept out of the very stones and crawled across the floor to pool at her feet and await her command.

"Oh. Oh no," he whispered, "Meggie . . ."

"Papá," she whispered, eyes wide as she stared at her fingertips and the liquid that leaked from them. "Papá . . . what is happening to me? I have no control . . ."

He shuddered but forced himself to take her tiny hands in his own. "You're . . ."

"An aba—abom—abomination?" she asked, raising her eyes to ensnare his before they darted away to hide under trembling and thick eyelashes.

He dropped her hands to place a finger under her quivering chin and tip it up, again raising her eyes to his. "No. No, darling girl," he said, fighting the tears stinging at his eyes. "You are still my bright and pretty daisy, Meggie—my dear little dove . . ."

Jordan fell to her knees then, her stomach rioting as realization struck. This sweet child, this tiny innocent had been damned by her own doing . . . Jordan bent, her broken heart racing, her stomach rebelling as she imagined every cruel thing that had been done to her being done to a child, by her father. She vomited until nothing remained in her stomach and her body shook with dry heaves, her head aching as everything came into awful focus and the pain of all the torture, and the torture of all the exhaustion of the uncertainty, took over, wrapped round her like the whip from before, and tugged her into the darkest place her mind had ever been.

Above them the cloud cover tripled, pulling in like a shroud to cover Jordan and protect its Conductor. Lightning danced from one black and roiling mass of clouds and reached out to embrace another.

The Maker gasped, cradling his child in his arms and trying to wipe away the tears that flowed from her and seemed to be never-ending. "You cannot," he said to Jordan. "You *are—*"

"No," she insisted, seeing what he saw high above. "No. I am Grounded," she whimpered before collapsing.

He watched one set of clouds, Jordan's clouds, whisk away to nothing and he simply knelt with Meggie, rocking back and forth as he stroked her face and said the only soothing words he knew. "It will be all right," he promised again and again like a mantra. But it was a lie. It was all a lie.

Jordan Astraea could not be a Witch. It was a scientific impossibility based on her heritage and Bran's knowledge. Impossible. And yet, the storm had come when she realized Meggie was a Weather Witch . . . If Jordan Astraea had, against all scientific reason, been Made a Weather Witch out of sorrow . . .

His work, his proud tradition, the idea that the little dove quivering in his grasp would not be discovered and that only those of a certain taint in their bloodline could be Made . . . He shook as hard as Meggie then, knowing the truth of it. That anyone—if taken far enough into the darkness—could be turned and Made.

And if anyone could be a Witch . . .

Then all of society's structure was at risk. The New World would not be saved through his effort, but ruined. And that was how Bran Marshall would forever be remembered.

Unless he could regain control. Somehow.

The airship was the easiest solution to most of his problems and Bran called down to the kitchens for Maude, wiped the last of the tears and mucus from Meggie's face, and set her in Maude's welcoming arms with the instruction, "Take her, pack two days' clothes and meet me with the bags in the library. I will not be long—I just need to clean up a bit of a mess."

Maude only nodded. Carefully she began the descent down the stairs and Bran waited until he could only see a bit of her before he closed the door and made his next call.

It was not long before the Wardens emerged from the doorway to lift the dead weight of the unconscious Astraea girl and carry her downstairs, across the street, and up the steps of the Western Tower, Bran following behind and watching her the whole time. She only began to rouse when they reached the top landing and stood by the broad doorway that led onto the balcony and to the ship beyond.

So close, they could hear the great airship groan as it

shifted and pulled against its cables. It flexed within its own odd netted exoskeleton, the ribbed and articulated sail-like wings stitched in Fell's Point tucked up along the basket manufactured in Boston's glass- and metal-crafting shops and outfitted with Philadelphia's finest lumber. Bran paused on the balcony, wondering just where inside the airship's gut the Conductor completed training. He spent less time wondering how.

The captain stepped out, dressed in a fine woolen suit adorned with big brass buttons that were as polished as his glistening black boots. "Welcome, Maker, to the *Artemesia*," he said, extending his hand for a friendly shake. "Is this the new Conductor?" he asked, his eyes wary.

"Yes," Bran assured. "She is quite capable and freshly Made—full of vim and vigor."

"Better than being full of piss and vinegar," the captain joked. Touching Jordan's cheek, he turned her face back and forth, examining her. "She looks as if she has yet to receive Lightning's Kiss."

"True enough, but I do not doubt it will come."

"Are you sure she is quite ready? She looks a bit out of sorts . . ."

"Her breakfast disagreed with her. And she was so suddenly ill it is possible her memory of the morning's events may even be tainted. If she says strange things, just disregard them. She will train up quite nicely. Of that I am certain."

"Excellent well," the captain said. "As long as she's not who the newest rabble-rousers predict is coming *like a storm* to change our pleasant way of life, I'll take her. Take her aboard," he commanded the Wardens. "Always a pleasure doing business with you, Maker."

"It is my pleasure to serve such fine individuals as yourself," he returned. Bran stayed and watched as the captain turned back to his ship and Jordan was carried out of the dim tower and onto the edge of the balcony.

The light hit her dress and dazzled everyone, the sun sparkling across every stitch of fabric. In a dress like that it was no surprise she always got quite a bit of attention.

Rowen, Silver, and Ransom burst forth underneath the open portcullis, flying past the watchmen, and came to a stop only when the dazzling sight of Jordan's dress showed up in the edge of Rowen's vision. The horse's hooves sparked on the cobblestones and Silver slid into a watchman as Rowen stared, transfixed for a moment. They were loading her onto an airship and—his gaze tracked the only imaginable path to her—across the square and up . . .

The watchmen shouted at him but it was all like an annoying buzz in his ears. He saw the glint of steel as they drew swords and he nudged Ransom into a trot toward the Western Tower's base.

More watchmen burst down a side street; these were mounted.

Rowen pursed his lips and rubbed his growing beard just a moment before drawing his sword. This was about to get ugly.

They came at him and Ransom danced backward, the most elegant fighting partner Rowen could imagine. But they were pressed in on all sides and he realized they had retreated until they were pinned in an alley, Rowen's left foot and stirrup nearly knocking on a door. Still holding them back, he assessed his position in relationship to the tower.

If he only . . .

He slid out of the saddle, using Ransom as a shield, and pushed through the door, locking it behind him.

Standing in the dark building, he bolted the door and caught his breath, nearly laughing at the rising volume of the watchmen shouting outside. If he passed through the back of the building and came out in the next alley . . .

He heard a click and stiffened as a stormlight came on, flooding the room with light. He shielded his eyes a moment, his sword still in his hand.

"What the hell are you doing here?!" someone shouted, and Rowen said, as calmly as he could, hearing watchmen pounding on the door, "Just cutting through."

"We'll do the only cutting that's to be done," the voice retorted, and the light was lowered so that Rowen could see nine men standing with their backs against the opposite wall. Nine men dressed in mismatched outfits, the fabric worn and the men's eyes hard.

As one, they drew their swords.

"I need to get to the airship and I want no trouble—" And then he said the only thing on his mind: "Where can I go from here?"

Someone slipped out of the shadows to stand beside him, disarming him neatly. The smell of lavender and spices washed over him and a rough yet distinctly feminine voice whispered in his ear, "You, my pretty young thing," she said in his ear, "will come with us. Lower your weapons, boys!"

Bran pounded on the door and waited. Then he pounded again. He wanted to see them—wanted to know his girls were safe.

Maude opened the door and stepped back into the library, holding Meg tight to her, her eyes never leaving his face. Bran rushed past them both and fought briefly with the laboratory door before pushing inside. He'd realized there were things he might need if he was to make good their escape from this life of threats and disappointments, and he shuffled through the laboratory, gathering odds and ends and shoving them into his father's rifleman's pouch. He grabbed a second bag hanging nearby and put it over his shoulder as well.

He had devised a plan of sorts as he made his way down from the tower's top. They would board an airship as he'd promised, and leave Making behind forever. He'd never have the immortality he always thought he wanted, but he had the girls. He had love and people to care for who cared for him as well.

Love gave a man a feeling close enough to immortality for Bran's liking.

He popped open the drawer where he kept the confiscated items from Reckonings. He could use a few in trade to get them where they needed to go. And once he was gone? If he took his main journals Holgate would have no choice but to release the Tanks' inhabitants. There was no other Maker and no Maker's apprentice.

There would be no other Weather Witches. There would be no more torture and, although the abolitionists didn't know about the treatment of Weather Witches, he would change the lives of at least one set of slaves. The entire world on this side of the Western Ocean would have to change. It would end where it began. With him.

The butterflies in the bell jar caught his attention. He would start granting freedom here and now. He lifted the bell jar and then dropped it to the floor. Butterflies soared past him, colorful wings whispering along his face as they sought an exit.

He quickly chose the items he still needed. They would travel light. A jar on the counter began to bubble. And another's contents rippled with life.

The strange sensation of being watched made the hair on his arms rise up and he turned to where Sybil's skull sat, covered in the beating wings of butterflies. He had no conscious thought of what he was doing until he picked up the child's gleaming skull, the butterflies abandoning their eerie ivory perch. "I will find you a place you are finally happy to sleep in death," he promised, tucking her into the bag at his side.

He strode into the library, slung open his desk drawer, dumped its contents, and withdrew the two journals: the one everyone knew he had and the private one that held his most intimate thoughts.

And fears.

These he slipped into the bag beside the tiny skull.

He crossed the library's floor to Maude and Meggie and wrapped them in his arms.

That was when he heard the other man.

"Wait."

Bran froze, looking to Maude.

"Do as he says," she suggested, her voice strained.

A man stepped out of the shadows and said, "I think it should all end where it began. With you, Bran Marshall."

Meg wormed out of Maude's grip and stepped in front of the Maker, her expression indignant, a fire so fierce in her eyes Marion thought she might be capable of melting all of his ice just with her will. "You cannot hurt Papá!"

Marion's eyebrows shot up. "Papá?" He squinted.

The Maker pushed the girl back behind him, shielding her with his legs and warning, "Do not get involved in this matter, dear little dove . . ."

Marion said, "Oh. Oh no, I think she is already quite involved in this matter." He crouched down and smiled the smile he had always used with his little brother. "How old are you, sweet child?"

"Very nearly six," she answered, peeking warily around her father's legs.

"So you were Made the same time I was," Marion whispered, slowly rising back to his full height. "We are like brother and sister—we share a creator. So it is best we are both here—quite the little family—to bear witness to what happens next. Because our world? It's about to be set right as rain, to be changed. Forever."

Bran merely looked at him, his eyes as sad as they were dangerous. "You have no idea how right you are."

"You are coming with me," Marion said, his eyes flashing. "I have packed your necessities," he explained, motioning toward a makeshift bag made of a sheet tied together. "It did not take me long," he mused. "You will not require much as you will not be of this world for long."

Maude choked, stifling a cry.

"Leave them be," Bran insisted. "They were no part of your Making—they are innocent in all this. Take me—only leave them be."

"No, no," Marion said with a chuckle. "I am not the sort of man to break a family apart." He grabbed Bran by the arm. "Pick up that bag and move to the door. Make no suspicious moves or I will be forced to"—he shoved Bran forward to grab Meggie instead—"do something to your daughter that would make her believe I, too, am a Maker."

Meggie cried, looking at her papá, eyes pouring forth tears.

Bran hefted the bag and became as docile as ever he had been. He allowed the man to move his entire family down the hall and the stairs, out and across the main square, and up the many stairs to the Western Tower's docks. "I have taken the liberty of booking us all passage," Marion explained. "We shall have one fine family escapade abroad before all the pieces fall the way they should."

Sunlight burnished the dock before them, two ships bobbing on their cables and chains. One the *Artemesia,* and the other's side was painted with the word *Tempest.* Before the *Tempest* her questionable-looking crew, led by a copper-haired woman, loaded a wide assortment of goods while guards looked on, eyes full of doubt.

"I have never been so distrusted," the redheaded woman said, clucking her tongue at the way the watchmen watched her crew's every move. "You appear not to trust me nor my crew," she protested to the lead watchman. "And I am a captain!"

"When I see a reason to trust you," the man said, "I will reexamine my entire world view."

Laughing, the *Tempest's* captain feigned a gasp.

A young man straightened from where he had been awkwardly loading oddments, a man a small bit younger than Bran, if he judged right, but taller by a good amount. The young man's hair was blond, his features striking—making him stand out among the rough and far from handsome crew. He rubbed at a ragged-looking beard. As Marion moved his unwilling *family* forward to produce their passes, Bran saw the young man sneak away from the crew and move around them to come up before Marion.

"What wish you for one pass aboard the *Artemesia*? I want nothing more than to book passage but . . ." The red-haired captain seemed to be looking for someone. He ducked his head and tried to blend in. "I have thus far been unable to . . . break away."

"Sorry, friend," Marion said, his eyes small. "We are a tightly knit group. I cannot help you. It seems, though," Marion added, casting a look to the frantically searching female captain "you are quite a wanted man."

The young man turned away to address another person in the crowd—this one tall, masked, and dragging a colorful trunk, a midnight-black fox at his feet. "You, good wanderer," he said as Marion and his small group shuffled past, showing their passes and pushing aboard.

Behind them the red-haired woman shouted, "Dear, dear Rowen, it seems you nearly boarded the wrong ship! Trust me, you do not wish to board that bloated belly . . ." Bran glimpsed movement and guessed the captain had again found her wayward crew member.

Bran glanced one last time behind him, at Holgate, his home for so many years . . . before he was again shoved forward by Marion, nearly trampling Maude.

The fox slunk through the crowd, never far from her masked master, and rubbed herself, catlike, around Meggie's little legs until the girl smiled through her sniffles.

The ship's door closed with a groan. Bran could do nothing but watch and wait for an opportunity. With Marion Kruse—the Frost Giant—guiding both Meggie and Maude now, his dangerously cold grip in constant contact with them, Bran had to be careful. He had wanted to escape his life of Making but hadn't thought it would happen this way.

Marion was right: Meggie and he had been created at nearly the same time. They were as close to family as Marion probably had as an escapee from Holgate. Bran might use that to connect with Marion . . . to set things straight.

No one had to die here. No one even had to get hurt if Bran handled things well.

Marion was a problem he'd Made, so he'd correct that problem. Somehow.

Ahead, the captain paused by a bank of windows lining the inside of the ship's belly, Jordan's arm firmly in his grasp.

Marion steered Meggie and Maude that direction, too, Bran following. Marion had recognized the look of a battered Witch. "I hope you don't intend on using that Witch to Conduct this ship," Marion said, addressing the captain. "She hardly looks airworthy."

The captain rounded on him. "You a Dissenter? I'll take none of that type aboard," he warned.

Marion shook his head. "No, no, not a Dissenter, merely a curious observer."

Before the captain could grunt a reply, another voice called, "I had similar concerns." A masked man approached, a fox the color of ink weaving in and out between his feet as he walked.

The captain smiled, his silent captive staring blankly out the window at the other airship still docked alongside. "Well, the Wandering Wallace, isn't it?" He reached out and shook the masked man's hand. "I doubt I'd recognize you without some strange mask on." He nudged Jordan.

She didn't react.

"She'll do fine," the captain assured. "Young. Feeling a bit off just now. Needs a bit more training is all. The Maker himself assured me of her fine capabilities."

Bran ducked farther behind Marion and away from the captain's immediate sight, fortunate a crowd was milling in the boat's bottom as they readied to detach from the Western Tower's dock.

"The Maker only Makes powerful things," the captain added.

"True, true," Marion said, the words so cold Bran felt them.

"So long as you are certain she will serve," the Wandering Wallace said. "Perhaps it would help if the young lady had a bit of first-rate entertainment? A little something to lift her spirits so she can better lift our fine, fine ship?"

"Are you offering to come Topside and entertain us?" the captain asked with a grin.

"Of course, of course," Wallace declared. "I want her feeling right as rain!"

Hearing those words both Marion's and Bran's heads snapped up, their eyes meeting with those of the man behind the mask.

"And might a curious observer perhaps be invited Topside to see how the operation truly works?"

The captain regarded Marion with a long appraising look before nodding. "Certainly. We will make arrangements to gather all of us together to enjoy some food and fine entertainment before our next port of call."

Jordan suddenly jumped, reaching out a hand to press her palm flat to the window glass, and Bran leaned around Marion to see what had excited her so much and so suddenly.

In the belly of the other airship was the same young man with the ragged beard and blond hair who had asked Marion for a ticket aboard this ship instead of the one on which he now rode. He seemed as much an unwilling captive as Jordan, and her attention was absolutely fixed on him.

And his attention was likewise fixed on her.

What had the captain called him?

Ah, yes: Rowen.

Across the distance Bran watched as Rowen reached up to his chest and touched the spot where his heart resided before pointing to Jordan and then touching his sleeve.

Cables and ropes slithered across the *Artemesia*'s body, dropping past the windows and slapping as loud as gunfire against the Western Tower. The *Artemesia* drifted away from the dock and out of sight of the anxious young man peering out at Jordan from the gut of the *Tempest*.

Stay tuned for the next book in
the *Weather Witch* series

STORMBRINGER

Available 2014

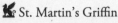